FIRST QUEEN

LEGACY OF RIVERFALL

AMABEL DANIELS

Disclaimer

This is a work of fiction. Names, characters, businesses, places, events, and incidents are either the products of the author's imagination or used in a fictitious manner. Any resemblance to actual persons, living or dead, or actual events is purely coincidental.

No part of this publication may be reproduced, distributed, or transmitted in any form or by any means, including photocopying, recording, or other electronic or mechanical methods, within prior written permission of the publisher, except in the case of brief quotations embodied in reviews and certain other non-commercial uses permitted by copyright law.

Copyright © 2023 Amabel Daniels, All Rights Reserved
ISBN: 9798396270534

Editing: Expressions Editing; C.J. Pinard at
www.cjpinard.com
Proofreading: PSW
Cover Design: Kellie Dennis at
www.bookcoverbydesign.co.uk
Map Design: Tyler Rose

Map of Contermerria

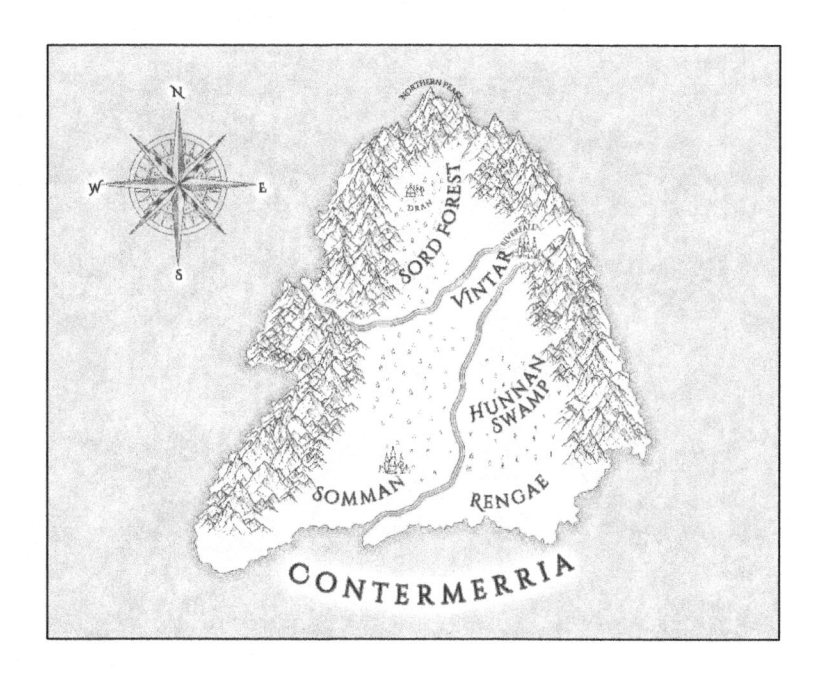

Courts of Contermerria

Court of Vintar
King Vanzed
Heir Prince Isan

Court of Somman
Prince Lianen
Princess Devota

Court of Rengae
Prince Baraan
Princess Sadera
Princess Amaias

Chapter One

Four months.

After the frecens attacked the village, I was locked out of the safety of Dran's caverns for four months. For all those days, I was parted from my sister. Each one passed with a gnawing pain of worry about her.

If I'd attempted to stay there in our windowless basement—a pathetic excuse for a home—I might have survived. Hungry, desperate for food and sunlight as I hid, I might have eked it out waiting for the magistrate to declare the village safe.

Instead, I'd met Kane.

Kane.

Another searing tear streaked down my cheek as the pang of missing him sliced me open and raw. I thought I'd cried myself dry. Every hour I lingered here—trapped, bound, and imprisoned—I lost myself to the misery and never-ending heat.

I'd met him in the unlikeliest circumstances four months ago. Thrown together, we'd formed an alliance. He'd been cryptic, wanting my help to find a royal's sword he'd stolen *and* lost. Me? I'd only wanted to survive. To live another day so I could search for the kalmere plant to cure my sister's longuex infection. To give her a better future. To save her from the chronic suffering.

It felt like so long ago that I'd made that life-altering decision to set out on a journey with Kane away from Dran. I couldn't have imagined the trials I'd face and the errors I'd make, the riddles and deception I'd encounter.

I hadn't found any kalmere, not in the monster-ridden swamp south of the castle I was locked in. Nor had I managed to obtain any growing in the sheds in the Somman Realm to the east. And I'd lost Kane when he was carried over the waterfall from this royal chamber.

Empty-handed, broken-hearted, and barely alive under the torture Devota administered here, I had truly failed. All I'd managed to do was get captured by the queen. After stabbing me in the back for trying to thwart her, to stop her from killing King Vanzed, she healed me. She'd brought me back from the brink of death only to torture me.

Four months had come and gone, and I was *still* apart from my sister.

Still stuck under a powerful binding that prohibited me from escaping this dungeon.

Still trapped under a taxing spell that hindered my fae powers.

And still burdened under the overwhelming grief and regret of losing the one man my heart beat for.

Kane. I'd never see him again.

I sniffed and blinked, holding back another tear. To show weakness in this place... I glanced up at the dungeon master to check if he'd witnessed my moment of vulnerability.

Revealing any emotion was fodder for abuse. Sadness welcomed taunts, teases, and harsh insults that cut to the bone. Slacking in the nonstop labor of moving ice from this subterranean colosseum was a cue for a whipping. A beating. Or worse, branding. It wouldn't be so bad if they allowed scars to scab over. With their Somman magic—more potent now that Devota had taken the throne—wounds remained open. Festering with demonic licks of fire that claimed the soul, those injuries they inflicted daily posed a battle of wishing for mercy in the most fatalistic way out of here.

The dungeon master hadn't noticed me. Lumbering side to side, the only gait this man's bulky form could manage with too many muscles bulging unevenly, he grunted and turned his eye to another prisoner struggling under the weight. I was spared a second glance for now.

Chin up. Face forward. Lock it down. Masking my power was a wasted effort. *Lock* what *down?* Devota and her highest fae courtesans had already spelled me to be nothing more than a numb, useless shell. I had no power to mask, no temper to tamp down. They'd well and truly beaten my spirit to nothing.

Since the day I tried to stop her from murdering King Vanzed, the same day I'd understood the scope of her deceit and how she'd used me like a pawn, I'd been stuck here in what was formerly the massive, ice-blue palace of the Vintar court.

Ice had melted, baring stone walls Devota quickly festooned with gold, fire, and trappings of wealth. Gaudy rubies and topazes glittered where simple frosted scrollwork once mutely sparkled. Crimson and golded light flickered and flashed where the dull brightness of snow used to dominate.

Winter had been chased out by summer, the snow lost to the heat.

King Vanzed's reign had been ended with *Queen* Devota's blade through his heart, and with it, her Somman fae power of heat terminated his Vintar might of cold.

In this heat that snaked through the air and into my body, I was thrown in with the other prisoners to move melting bergs of ice from the colosseum. Every day and into each night, linked together by ankle shackles, we picked up the chunks and hefted them onto carts. From there, we manually dragged the cumbersome loads to the river that cut through Contemerria's highest peak, the stream that rushed through the base of the castle, higher now with the melting ice and snow outside. Without rest, we labored and hauled massive boulders of ice. Until we collapsed, our arms and limbs numb from no rest, we could do nothing but force our bodies to keep up with the strenuous tasks.

I'd passed out yesterday—or was it today? Time had no meaning down here anymore. It was endless heat and agony. I'd only tracked the months passing by tying small knots in a strand of my filthy hair.

After my rest, once other prisoners dragged me to my cell in the Riverfall Chamber, I'd woken up with a slab of suspicious dried meat, supposedly recharged to start it all over again.

"Get up!" the dungeon master bellowed now.

I flinched but didn't turn to witness the prisoner behind me. The metal links that bound us in a line of slaves tugged, telling me enough. Another had fallen. At the first smack of the smoke-curling fire whip on flesh, I winced and sucked in a gasp.

Chin up, Maren. I heaved in a deep breath, the burn of smoke irritating my throat.

"I said get up!"

Another crack of the whip. Then a harder pull on my hands as the man fell back. I dug my bare feet into the jagged stone floor to avoid being knocked down.

Face forward. I tuned out the guttural cry from my fellow prisoner.

"Get—"

A second dungeon master's voice joined in. Two of them beat on the same person, halting their commands of marching us toward the cart. We stood still, our legs restrained from the interruption. Ice water flowed over my arms, challenging my grip on the frozen chunk larger than my torso. My biceps burned, and my legs quivered. Straining under the weight of my block, I tempered my breaths and willed my body to stand firm. The last time I'd dropped a piece of ice... Shivers wracked me at the memory of the fire whip on my knuckles.

We remained stationary, holding our ice. With jerks and tugs, the central chain that held our ankles together tried to fell us all.

Finally, "Drag him to the cells." More shuffling came through the scalding hot chained length. A dungeon master appeared at my side. He arched back, kicking the ice out of my arms and slamming his boot against my forearm in the process. "Drag 'im to the cells." A whip of the fire cut through my ankle shackle, sparking blisters up my leg. "Now!"

I was free to move. Without looking at the prisoner's face or his wounds, I turned and kept my face as blank as possible. I was a healer. It was in my nature, more so than the locked fae powers, to heal, to help, to care. Yet, I ignored it all for the sake of sparing myself abuse for holding up the line or showing disobedience.

"You." The dungeon master pointed his whip at a parallel line of newer slaves. Recently captured, these unfortunate souls still had their boots, still wore some semblance of clothes, their skin unblemished from demonic burns.

"You!" He repeated the order to one hunched-over body struggling to grip a chunk of ice. "Help her."

The other was unlocked, and together, we each grabbed a limp hand and began the long trek of pulling the fallen one to the cells.

I resisted limping on the broken bone that hadn't healed properly in my right foot. If I jerked too far to the left, the other prisoner would be thrown off their shaky equilibrium, shuffling as unevenly as I was, and we would tumble down.

"Keep going," I said. My voice was dull, a flat, lifeless whisper from my abused throat.

The first week after Devota imprisoned me, she administered dragon's teeth venom orally. Forcing my mouth open, she poured the toxins into me. Only in small doses to drive me to the brink of insanity, but never to kill.

The following week, I'd learned the hard way that screaming during whippings made these Somman brutes lash out harder and longer.

My voice, just like my hope of ever escaping, had withered into nothing.

The prisoner at my side stumbled over a thinly spread-out pile of embers. Hissing in sharp breaths, they hobbled more lopsidedly as they tried to bat at the sparks bouncing up at their legs. They let go of the fallen. Before the guard trailing behind us could notice, I grabbed both hands and lugged him along.

Harsh orders spewed from the guard's mouth. The prisoner once again gripped the fallen's hand, muttering darkly with their hood covering their head in that bowed posture. Turning a deaf ear to the guard berating this newcomer who'd soon learn to shut up, I trudged up the stairs, down the narrow corridors, and all the way over the thin, precariously balanced strip of a walkway toward the Riverfall Chamber where cells awaited.

I noticed the oddity of silence after we entered the hallway nearest Devota's lair. She wasn't in the palace today, likely gone on another raid. That woman loved malice so much she couldn't get enough of a high from torturing us in the castle. It was why we dragged this fallen prisoner toward her lair—she'd erected cages of fire to further agonize those who'd fallen. A favorite pastime of hers.

No prisoners ever entered or left the chamber without a guard, but as I looked back, the guard was nowhere to be seen.

"Ain't going to last long," the prisoner paired with me uttered.

A woman? I couldn't tell with that low, raspy voice, but it sounded feminine. I had to agree. She wouldn't survive at length in here if she was already physically hindered.

Despite the guard's absence at our backs, I knew better than to delay. I certainly knew better than to attempt escape. For one missing or errant guard and dungeon master, another ten would be waiting nearby to remind me of my station here: a slave.

Huffing and gritting my teeth, I took over the brunt of the work dragging the fallen toward the cells. Bars of fire licked up and down in vertical poles, tiny taloned fingers clutching the post as the spell of Somman warded the cells to remain upright. My so-called partner had ceased dragging the body. Instead, she roved her head back and forth, peering at the vast openness of the chamber. Furious heat flared in our faces as we crossed the patio space. In the middle of the room, the river rushed through at a tremendous speed, churning thawed water so fast, it created a suction of hot air in the large room.

Pushing forward, I blinked and shook my head to free my hair whipping into my eyes. It didn't matter if I could see. I'd forced my aching feet over this path so often that I knew it by heart.

And this time, I dragged this fallen alone. With each step, the body felt heavier, my every footfall more difficult to place.

Glaring at this newcomer, I bit my lip. She wasn't looking at me, wasn't attempting to help drag the fallen slave like we'd been ordered. To disobey the guard was asking for more abuse. But then, she'd only arrived with a new shipment of people Devota deemed unworthy of an ordinary life.

Was it my job to explain it to her? *No.* Yet I couldn't resist wanting to help. "They'll beat you if they catch you dawdling," I warned as we passed the first cells. Moans and cries mixed with whimpers, but it was the silent rooms I noticed. More dead? I swallowed hard, my mouth too dry. The Somman fae would only revive them to torture them further. How cruel, to be near the freedom of death only to return and suffer more.

"I ain't dawdling." She stood peering around the guardless chamber. Paused at the threshold, she seemed to be on the lookout.

She's in for a rude awakening. There was no safe place down here. No refuge to hide. No—

I stood up from dragging the body into the cell. A cramp spliced through my back from straightening too fast.

Tiny tips of flames heated my skin as I hesitated too close to the wall of fire bars.

What is *she looking for?*

I glanced around, peeking through the hazy gaps of the bars as she stood there intently studying the chamber. As she waited, staring across the rushing river, my jaw dropped.

Guards. They were *all* gone from the chamber. It was mostly empty since Devota was away, but they were always present in passing, walking around and ordering us somewhere. Except for now.

A thunderous crack sounded from the other side of the hot, cavernous chamber. The room echoed the noise that didn't belong. Grunts and growls of a fight came over the roaring din of water rushing in the narrow river splitting the halves of the patio.

She nodded once. "Aha. There."

There what? She'd been waiting for that noise? I couldn't stomach another attempt at rebelling. The last time several prisoners teamed up to resist—*please, no.* I feared I'd never forget those screams.

Her grunt almost sounded like a laugh. "Last thing I'm gonna do is *dawdle* down here. So, come on." She faced me then. After a brusque flick of her hood, she freed her ancient, leathery face from the shrouding shadow of her cloak's hood.

Recognition hit me so hard, I refused to believe it.

Ersilis? *Here?*

I closed my eyes and shook my head. Was this it? I'd finally cracked? At last, I'd gone insane, imagining the cranky Rengae healer who'd once kicked me out of her rental room. That onerous old woman who'd healed me at Kane's bequest before teaching me—barely—how to mask my power. Ersilis couldn't possibly be here.

"You ain't got time to dawdle either," she told me in that throaty bark of impatience I hadn't forgotten. "Come on!" She squinted her one eye at me, her brow etched in lines beaded with sweat.

I stared at her outstretched hand, daring to hope. Daring to believe it.

She grunted, limping closer to grip my hand and tug me forward.

At the contact of her wrinkled flesh so cool to touch on mine, a blast of power smacked into me and robbed me of speech.

AMABEL DANIELS

Chapter Two

Ersilis. She was here. *Here*, in Devota's dungeons of misery and fire.

I paused shaking my head as she dug her fingers into my wrist. Another balm of chilly air rocketed through me. So cold. So soothing. A cry slipped past my lips as I was flung back from the force of her fae magic bursting through me. It raced along my veins and set my wounded heart to beat harder, faster. Stronger. She sent out such a mighty gale of healing power that I fell to one knee. Had she not held on tight to my arm, I would have been wrenched free and blown back to the bars of fire lining this cell.

Rapid and insistent. It was a bludgeoning punch of an energy that I feared it would overwhelm my battered body.

Wounds closed over, bruises faded, and cuts ceased bleeding. Bones cracked anew to reset properly. My muscles quickly knitted together firmly. And the aching inflammation that had set in everywhere closed up to a dim warmth, then smoothed to nothing at all.

"Ers—" I couldn't speak as she shook, holding on to me with a fierce pinch of her lips. Her watery eye flickered pulses of blue, and her one pupil dilated then closed, back and forth.

"Ersilis!" another cried out.

Leaning on my knee, I craned around the old woman. Just as I blinked away the stinging tears of so much magic racing through my body, I witnessed a geyser of water falling onto the patio opposite me on this side of the chamber. Waves plopped down, sizzling and misting on contact with the hard, hot surface. Through the steam, a woman battled a Somman guard.

Red tresses whipped back as she was nearly pushed down to her knees. Before a guard could slice his burning blade across her neck, another figure burst forth. This bulky frame, dressed in ragged, charred scraps, tackled the Somman guard in the stomach. More grunts followed. Fists were raised and aimed as they all three scrambled into a wrestle.

Ersilis whimpered a weak sound of protest. It tore my attention from the battle across the river from us. That a battle, a fight was breaking out here, was enough of a shock. But finding *that* redhead here?

The last time I saw Princess Amaias, she'd been in the throes of another fight. Devota had merely been a princess when she and Amaias clashed in the Hunann swamp, but that fiery red hair was unforgettable. It had to be the Rengae princess.

Amaias slumped down, coughing hard on top of the prisoner she'd broken out. Another "special" guest of Devota's. In all the months I'd been captured here, I hadn't witnessed the occupant of the cells across from me. I'd heard cries, screams, and sobs. But whoever had been held over was never dragged to the colosseum to move chunks of ice with the other slaves.

Strength shot through me, my muscles tensing and bracing. Ersilis slapped her other hand over the first one, doubling up her hold me on. "Ain't no time to dawdle," she croaked out.

Was she mocking me? Agreeing?

Ersilis—and the princess—had shown up so suddenly that I struggled to keep up with reality.

I'd given up hope anyone would come for me. Of all the people in the world, I thought Kane might be my savior, no one else. No one else cared. No one else would risk coming to the ruling castle.

And if Kane wasn't here...what did that mean for his fate? I'd watched as he'd fallen over the waterfall. But I also heard him call out afterward.

"Where is Kane?" I asked, desperate to know.

She shook her head. "You have to help her," Ersilis said.

"Amaias?" I asked, standing now. Gripping Ersilis's arm, I gave her support to lean on me, too.

She nodded, refusing to cease this healing effort until I was back to normal. "The...princess. Yes."

"Where is Kane?"

Her hood flapped to the side and stayed there in a bunch over her shoulder. Spending her all on healing me, she lacked the strength to shake her head. "You'll never forgive him..."

Dread cut me down to the core. Forgive him? I dug my fingers into her arm. What could that mean? What had he done? *Is he alive?* I wanted to scream the question at her, but she struggled to stand, her chapped lips moving.

"Help the princess—" she snapped, seeming to reach an inner reserve of energy to order me until she coughed. "— said you would." With that, she flung my arm free and breathed fast and hard. Leaning over, she hunched her back and strained to catch her breath. I caught her, a hand on her side.

I was healed. Strong. *Alive.*

My existence had been reduced to suffering and agony, teased to wish for survival in this dungeon. Now that I wasn't clinging to life, I was ready. Primed and eager to get out of here once and for all.

"Help her," Ersilis ordered weakly. She kicked off her boots and toed them to me.

I looked up just as Amaias fell again. That prisoner was a lump on the ground, unmoving. If Amaias wasn't bent over coughing, she feebly hoisted a sword.

"How?" I shook my head, stepping into the boots. I was healed, but I wasn't whole. As long as I remained in Devota's prison, my body and fae powers would be bound to the perimeter of this chamber. My magic was locked. "She's bound me here. I can't *do* anything—"

"Then break the bond!" The Rengae fae stood up straight, shoving me back with the suddenness of her move. Clumsy from being so weakened and abused, I was slow to correct myself. My left foot landed close to the river's bank, and I spun my arms to regain balance.

"Break free!" Ersilis shouted at me once more. She stood mere feet away, but with the rushing roar of the river inches behind me, and the echoing clashes and shouts of Amaias's fight, her words sounded muted.

They weren't. She'd yelled loud and clear to be heard. Her words were fuzzy, my ears ringing and my brain slow to adapt.

Her order carried well, though.

After she snarled and shouted at me, vibrating growls shook through the chamber in reply. Starting at my feet, then trembling up my legs, the warning rumble spread for a long moment.

Ersilis turned, grimacing. She faced the double doors behind Devota's throne as another reason for my lack of escape was revealed. Even if I could break this binding spell, I'd need the strength to escape *that*.

A dragon. No. *Them*. A pair of them. Growling and panting hot, smoky breaths, the monsters prowled into the Riverfall Chamber.

No doubt awakened by all the noise.

"No!"

Princess Amaias had cried out that single plea, tearing my stare from the two beasts who'd been roused.

"Go!" Ersilis yelled at me. "*Go!*"

Bracing myself in a low crouch, I watched as the sable, scaled monster narrowed its red eyes on me. I was healed, but that was it. I had nowhere to run. No weapon to wield. I didn't have my tribis fae powers for defense.

Before I could panic, the dragon lunged at me. Fire plumed at me with its dive. Red waves of fire spanned my vision with its advance, and I jumped into the river cutting through the castle's chamber.

Water rushed at me with a punching force. Despite my drop into the fast-moving current, I sank straight down, spinning. Tossed and turned. I was forced deeper yet, rather than along the stream, when the dragon's mouth dipped into the river after me. Teeth cut through the water as it snapped its massive jaw shut. I slipped clear of being torn—or poisoned from its venom—by tucking my legs in and twisting to the side.

Another impact broke the surface. Wrenching my eyes open, I found it hard to see through the cloudy liquid. But there was Ersilis. She'd jumped in as well, but she didn't flail from a dragon seeking her out.

She raised her arms, using her power of water to form a bubble. Protected from the churning current, she was safe. And inside that sphere, she was quickly washed away.

Before I could be carried away over the edge with her, I reached out. Fingers splayed, I groped for something to anchor me. Anything to ground me. I wouldn't survive that fall, not without protection. Ersilis could use her Rengae magic to manipulate the water, but my powers were locked. I had no options for safety in here, and I had no means to break the binding spell Devota issued on me.

Another dragon bit into the surface, sending me deeper and to the side for the force of it dunking its head underwater. I closed my eyes and whipped out my arm to block myself from crashing against the rocky bottom. As my fingers slipped over the stones, I felt a pattern that didn't belong. Smooth. Linear. Engraved with lines. It was a handle?

A sword's hilt! I forced my eyes open as my lungs screamed for air.

A *sword*. I'd found a sword at the bottom. Turbid water prevented me from identifying it, but I suspected I'd seen it before. As I curled my fingers to clutch it, it was loosened from the rocks and was taken down the river. I spun in a spiral, tossed aside again from a dragon lunging in to bite at me again.

Whatever it was, that blade was gone.

If I followed it, I'd be carried over the waterfall to sure death.

When the next dragon bite came, I reached up. Avoiding its open mouth, I hugged its snout. In a whirlwind of water, much-needed air for my lungs, and its hot growls, it raised its head. Shaking from side to side, it tried to dislodge me. It finally did, flinging me into a column when its smoky breath burned my thigh and I'd let go.

I cried out as I smacked against the stone column. Sliding down, I scrambled to see where I'd fallen.

Not on my side of the chamber. It had tossed me close to Amaias's fight.

The princess lay there on her side, heaving for air. A Somman guard reared his arm back, a flaming whip sparking in the air.

In that moment of life or death, we made eye contact. I climbed to my feet, and the princess stared at me. Just like she had in the Hunann Swamp. She'd saved me and Kane from that tentacled lernep monster, but when she realized *who* she'd rescued, she'd glowered with disbelief. With scorn.

I didn't have time to ponder her problem with me. I grabbed a staff. It was only a busted portion of one of Devota's gaudy candle holders. I swung it at the guard before he could whip Amaias.

She tensed, bracing for the impact. Without pause, in the same forward motion, I reached down to grip her thin armor, lugging her back to the river with me.

"No!" she protested.

"More dragons will come," I argued.

As the words left my lips, three more ran out from the double doors that had locked them in.

She stretched her hand back toward the prisoner, but I pulled her with me harder.

"No!" She wrestled my grip. Only with a deft kick to the back of my knee did she lose me. From the momentum of dragging her to the river—the only safety from the dragons swarming the Riverfall Chamber—I once again fell in.

This time, I dropped in but didn't sink. Ripples of magic surrounded me. The pulse of magic was unmissable. Through an opaque curving sphere, I gazed up at Amaias on the bank. Leveling me a lingering hard look, she glared at me from up there in the chamber.

A bubble. Just like Ersilis had given herself for protection.

Princess Amaias used her Rengae force to shield me inside a bubble while she stayed behind.

I couldn't make sense of it. Wasn't I supposed to help her? To get her out of here?

She'd have no chance of survival once Devota returned. She might not live long enough for that. The dragons showed no mercy.

All for what? That prisoner?

I didn't have time to try to understand. As the bubble picked up buoyancy in the slim river, I was tunneled away with too great of a speed. Holding my breath, I pressed my hands against the formation.

Would it hold? Would it burst?

Am I going to die?

I floated faster. Faster yet. I rocked in a violent sway, cast along the stream.

Over the edge of the falls I went. Air was suspended. My heart raced at the topsy-turvy sensation of flying. Of floating. Of being flung into furiously fast torrents of the river charging over the earth's slope.

I didn't need to fret about the bubble holding. It couldn't matter now. I was powerless to think because I was smacked unconscious anyway.

I fell over the waterfall, housed in a bubble, and left the Riverfall Chamber I'd been bound to. Princess Amaias's spell held. Water was repelled in a spherical push around me. And as gravity forced me to fall with the river, Devota's binding hex broke.

Darkness swiftly followed.

Chapter Three

In and out. Darkness claimed me, a simple nothingness. Then just as quick, bright, blurring swirls of water threatened to blind my eyes in slips of lucidity. One moment faded into the next in this jagged transition of time and space. Awake, then asleep. Gasping for air, then snoring.

I couldn't track how long I shifted back and forth. The only constant was the swift current. Flowing, floating, rolling. It wasn't always a gentle wave I rode. In the mere blips of awareness I was allowed, I registered hard, full-body punches against the bank's rocks. Some dips felt deeper. Turns and curves pushed me into spinning cycles until the elevation smoothed out in my favor.

Over the waterfall, along the river, and into the swamp, I could barely register where I was.

But I was alive. As I recovered from the strange dream-inducing haze that came after being broken from a strong binding spell, I was aware I lived. Nausea competed with calm. Dizziness mixed with sluggishness.

But I was whole.

This wasn't another twisted mirage of wondering if I'd escape. I wasn't loopy and disoriented after a cymmin branding or the noxious torment within Devota's dungeons.

I was out of that hell. I'd survived.

As the morning sun rose, the warmth blanketed my back. A gentle, comforting spread of heat unlike the fierce fires in the castle's cells. Mixed with the slow breeze of fresh air, I tried to make sense of the contradiction.

Real? Or another dream? I'd only ever endured heat in the castle. Somman fae ruled the power of summer. The last time I'd been outside, it was a frozen, ice-bitingly cold winter. Ice. Sleet. Snow.

The absence of the chill jarred me, and I woke up on this muddy, slippery slope. Whatever spell Amaias had cast on me in the Riverfall Chamber was broken. Or more to the point, the bubble she'd enshrouded me in had popped. Lying on the odorous bank, I lifted my shoulders, testing my range of motion. I'd lain on my arms beneath my chest. Clawing my fingers into the surface, I frowned at the sensation of slimy ooze squelching them deeper into the earth. I tried to push up, to rise to my feet, but after the slumberous effects of no longer being bound, I was clumsy. My cheek slapped right back down to the brown mud.

Chin up, Maren. This wasn't my first time recovering from a binding. I'd been bound to Dran, trapped there and never able to leave the village's perimeter until Kane carried me over it.

Kane.

My heart beat faster at the reminder. The mere thought of his name roused me.

He'd broken me out from my home. I had no clue where he was now, and I imagined if I hadn't been secured in a bubble that floated down the river, I never would have been forced out of that binding spell either.

Just like the first time, I was tired but free. It wouldn't last long. Breathing steadier, I eased into consciousness and waited for my limbs to react to being mobile once more.

Kane. I refused to lie here until I knew. Until I could discover what happened to him. Thinking of him pushed me to move.

I rose to my knees, still shaking from the atrophy my body had while I floated. How long was I in the river? Hours? Days? I'd only managed a flimsy grasp of time passing by tying those miniature knots in my hair like a calendar. Each knot marked a day, but since I'd fallen out of the Riverfall Chamber, I was lost. In time and location, I was so utterly lost.

I stood, slowly and cautiously as I tested out my body. Ersilis healed me, but rolling over a waterfall and along a mighty river earned me more bruises and scrapes since.

How far had I gone?

Spinning in a steady circle, I took stock of my surroundings. Humid mist clung to the ground, swirling around me in a thick cloud. Trees stood in a thick wall from the bank I looked out from. Behind me, between a low branch of a heffen tree and a fat trunk of a cypress, I thought I spotted something in the murky distance.

A turret. The castle? The blurry sight was of something higher than me. The mainland's biggest castle had been built into the highest mountains on the eastern coast of Contermerria, but I stood at a lower elevation here.

I straightened my back, listening for threats and waiting for an ambush. All was quiet. All was still. But I couldn't be alone. To assume so would be stupid. I had no map to confirm my guess, but I'd trekked through this swampy area before. If I was south of and lower than the former Vintar lands, there was only one place this dank, wet forest could be.

I'd washed up on the shores of the Hunann Swamp.
I think.

Reaching up, I pulled back a braided mess of vines. Warm to the touch, the coarse fibrous strands stung my skin. I frowned and jerked back, peering at the minute thorns pressing into my skin. After I wiped my hand over my skirt, I tilted my head to better peer through the opening in the canopy.

A tan face with large eyes punched into my view. Opening its mouth to show tiny, curved teeth, it screamed at me as it swung down from a tail wrapped around the branch.

I stepped back, startled at this thing so near my face. My feet slipped in the slick mud, and I gasped in too big of a breath of warm air. Stagnant water stank everywhere, the rank filth heavy and cloying in this forest.

It blinked its dark eyes and assessed me. Staring me down, it cocked its chin up as its shoulders drew back. It heaved in a breath. As it pried its mouth open again, wider, it dropped lower from the branch and lurched toward me.

I cringed at the howling, scathing hiss it released. Before it could nip me, I raised my fist and punched it between its wide-spaced, inky eyes. It choked on its tongue, perhaps not expecting a blow. With my forceful jab, it wheeled back, then again, wrapping in a rotation around the tree and too stunned to stop.

I shook out my hand, unused to combat after so long in prison. Flexing my fingers, I dismissed the blood trickling from my knuckles. Brown knobby bumps had at first resembled mud-caked scales, but after making contact with it, I realized his hide—or skin—was instead composed of gravel-coated horns.

Clamping my lips shut, I held back muttering or screaming in pain. It stopped spinning and hung limply, its eyes droopy and unfocused. I'd knocked it out, all right. No bigger than a turbbit, it wouldn't take much to be rattled unconscious.

Still, I nursed my hand, rubbing the ache from punching those nubbed horns. I frowned at the creature. It had no hide, no shaggy hair. Smooth, horny skin covered its body. No coverings to protect it from the cold.

What cold? When Devota killed King Vanzed, she ended that royal's reign. Vintar—the fae of winter—no longer ruled. She'd replaced the winter with summer, and it was with that drowning numbness that I realized what this meant.

Sunshine baked the earth, causing moisture to rise and cloud the lower canopy and ground of the swamp. Trees stood green and free of frost. Water rushed by in the stream that had delivered me here—an abundance of liquid from so much snow and ice thawing over the last four months.

I'd landed in a surreal vision. No snow? No ice? It was such an unbelievably odd concept that my first instinct was to refuse it. Had I not punched that humanoid creature, I wasn't sure I'd trust that I was standing and that my eyes revealed *this* environment. Had I not given myself a smarting injury on my knuckles to know I was indeed awake and lucid, I would have dismissed my sanity as a lost cause.

Summer. Not winter.

Here in the swamp, I saw and felt the effects of the massive thawing. Plants unburdened from the snow. Roots exposed with the absence of ice. And the warmth. It was a cloak of unyielding heat. Sweat trickled down my back and along my temples. My skin buzzed with the exposure to the air. Flesh no longer covered and protected but able to breathe and soak in the sunshine.

Realm above. It was *summer.* I couldn't have felt more like a foreign displacement if I tried. Born in the age of iciness, I struggled to adapt.

As I removed my outer shirt, charred and burned from the dungeon, and ripped and torn from the river, I flinched. The horn-skinned creature gurgled, hanging upside down.

I had no time to stand here stupefied. Gawking at this warm swamp was a pastime I couldn't afford. If one creature wanted to surprise me with a hiss, others would be lying in wait too.

After I tied my long-sleeved garment to my waist, I pulled my feet from the mud, kicking the excess muck from them. Eyeful of my surroundings, ears listening, I turned again to survey where I was. I'd stick to the river. Going into the depths of the swamp wasn't a rosy alternative to consider. Some meager opening in the canopy was provided in a route where the river cut through the marshy ground.

I adjusted my skirt, wishing I could lose it. Striding through the low, thick brush and soggy yet stiff grasses would be easier with a man's trousers. In this state, though, I couldn't complain.

I'd managed to escape Devota's dungeon. Nothing could be worse than what I'd faced there.

As I walked from the slope where I'd washed up, I stretched and took stock of my injuries. All the while, I remained alert. I didn't know where to go, but I wouldn't be aiming for a return to the palace—ever.

Where is Ersilis? She'd shown up so unexpectedly. And she'd left abruptly too. I saw no sign of footprints, no marks that anyone else had passed through here. We hadn't left the castle in a similar fashion, though. Yes, we'd both dropped over the falls in bubbles, but she'd controlled hers. I'd been cast away in one from Amaias, and then was forced asleep after the binding hex was broken.

Ersilis could have planned her escape and manipulated her course through the river. She must have premeditated going *into* the castle. Not only making a deliberate strategy to enter the Riverfall Chamber, but also with the express destination of freeing and healing *me*. With Princess Amaias.

I'd left her— *No.* I hadn't willingly abandoned the royal woman. I'd tried to follow Ersilis's command, as sketchy and sudden as it had been given. I'd attempted to pull Amaias to the river with me and save her from the dragons, from Devota's eventual return. She'd refused. My last image of Amaias was of her standing there so stubborn, defiant to send *me* away.

Once again, others decided my fate for me. I rolled my eyes as I walked, unamused that the minute I could hope to have a fate other than endless slavery and torture, someone once again dictated my purpose.

Swaths of vines hung low, sopping wet with sticky gel. I'd learned my lesson by touching that first plant. Without ice and snow as a barrier to my skin, it seemed any number of defensive exteriors could harm me.

Quickly, in the briefest burst I could control, I sought the fae magic coursing through my blood. After months of nothing, I wasn't prepared for the hit. I'd long since dismissed the idea of masking my power, of keeping it on a leash so others wouldn't detect me using it. As soon as I opened myself up for the charging pulse of my Vintar power, I flinched. My shoulder jerked to the side as though I'd physically taken a punch. My fingers trembled, and my heart raced. Fisting my hand, I concentrated on that innate mask I'd mastered before Devota used me as a pawn. Intangible, it was nothing more than a mental effort to wrest control over this magic. Before it consumed me unfettered.

"Ah," I gasped in a breath as I winced, unused to this raw, vibrating energy spiraling through my arm. Rusty. I was without practice to attempt anything more than a jagged, mostly flat blade. A nub for a hilt, an almost-sharp point. Fashioning a simplistic weapon from ice, I held a mediocre dagger.

Nothing like *my* dagger.

"You're going to pay..." I seethed in a low whisper. That promise was for Devota. She'd used *my* father's dagger to stab me in the back. I could have sworn I saw the sheath slung from Xandar's waist. Knowing the princess's right-hand man had my weapon didn't make the situation any better.

Stabbing me in the back was bad enough. Binding me to the dungeons for slavery was worse. But taking my fae blade—a tool I never ceased to recognize as a part of me that was missing?

No forgiveness would ever come for that transgression.

Anger fueled me, the mere thought of Devota and Xandar enraging me. I rotated my wrist, acclimating to holding a weapon. Primed with my combative emotions, I produced a second, longer blade from my other hand. Smoother, sharper, with a better handle.

Practice made perfect. I'd feel more like myself again soon—

And I did. Using my magic without masking it was foolish. I hurried to conceal my use of power, threatened by a welcoming presence of another charge of magic.

I paused, listening carefully and raking my stare through the dense, wet greenery.

Nothing moved. Not a squeak sounded.

I'd felt it. I sniffed, although it wasn't a *smell* I'd sensed. But I felt it. I might be readjusting after such a long binding, but there was no mistaking that inner warning.

Danger was near.

A monster?

I glanced up, wondering if a dragon circled closer, hunting me after detecting my use of fae ability to mold blades of ice.

The thick canopy blocked the skies. No. It had to be something in here, in the swamp...

Water trickled along my fingers, my ice daggers melting in my grip. My fingerprints caved in on the ice, and I drew in a deep breath to relax. To ready myself for whatever approached with the wickedly foul odor of danger.

More. And more. Strikes of the scent assaulted me, like barbs piercing through the air. Something—many things—charged for me in this forest. I cleared my mind to focus on a fight.

It'd been a while. It'd do my soul good.

I was a healer at heart. But a woman could only take so much.

It was time I fought back.

I raised my hand and slashed my dagger to the right, cutting clear through the curtain of vines. Running forward, I stayed ready and low to the ground.

"Halt!"

I ignored the woman's order, throwing my dart at the beast dropping from the trees.

AMABEL DANIELS

Chapter Four

"I said *halt!*" the woman ordered again, a battle roar of an instruction.

I tuned her out, rearing my arm back to throw my dagger.

My aim wasn't great. The ice dagger was shoddy. But it had a point and it drove into the beast's stomach as it fell from a branch.

Shiny brown. Its shell-like armor of exoskeleton protected the mammoth scorpion's back and neck. My ice stabbed into its thorax, and it spun in its descent. Fat, clacking claws shuddered with its plummet. No longer able to control its movements or direction, the large form crashed down on the woman. Larger than a man, the scorpion knocked her to the mud.

I'd already formed another ice dagger—faster than before—and masked my power as I braced for more to attack.

She grunted, rolling out from beneath the massive scorpion.

"Watch out!" I flung another ice dagger at a smaller, skinnier, yet faster mutant as it dropped from another branch.

The woman growled, on her knees and glaring at the second fallen enemy. It, too, had come too close, pinching its claws a mere foot from her leg.

She blasted water at me, a tunnel force of a wave from her hand. "I said—"

Unprepared for her strike, I fell back. Squished into the mud from the rough hit, I scrambled on my hands and knees to scoot up as another beast fell to the ground. It clicked its pincers as it turned to me. On my butt, I gritted my teeth and formed another ice dagger.

Forget about shielding my power or masking anything. I was under attack. From these swamp mutants *and* this woman who wanted to tell me to stop among the danger.

I wasn't obeying *her*. I'd survive regardless of what she wanted.

Seated in the mud as I caught my breath, I was at a lousy angle to throw my dagger. The scorpion charged forward. My ice blade bounced off its shell, and I retreated again.

The scorpion ran, small feet eating up the distance. I thrust my back against a trunk, losing my breath.

Panic threatened. The ache of missing my dagger tugged at me. If I had it, I'd *know* how to fight. It would intuit how to defend me.

In the mud as not one but now two scorpions rushed at me, I was stuck.

I growled, relying on my anger to catalyze my magic. Shifting to my side, almost lying face down in the mud, I slapped my hand to the wettest part of the mud and froze it.

Tan chunks of frost flickered up in a spray rippling outward. I dug in harder. Faster. I let my fae power burn through me as I froze the mud, with the scorpion in it. Feet were caught and remained immobile. Clacking their pincers, they tugged and wiggled to free their limbs.

I stood, pushing off the mud with my hand. Five of them remained in place, legs wedged into the thick iced mud.

"I said—" the woman shouted.

As I formed two swords of ice, I glanced at her. Stuck in the frozen mud I'd controlled, she placed one free foot on a log and squatted, trying to bust her other leg free of my spell.

"Halt?" I mocked her as I strode to the scorpions. One by one, I walked on the frozen mud and sliced them in half.

I'll tell you to halt.

"You—" She jerked to break her leg free. Hard mud locked her at the ankle. With a full-body arch of her back, she strained to get out. Failing that furious motion, she growled again. Her helmet fell off, showing a short cut of bright-red hair. Fidgeting, she cursed in a language I couldn't understand.

Calm while she fumed, I killed the scorpions and caught my breath from the fight.

On a frustrated cry, she glared at me, then raised her hand.

I might have been slow, but I wasn't stupid. She'd already blasted me with water once, and I wouldn't give her the chance to surprise me again. When she shot a geyser of water at me, I used my Vintar power on her and sent the water back at her as a cyclone of frost from my hand. It spiraled around me, not a flake touching me, as she watched it slam back into her.

On *her* butt, now, she growled and grunted, shivering. "Sadera!"

I raised a brow at a man yelling in the distance. Glancing around the swamp for more scorpions rushing at us, I was curious that *she* would be here. Were those swamp monsters here for me? Or her?

If the other Rengae princess was lurking in the swamp and assuming she had any right to tell me to halt, I must have washed ashore closer to Rengae, the land of the sea. More south than what used to be the realm of Vintar. Again, I looked back, to the north, to gauge how far I was from the castle I'd fled.

As I gave the irritated princess my back, though, she sent another burst of water at me. "Get me out of this—"

Without facing her, I changed her water strike into ice, slamming it into her face.

"You Vintar scum," she spat, growling and straining to get out of my muddy ice. "Get me out. Now!"

Once more, she resorted to her fae magic to attack me. Her water did nothing more than annoy me. But her insult intrigued me. She thought I was *only* a Vintar fae? She was ignorant of the fact I was tribis, possessing fae magic of all three realms.

"Sadera!" the man called again, his voice closer now.

I squinted into the distance, giving up on trying to guess how far I was from the castle. Those spots in the sky might have represented dragons circling close by. I wouldn't take my chances.

Again, and again, Sadera blasted water at me, and each time, I froze them and pushed it right back at her. My spell wouldn't last. It was no longer Vintar. Winter wasn't the norm. Any minute now, I imagined my muddy ice would crack and melt from the heat surrounding this rank swamp.

"My brother is coming. You better get me free before he finds me like this," she warned. As she sat back, her hands on her calf as she tried to pull her foot free, her armor plates shifted and clinked.

Another scorpion rushed at us, having dropped from a tree. It zeroed in on her, feet skidding on the muddy ice. I waited until it almost reached her and sliced its head off.

"You don't want the wrath of a prince. Not my brother," she said, chin thrust out.

"I hardly care what a prince thinks," I retorted dryly. A bigger scorpion ran up, and it took two swipes of my ice sword to kill it before it reached her.

"Besides." I leaned the tip of my ice sword to the muddy slab trapping her. "You're welcome, by the way." Gesturing at the scorpion corpses, I dared her to sass me.

Sadera shuddered as the dark-green blood streaked toward her from the head of the small one. She swallowed, then clenched her teeth to glower at me. "Get me out of here!" Once more, she blasted water at me, and I froze it into pellets. Each time I countered her magic, I masked myself. Yet I could have sworn I smelled a dragon's approach.

"Stop," I ordered her. "Stop using your power."

She groaned, her face red as she sent blast after blast of water at me.

"You'll attract—" A spray of water hit my face. I was done. I was finished with this nonsense. As pounding hooves approached, I froze the princess silent. Using her water strikes, I immobilized her hands mid-air, arches of ice keeping her still as she sat there.

She was a royal. No doubt trained and at least educated in how to use her magic. Maybe all royal fae were by default stronger than others—even an ignorant tribis fae like me. Yet, she sat there, fuming under my spell, locked into ice and unable to move her hands.

Could she break free? I bet she could, but before she'd try, others approached.

I formed another ice dagger as a troop rushed into this clearing. Elkhorns skidded on the muddy ice. A shorter steed whinnied as it slipped in its stop, crashing into a tree. Astride another interesting mount, though, was the person I needed to see.

Not Kane.

But someone who owed me an answer.

Ersilis dismounted the sleek and furry creature's saddle. She frowned at me, then at Sadera in the ice.

"Don't, Maren," she croaked in warning. "Don't use your power. It's too close to the castle. The dragons and Sommans will detect it."

Once her words floated into the air, proof was provided. A dragon's scream cut through the swamp's quiet.

We *were* too close, and those dragons had to have scented our use of fae magic here. I glared at Sadera but focused back on Ersilis.

"What did you mean?" I demanded of her as she inspected the carnage I'd caused. "Why won't I forgive Kane?" Since she spoke that line, it nagged at me.

Scorpions lay in bloody heaps. Ice had four Rengaen fighters slipping and sliding. A muscular man gaped at Sadera, amusement dancing in his eyes. Another rushed to her, falling to his knees to chip at the arch of ice locking her arm in midair.

"Get me out of here," she insisted of me. As soon as her hand was free, she sent water at me.

The redheaded man striding forward from an identical animal as the one Ersilis rode raised his hand. He reflected the water at Sadera in a drizzle. "Enough, sister."

Sadera winced as another Rengaen struck at the ice. "She dares to disobey—"

"I don't bow to you," I snapped. When the man grunted, I sneered at him. "Nor you." Facing Ersilis as she surveyed the scene, I asked again, "Why won't I forgive Kane? Did he survive?"

She scowled at me, sniffing as she lifted her face to the sky.

"*You* won't survive," Sadera retorted. "A *Vintar* thinking she can come through here and—"

On another growl of frustration, she wrenched her elbow out of the ice arch. Hand free, she pointed a spray of water at me.

The man and I reacted at once. Me turning her strike to ice and him reducing it to a drizzle.

"Enough," he ordered at the same time I said, "Stop attracting the dragons."

"I won't take an order from *you*," she hissed.

I looked at the broad-shouldered redhead. His frown was almost hidden in his thick beard, but there was no missing the disappointment in his eyes. The emblem representative of the Rengae realm was barely legible from a sash tied around his upper arm, but it told me enough. This was Prince Baraan, Sadera and Amaias's brother—but it seemed he held more wrath for his sibling than me. "Then listen to the prince."

Sadera snorted, straining to get free.

"Baraan," Ersilis said, her frown ever-present as more dragons cried from afar. "This isn't safe. It's a fool's errand, and—"

I stood at her side, at least familiar with her. Ersilis had helped me in the past. I didn't know why she'd aligned with these royals, but she was my direct link to answers for what mattered.

"Kane," I repeated to her, ignoring the others. "Is he—"

"You must help him," Baraan replied for Ersilis.

I straightened, giving this prince my full attention now. He'd shared that clue in a calm tone, but the worry in his gaze wouldn't dissipate.

"Kane's alive?" I asked him, since Ersilis was so recalcitrant to answer me. What was it? What was she searching for here? Peering at the scorpions, frowning at the ice lock I'd given Sadera... Then again, she'd jerk her face up at the sky. If Ersilis was on edge, I would be too.

Baraan nodded, leading me away from his sister. He dragged back the unruly red locks that fell over his face with the action. "Kane is alive. After the reign ended, we found him in the swamp."

I swallowed, my mouth so dry with this news. My eyes stung, and I breathed faster. Tears of joy threatened to spill as I tried to believe him. The impossible. That Kane was alive after all...

Elation dared to burn hotter. Kane was *alive*. Someone had witnessed it. He'd survived the fall from the palace.

"Barely alive," Ersilis muttered.

Ever the downer. My shoulders dropped.

Baraan raised his hand as though to silence her. "He wasn't armed to defend himself from the swamp, but he lives. And you must help him, Maren."

"Help him?" It wasn't a novel notion. When I first met the infuriating thief, we'd allied with each other. He guided my departure from Dran to help me find a kalmere plant—I hadn't. In exchange, I was to assist him in finding his grandfather's sword—we didn't.

Sword.

I blinked, a phantom tease of a vision hitting me.

A hilt? I'd fallen into the river, and I'd reached for it. *Didn't I?* Was *that a sword?*

The haze following my plummet to the moat had me doubting myself. Was it a dream? A memory? Wishful thinking as I feared imminent death?

I couldn't tell, and I couldn't trust my mind either.

"Where's Amaias?" Sadera demanded, interrupting both Baraan's words of Kane's survival and jarring me from the foggy memory. If it *was* a memory.

"You left her there?" Ersilis guessed.

I shook my head.

"She's—" Baraan cleared his throat. "They're dead?"

"Devota ain't there," Ersilis told him. "But them dragons came out and..." She flipped a hand toward me. "Well, ain't she or is she? I escaped before you."

I shook my head again. "Amaias was alive when I fell in."

"You *left* her there?" Sadera said, now free and limping toward us. She slipped on the ice, fury clear on her face. Her nostrils flared as she fisted her hands.

I raised my ice blade. "Amaias refused to come."

Ersilis huffed, muttering as she walked off.

Baraan shook his head. "She'll..." He closed his eyes and drew in a deep breath. "Amaias can handle it. She'll—"

Sadera reached me, shoving at me with both hands. "Amaias broke in there, just so only *you* could come back?"

I caught her wrists, this dormant awareness flaring to life in me. Xandar might have my dagger, but I wasn't helpless without out. I was fae—a warrioress at heart.

Pulling Sadera with me, I somersaulted back. After a twist, then a flip, I was on my feet as she lay on the icy mud. I pointed a blade at her neck, and she scrambled back. Baraan intercepted, shoving my ice blade aside and putting himself between us.

"Enough!" he ordered her.

Sadera bared her teeth, pointing at Ersilis. "She was supposed to get her in there so Amaias could free the prisoner."

Ersilis marched close again, her gait wonky from her gimp. "I did!" She thrust her finger at me. "And she's free!"

"She doesn't matter!" Sadera yelled at them.

"She *does*," Baraan argued. "Because she can help Kane."

"I don't care about him! Or her!" Sadera winced as she stood. "We need to retrieve Amaias and—"

I stabbed my sword into the muddy ice, wedging it firmly between the siblings.

Baraan stilled, staring at my interruption. Sadera curled her lip, mouthing her annoyance as she looked away.

"*Where* is Kane?" I asked.

That was all that mattered. These water fae could argue all they wanted. It was no matter of mine. I was done being a pawn. Or bait. Or whatever else they fought to agree upon.

Baraan licked his lips. "When we found him, he wanted to go for you, in the castle."

I nodded, uneasy at his hesitant reply. I knew nothing of this man, only that he was one of three royals for the southern coastal realm. His tone was firm, a deep baritone that *sounded* regal, but his reluctance to speak bothered me.

What is he hiding?

"But word came of...danger. I promised him we would help break you free. Amaias volunteered."

I shook my head. *Spit it out.* Kane wanting to rescue me made sense. We were allies. We were... I drew in a deep breath. He was mine and I was his. That connection *had* to be true. My heart wouldn't lie.

But why would he leave it up to someone else to break me out of that dungeon? Why would he trust someone else with my life when he'd taken it upon himself to be my protector all across Contermerria?

"Where is he?"

Ersilis whined quietly, rubbing her forehead as she paced. "You'll never forgive him..."

For what? A scream waited on the tip of my tongue at her worried tone. I forced my dry throat to swallow. *I'll never forgive him for what?*

"Where is he?" I demanded.

Baraan furrowed his brow. "He left to go up north."

I frowned, trying to understand. *North? Of here? So...he went to the castle after all?*

Sadera scoffed. "To save *your* sister."

Chapter Five

Thea.

My lungs seized on the air I held in. I blinked, deafened by the drone of my pulse in my ears. Panic—dread—settled in swiftly.

Thea.

My sister. These Rengae royals were bickering about *their* sibling. How I'd somehow been expected to play a hand in rescuing Amaias.

But my sister...

Sweet, innocent Thea who wore her heart on her sleeve. Caring about books and wanting to teach others how to read. Weak and helpless from her longuex infection.

Thea! She couldn't suffer. I hated the mere idea of her in pain.

"Save—" Words wouldn't come, not easily as I drew in shallow breaths of panic. "Save her from what?"

I'd only left her in Dran because we were split up. She was safe in the village caverns—locked up safely as the frecens attacked. I'd taken off to help her, to find a remedy for her, knowing she'd be protected with the others in the caverns while I was gone.

But months had passed. She'd be out now, repairing the village since the threat of the frecens no longer lingered.

I gripped the prince's shirt, pulling him to face me directly. No more evasion. I wanted answers *now*.

He stared me down. Still and blank with his stony face.

"Save her from what?" I bit out.

"After we found Kane, he asked for her to help." Shifting out of my grasp, he gestured at Ersilis, who still muttered and paced.

"I had my men fetch her among the refugees fleeing the coast, and we planned to break into the castle. It has been hell since Vintar ended and Somman took the throne. Kane wouldn't budge from going after you. When we neared the castle, the closest we'd gotten, I captured a Somman. A guard." He licked his lips. "We got him to talk."

Tortured him. I didn't care. I couldn't. Not when my sister's safety was challenged.

"The guard shared that Devota was sending elite troops of fae with dragons. To Dran," he explained.

To get Thea. I didn't need to ask why. After I'd thwarted Devota, I'd earned her everlasting wrath. Her hatred.

Queen Devota wanted to get Thea to further torture *me*. To hurt *me*.

I didn't need to wonder anymore. It was clear. Queen Devota would capture Thea and use her as bait. As a punishment. Or to simply kill her to get back at me. Any harm done to my sister would strangle my soul. To allow anything to happen to the only family I had...

No!

I bit back a sob and went to Ersilis. "Why would I never forgive him?"

She shook her head. "Kane wasted all that time trying to get to *you*," she spat. "While you're fae, a tr—" She clamped her lips shut, darting a glance at the Rengae royals behind me. "You're fae," she clarified carefully.

I understood at once. She'd almost called me out, identifying me as a tribis fae, empowered by all three realms. It seemed Baraan and Sadera didn't know that and Ersilis deemed it a secret to keep.

"Your sister is weak," Ersilis scolded needlessly. "*She* needs rescuing more than you. If Kane doesn't reach her soon enough. If he can't beat Devota and the dragons she sent up to your village..."

I'll never forgive him for not saving her. For not saving her when I couldn't.

"Your sister, this commoner, is *weak*," Sadera scoffed. "And therefore, cannot matter."

I lunged at her, my hand around her throat at once. Whatever water she sent at me in defense turned to ice at my magic. Shards dropped to the swamp floor, and I squeezed harder.

Her hands gripped my forearms as she strained to breathe. Ersilis tugged at my arms. Baraan banded his arm around Sadera's waist to free her. Both shouted at us to stop as Sadera repeatedly sicced feeble bursts of watery magic at me.

A dragon cry sounded closer, and I gritted my teeth, knowing better.

We couldn't be detected. Not this close to the castle. I refused to return there.

With a violent shove, I released Sadera. As she fell back, she kicked out at Ersilis standing at my side.

The old Rengae fae fell, grunting, and I caught her.

"You," Sadera said, pointing her finger at Ersilis while Baraan held her back. "You agreed. You were supposed to get Amaias in there *and* back out."

"So long as we freed *her*, too," Ersilis growled, holding on to my arm as she panted.

"Yes, because we promised Kane we would free Maren for him," Baraan cut in roughly, slanting a hard look at his sister.

Sadera pursed her lips, scowling as she pointed at Ersilis again, her finger trembling. "She was only supposed to free the Vintar to help Amaias with her mission—"

"What was her mission?" I asked. She hadn't gone there to rescue me.

"To get Isan out," Baraan answered, gritting his teeth.

The Vintar prince? I didn't want to know why. That had to have been the lump of a prisoner I'd spotted across the river.

"I don't care about her sister," Sadera shouted at her brother. "Or Kane. Or whatever you and he conspire about."

"It's not a conspiracy but the truth," Baraan shouted at her. "And Maren must help him before it is too late."

"Help Kane with what?" I snapped. It didn't matter what these Rengaens wanted. What any royal fae wanted. I was done with them. I'd hear out this prince, but my mind was made up. I would travel home and see to it that my sister remained out of Devota's clutches.

"To end the Somman rule," Baraan said.

I laughed bitterly. "It *just* started."

"It cannot continue another day," the prince vowed.

I threw my arms up, sick of this game. I'd gone from one urgent, confusing mess of everyone wanting the Vintar reign to end. Everyone had plotted to assassinate King Vanzed—even Kane had at first.

And now no one wanted Somman to rule either? I didn't care. They were all horrible.

But Queen Devota was a sadist. An evil being.

No one wanted to kill that woman as much as I did.

I shook my head. Why *me*? Why was this burden on *my* shoulders?

"*Queen Devota* cannot sit on that throne," Baraan said.

I spun back to him, pressing my lips together as hard as I could. Ending a reign was only accomplished with one action—driving a fae blade through the ruler's heart. I'd *just* witnessed that ordeal. I'd tried and failed to save King Vanzed from that very fate. Because Devota's blade murdered the Vintar king, she was now in charge and the season of summer—of Somman—commanded the mainland.

"Then who should?" I spat back. "You?" I pointed my ice blade at Sadera. "Her?" *Prince Isan? Is that why Amaias went there to get him out? To restore the Vintar Reign?*

Baraan shook his head as he told me, "You must help Kane find his grandfather's sword—the Ranger's sword."

I groaned, rubbing my hands over my face. That sword. The "item of importance" Kane had so deceivingly asked me to help him find. His adoptive grandfather's sword—the tribis fae blade—that had been lost during King Vanzed's reign.

I shook my head. "No. *No.*" After spending months wondering where that weapon was, and with all the secrets about fae blades, I was in no mood to entertain a repeat of the very search Kane never shared details about until it was too late.

He'd had the sword in his hands. And lost it to Heir Prince Isan. Then *stole* another royal's sword—and lost that too, again, to Heir Prince Isan. In a swapping chaos of weapons, too many swords had clashed in the Riverfall Chamber at the king's death.

Did I grip this Ranger sword in the river? I didn't know, and I didn't care. I was done with this mess. They had no right to expect this of me.

"No," I repeated, lowering my hands and facing Baraan again. "I won't. I'm going to save my sister. I've sacrificed enough of myself, and I won't be a pawn in any other hunt for a sword again."

Sadera strode forward, her back straight and her eyes fierce with loathing.

"You need to get *my* sister." She slashed her arm at her brother as he rushed up to argue too. "Forget those damn swords. You need to go back and get Amaias out of there."

I pointed my ice blade in the direction of the castle. Water dripped faster from the edge, and rivulets streaked along my arm. "I'll never return to that castle."

"Amaias helped you escape," Sadera argued. "She had *your* back."

I bit my lip, afraid of what I'd blurt out as guilt hit me. Amaias *had* defended me. She'd saved me—twice, actually. First in the swamp against Devota, and again in the castle, sending me away from the dragons.

But Amaias hadn't broken *me* out. She'd gone straight for Isan, not me. Ersilis was the one who'd healed me in the chamber.

I looked between the two Rengae royals, feeling like I was missing something. Which was a sensation I didn't care to experience any longer.

"You must go back and get Amaias out," Sadera demanded. "You owe us."

"I owe you nothing," I retorted, glancing at Baraan as he stared me down. "I won't be your pawn. I won't go looking for that sword again."

"Devota needs to be stopped," Baraan insisted.

"Tell me something I don't know!" I paced away, then back toward him. "*You* end her." I tipped my hand toward his waist, spotting no sheath, no blade. "You're a royal." I jabbed my finger at my chest. "I'm not. Use *your* fae blades to end her reign."

Sadera sucked in a deep breath, grunting as she exhaled in a long rush.

"No?" I mocked when the prince didn't reply. "Not a good idea? Where are your blades? Huh?"

Baraan licked his lips, not making eye contact with me. Instead, he turned his head to the east, staring absent-mindedly.

"Stop this bickering," Ersilis argued. "Where's yours, Maren?" She tugged on my arm, coaxing me to look away from the prince. "Where is your dagger?"

"Her healer—her—" *Xandar.* I snarled at the thought of the Somman fae who carried out Devota's plans. "They took it at the castle," I said, stating the obvious.

"Then you go back for it." She nodded curtly, once.

"No. You go back for Amaias," Sadera interjected hotly. "You go back and get Amaias and Isan out of there."

Why does she care about the heir prince making it out of Devota's dungeons alive? When Kane was extradited to the Vintar castle, it seemed that the war of the land was fought between Somman and Vintar forces. But Rengae...what was their role in this? What was she referring to when she accused Baraan of conspiring with Kane? Just to get that sword?

It wasn't my business. It could *not* be my concern.

Thea was my concern. Making sure she was safe was my priority. I trusted Kane to see to it. He understood how much she mattered to me. He wouldn't let me down after all we'd be through, but...

Devota cannot rule. I shook my head, torn by the burden that fell on *all* of the mainland now. If she could stoop so low to steal the throne the way she did...

She must be stopped. This was a fact no one could deny. A truth I felt deep down.

But is it my *war to take on?* I swallowed, hating the role I'd played in getting her in the position to have the rule of the land within her grasp.

"You will!" Sadera blasted a wall of water at me, interpreting my shake of a head as a refusal. Both of her hands were up as she stalked toward me, her brow lined and her mouth curled in a snarl. "You *must* go back to the castle and get Amaias out!"

"You don't tell me what to do—" I sliced my arm through the air, turning her wave into a sheet of ice. Before the opaque shelf could fall and shatter on the ground, claws cut through the wall.

Talons broke apart the barrier between me and Sadera. Then legs showed in the commotion. Scaled legs. A deafening roar. And so much heat. Fire streamed at me as I pushed Ersilis behind me.

A dragon plowed through the canopy, at last detecting our location as a result of Sadera using her power. I had, too, but in defense. If the hotheaded Rengae could just listen and mask herself...

I gritted my teeth as Ersilis cried out. She flung her hands out and fell, shooting up a geyser of water. I froze it instantly, shielding us from a brutal swipe of those talons.

"Halt!" Sadera shouted again from outside of the ice shield I'd cast over myself and Ersilis.

"Foolish, *foolish* woman," Ersilis grumbled, getting to her feet.

Telling a dragon to stop *was* idiocy.

"Baraan, stop her!" Sadera ordered.

Double blasts of water pummeled at the dragon that swung his tail around and cracked the ice formation. Brother and sister both shot their fae power at the beast, sending it screeching and twisting to get to the ground. I covered my face with my forearm, building a shield of frosted shards that fell on us.

Sadera was telling *me* to stop, not the monster. *Still*, she sought to control me? To keep me here to order me around?

"What does she want?" I asked Ersilis, hiding behind the shield. With my left hand, I sprayed up water, with my right, I froze it. It fell to the ground in front of Ersilis, and she picked up the flat piece, hoisting it in the same manner as I did.

"Don't tell them," Ersilis answered instead. "Tribis," she added for a blunt explanation.

Oh, I was no stranger to hiding myself. To concealing the fact I was the same as the now-extinct Rangers, a fae with all three powers. Kane—and Ersilis—were the only ones who knew. I'd keep it that way until I knew who my enemies were if I ever truly would.

"I ain't—" The wizened woman cried out as the dragon bit her ice shield and tossed it aside. I ran at her, forming another slab of ice as a sword. Fighting back the monster's snout, I winced as slices of my weapon melted off from its hot, smoky breath.

Ersilis cowered behind me as I battled the dragon. "I ain't—I don't know. I don't trust her. Any of them," she told me in a choppy breath, leaning around me to assist with sharp jets of water at the dragon.

"Sadera. She wants something," she mused.

"Who doesn't?" I snapped.

"Them royals..." She growled as the dragon spun too fast and knocked her over. "Always got a plan. Then 'nother secret plan. Always with them beasts and blades. You get yours," she advised. "Go back."

The dragon snapped my ice sword in two, and I gritted my teeth to form two ice daggers. "To the castle?"

"Go to the castle and get your blade," Ersilis urged. "Then find him."

I arched back, parrying strikes with the dragon as it bobbed its head from my hits. "You mean *them*?" Kane *and* Thea.

"Get your blade and find him," she repeated. "And make him explain before they come."

Getting answers from the man who had my heart was *not* an easy feat. It was precisely what I intended to do, though.

Faster and faster, the dragon busted my weapons. I was getting nowhere in this fight, clumsy and unsure unlike when I had my weapon. Each time I struggled to pierce the vulnerable spot on the dragon's neck, my frustration scaled higher. If I had my father's dagger... Knowing Xandar had helped himself to it angered me more.

"Before who comes?" I asked Ersilis.

Baraan cried out, and I wasted a precious moment to watch as he was flung into a tree. A smaller but fatter dragon swiped its talons at the prince, sending him flying.

I clenched my teeth and formed two more daggers. Then I jumped on the dragon's snout the next time it lowered to spray fire. In the middle of a fight, the Rengaen royals wouldn't see that I used my Somman magic. Too much commotion gave me the chance to spell the dragon's fiery breath back into his throat, protecting me from being scorched as I climbed on. It roared, coughing and seizing as it swallowed its inferno back down too soon.

My patience was shot, and I finished him. I stabbed my ice daggers into its scales. Cold splinters cracked free on impact, but I wouldn't kill him with petty pricks. Like needles. No. Every time my icicles snapped, I reformed short loops of ice blades to climb up. I clung to his head as he whipped it side to side to toss me off.

Closer, closer. I was almost there.

Sweat dribbled down my face, blurring my vision. Heat slickened my fingers, and the ice melting worsened my grip. Yet, I refused to let go. I ground my teeth together, dismissing the pain of his hard scales bruising my flesh and the ache in my muscles as I climbed.

Higher.

A little more.

Right there. I clutched a newly formed fat staff and aimed the point at the dragon's softer spot. In went my weapon. With a keening screech, the dragon flailed and fought weakly. It went down, and I jumped clear of its body before it could smash over me on the ground.

"Maren!"

I jerked my head around, spotting Baraan on the ground. Sadera lay next to him, a smoking heap.

He raised both hands, panting and begging me with his stare. Water plumed up, cascading down on the dragon diving its head down to bite him. I lifted my hands and froze his tsunami, locking the monster inside.

It shook and beat its wings, struggling to break free of this cube.

I don't think so. I didn't have time for this. It was different, fighting a monster with another fae at my side, but I couldn't trust this Rengae prince who made demands of me—ridiculous wishes like searching for a freaking sword again. Looking for *that* sword.

I *knew* I couldn't trust Sadera.

But Ersilis had come through for me. And with her warnings to be cautious, I doubled down, thickening the ice until it squeezed the dragon like a vise and exploded.

Chapter Six

I squinted to protect my eyes from the debris falling to the swamp's soggy ground. My feet squelched in the mud as I dodged larger chunks of body mass. A dragon tooth flew up and arced back down, and I stepped out of its way. Panting, I stood there and watched the remnants of dragon and frost filter through the swamp's mugginess.

Baraan shook his head, seeming to clear it as he stood. On his feet, he didn't look as vulnerable, as defeated, but his steps toward his sister were slow and cautious.

"The princess!"

Cracking out the kinks in my neck, I turned toward the source of the cry. Rengaens had come, hiding off to the side. A half dozen or so stood there beneath the vines draping from a cypress. Most were slack-jawed, eyes wide as they stared at me. The one who spoke was likely the tall woman who darted toward Sadera. Jewelry of bones and strips of scales adorned her wrists and torso. All of them sported the same grungy, ragged attire of mismatched, wet garments. No uniforms here, but they showed as a collective front. Dull metal hung at their hips, their swords filthy, and the shorter two of the group tensed with fat triangles of darts in their hands.

Was this the Rengaen royalty's attempt at an elite troop?

I coughed once, my throat raw from breathing in too much dragon smoke close up. At the sound, the Rengaens cowering beneath the tree flinched, rearing back as one.

Skittish, aren't you?

"She will live," the taller fae told Baraan once she reached Sadera. She skated her hands over the smoking body. Frowning, she took inventory of the foolish fae princess who thought she could call the shots around here. Sadera couldn't. Not with a dragon. Nor me.

"I will heal her—"

The prince set his hand on this woman's shoulder. "Not here." He stared woodenly at the sky hidden from view. "We're too close. Healing her would be detected..."

Speaking rapidly, the fae ordered the others to come close and adjust their transports. They'd move Sadera and heal her closer to their realm.

Coming down from the rush of fighting, I relaxed and steadied my breaths as I watched them hurry. Four more of those interesting beasts approached. Saddles waited over their sleek, short tawny fur. Their conical heads prompted me to think of a horse, but the rotund shape, with large, circular eyes, called to mind an otter. Taller than a standard wolf, but shorter than a horse, it was clear the low-lying animals were a steed. Muscles bunched as they waited with whinnying growls, shifted by the Rengaen hands readying a sling-like carrier.

"Too close," Ersilis said quietly for my ears only as she, too, watched. "But not close enough."

Her implication was clear. We stalled out here in the dangerous swamp, near Devota's castle but not within it—where everyone claimed I should be. I clamped my lips tight, irked at these constant orders to go. To return to the castle. I'd *just* gotten out of there! What about what *I* wanted?

"Get your dagger, and find him," Ersilis reiterated.

It was curious that she shared the same sentiment as the Rengaen siblings, yet she made no mention of retrieving Amaias from Devota's dungeons.

"And leave the princess there?" I asked quietly, watching with her as Baraan and that leading fae picked up Sadera to slip her into a carrier.

"She is...like you."

I raised my brows at her.

Ersilis shook her head and wiped the water from her eye patch. "Ain't gonna listen 'til she wants to."

Stubborn, then.

"If she ain't wanting to leave, she'll have her reason."

I understood her summary. I *should* get my dagger back and find Kane, but Amaias was her own boss. I preferred it that way. She hadn't listened to me in the Riverfall Chamber the first time, anyway.

I didn't need any further prompting to reclaim my dagger. As I shifted my weight on my feet, I winced at the searing burn of the smoke that laced my leg. I'd escaped the castle to slide right into a life of battles, and I needed the confidence that dagger lent me if I intended to survive to find Kane and Thea. Blades morphed of ice wouldn't last against constant peril.

"Are you working with them?" I asked, tipping my head toward the Rengaens. A couple still glanced back at me, unsure. They must not have ever met a Vintar fae, which made sense. King Vanzed had recruited and trapped them at his castle—or so I was told. When one tripped on a shard of dragon bone and gagged, I shrugged one shoulder. *Or perhaps they'd never witnessed a dragon exploding.*

Ersilis frowned at my uncomfortable stance. "With *them*?" She glanced at the ragtag group and shook her head, approaching me with her hand out. "No."

When she crouched to press her hand to my knee, I hissed. Healing power spiked hard and fast, and I breathed through the rush of energy. "Yet you're traveling with them. You're—"

She removed her hand and gripped my arm to stand straighter. A sign of weakness, it seemed, and my worry grew for her. Just how worn was she from all this? When her fingers firmly bit into my elbow, I realized her disguise. Leaning close to me, feigning the need for support, she pulled on my shirt to bring my ear closer to her mouth.

"Too many secrets. Too many wars..." She cleared her throat, the rumble low and wheezy. "Kane is fighting the *right* war, and it is *him* you need to align with." Rearing back, she looked me straight in the eye.

Not them. The message was clear: *Forget about the royals.*

I nodded once, and she released me. She didn't need to share that in confidence. I already knew who my priority was. Thea. And the one person who mattered was already seeing to her safety.

"The scouts are close," a Rengaen told the prince.

"For the camps," another clarified. "They've burned Tonias, and no one remains in Scellin."

Baraan looked at the ground, fisting his hand. "What of the refugees in Scellin?"

I strode closer. "What camps?" Ersilis told me to mind my own, to steer clear of the royals' problems. But this wasn't endemic to the fae. Camps? Devota's camps? I'd only caught a mention of them when I'd been a "guest" at the Somman palace.

"She captures them all," Baraan said, "to place them in internment camps." His rough-skinned hand gestured toward the west, toward the dry realm of Somman. "To purge Contermerria as she sees fit."

I held his stare, matching it with a somber expression of my own.

Devota must end.

I sighed, surveying these water-loving commoners and fae as they stared at me with their prince. Each one bore expressions of hardship. Life in Contermerria was always strife with danger and struggle, but it was clear that Devota had worsened it over the last four months.

He raised one brow at me, a simple emphasis of what he expected of me.

"The Scellin have traveled to the Poround Shore," one said to Baraan.

"Poround?" He shook his head. "When did they leave? It's most vulnerable to the sea now that she's—" A grunt interspersed his rapid shouts. "Between the flash floods and storms, the waters are too high and—" He raked his hand through his hair. "When? When did they go? They'll never survive it without my help."

"Two days past."

Baraan gritted his teeth, hurrying toward the animals. "Let us go. We must make haste. *Now.*" He glared at me, then at Ersilis.

"What?" I asked.

"Will the Vintar come with us?" one asked Baraan. "To aid us at the shore?" He peered at the largest chunks of the dragon I'd exploded. "Surely, we could use the help."

"She has other responsibilities," Baraan said. He reached into a saddle pack and tossed a rough-clothed sack to me.

I caught it as I marched up to him. "I'm not your citizen. I'm not yours to order."

"She can help us at the shore," the Rengaen protested again.

Baraan stared me down as I glanced into the bag. Clothes, boots, a flask, and dried meats. "But you are one of *us*. It is all of us against her. Against—" He shook his head. "We must all fight *together.*"

Impossible. A united force would *never* happen with too many secrets among the royals.

I stabbed my finger at my chest. "I must find my sister." Then I cut my hand through the air. "That is all."

"You'll turn your back on us?" he challenged me.

"I—"

Ersilis heaved in a deep breath as she hobbled to stand between us. "Take my ride, Maren," she said, gesturing for her animal to be presented. "And go."

A Rengaen led a creature toward me. Faint hints of pink showed among the sandy fur. At first, I feared it was blood. Was it wounded? It stalked with strength. Long, muscled legs touched the mud with certainty. Upon closer inspection, the rosy shimmers showed more of an ethereal metallic glint.

Sadera was bundled in a carrier, moaning faintly as they hastened to leave. As I took the reins to this saddled beast, Ersilis backed up, maintaining eye contact as she was helped onto another.

"The corga will follow you over the land," she said, "He will carry you well."

All the way to Dran? Because that would be my destination. Not the Poround Shore. Not the castle. I'd stop there to get my dagger on my way home. That was it. I'd embroiled myself in these politics too much as it was.

"Please," Baraan said as his people hurried to mount their corgas and horses. It was a simple farewell left to complicated interpretations.

I lifted my hand. Not in a dismissive gesture nor in a wave of agreement. Acknowledgment.

I'd heard him and what they wanted from me. But I was done serving others when none of them ever considered what mattered to *me* other than how much they could use me. The last time I was approached by royals, they betrayed me. The lack of trust they instilled in me trumped my compassionate nature. They'd hardened me, whether I liked it or not.

Most importantly, this sword, any of their fae swords, was their responsibility. Not mine. I was a common healer who happened to be a tribis fae. Not a royal. Just a nobody they wanted to do their dirty work.

I'd lean on what Ersilis whispered, instead.

Without a look back, the Rengaens parted, racing through the swamp.

I climbed onto the low saddle and balanced myself on the corga's back, registering how high I lifted with its deep, heaving breaths as it waited for my commands. Unlike the tall elkhorns and sturdy ashirs the Sommans used for transportation, this animal was patient, eager to receive my direction.

I'd go get my dagger. And see to my sister's safety.

Hopefully, forgiving Kane wouldn't be a matter to consider. Because if he didn't get to Thea on time and keep her safe in my absence...

I shook my head and steered the corga north.

I don't want to think about it. I couldn't. Dreading the worst and imagining Thea in Devota's clutches would ruin me. My heart already beat too fast, weighed by the burden of my one, true responsibility—Thea. All I ever wanted to do was see to her happiness. She was too innocent to not have that basic need.

And Kane...

"You can't fail me now..."

Emboldened by the news he lived, I wanted to take faith in him more than ever before. For him to race across the mainland to see to Thea's safety, it meant he *did* love me. He did understand me. I had to have confidence in him until I could reunite with him.

Riding on the corga's back, I crouched low to his coarse fur. My face pressed low, my cheek bristled from the friction of his short, choppy mane, I avoided getting smacked by the hanging vines and stout branches shooting perpendicular from the thick trunks.

At the first scent of danger—a monster—I redirected the corga. It leaped, bounding off the trees in another level of a speedy race through the Hunann Swamp.

Goblins chased, but the corga growled, nipping at the closest fiends while I shot bursts of fire at them. Further on, troll-like beasts lumbered after us, fat, rocky fingers groping at me to pluck me off the corga's saddle. It only ran faster, climbing and jumping from branch to branch where the blind monsters couldn't see or reach.

Panther-like, the corga proved to be a driven beast, its webbed paws light over the soaked terrain. Gripping the reins, I squinted to reduce the burn of sweat sliding into my eyes. Heat followed no matter what shadows we sprinted under. Muggy, rank air clawed at me near the point of suffocation. In such a blur, I couldn't catch my breath. I couldn't slow my mind to think, overwhelmed by the contrast to what I knew.

Green plants blended to the point of confusion. Bright varied colors of blooms. Mammoth insects buzzed and flitted too close. Animals of fur and scale, all of them so foreign I didn't consider what they were.

I couldn't afford stray thoughts about this new, surreal environment. All I could lock down in my mind was the need to find a way back to the castle.

"Easy," I murmured to the corga after hours of a dash through the swamp. It slowed to my command, panting, and I slipped off its saddle. After that nonstop pace, it needed a break before it fell into exhaustion. On my feet, I led it with the reins. Once it lapped at a stream of less-muddy water, I rummaged through the sack Baraan had tossed to me. I quickly changed into the dry clothes, not caring how some seams of the shirt seemed too tight and the trousers too loose. They were dry—for now. Best of all, these boots fit perfectly. The ones Ersilis had given me had fallen off in the river, too loose on my feet.

I kept a careful eye on our surroundings as the corga relaxed and drank. I ate and drank, saving the majority for later.

Eyeing the animal that had served me so well thus far, I strapped the pack to the saddle and placed a protective ward over it.

A dragon's scream immediately followed. I froze, waiting to hear more. If it had detected even that little bit of fae power...

I'm close. Dragons—smaller but potent ones—lined the perimeter of Devota's castle grounds. The corga pawed at the mud, circling with strange grunts. It was anxious to move. I couldn't blame it. My ward might keep it alive, but I didn't want to expose it to the hell within the queen's reach.

I hadn't placed many wards, and I didn't want to test if it would hold to dragon fire.

Creeping through the foliage, I peered up the best I could. Too many trees blocked my vantage. The castle had to be higher up, but the vegetation was too thick for me to orient myself.

A grunt sounded close. The coarse whiskers of the corga's snout nudged my side.

I lowered my hand at it, to urge it back as I explored on foot.

It didn't listen, bumping its head at my knees. Falling back slightly, I scowled at its persistence. It caught me. Slumped over on the saddle, I realized it wanted me to ride. So I did. I climbed back on. Before I grasped the reins, it jumped, nearly bucking me off.

I held my breath and clutched the reins tight. From branch to branch, it scaled the tree. Instead of standing on the ground trying to look up for sight of the castle as darkness spread, it changed my odds. It climbed so I could look out laterally at the land.

Finally, on a thick, slimy branch of a tall heffen tree, it slunk toward the sky. Air was clearer here, not as heavy and dense with the foul humidity of the swamp.

Near the tip of the extension, I hugged the corga, the pommel of the saddle a hard protrusion into my ribcage.

There, before us, was the castle.

I was back.

Chapter Seven

Fires danced from the turrets and dragons circled the towers. Looming dark and mighty, the queen's home did *not* express any semblance of welcome. But I dismissed the omen of death and destruction the structure suggested.

The last time I'd raced to this structure, I'd done so with a fevered rush to save Kane. I'd been so sure he'd be killed under King Vanzed's order, wanted for attempted assassinations. What I'd found instead, was how Devota had used me—used my concern for Kane—to break into the highly guarded palace and take the throne for herself.

I shook my head, anger rising anew at her duplicity.

That time, I'd barreled on the back of an elkhorn, storming right up to the front gates. I'd faced the elite guards, a herd of mutant hur-wolves, and then got lost in the maze of white and blue within the unadorned interior of the castle.

Tracking the turbid waves in the moat I'd floated along hours ago before I was dumped into the swamp, I knew I'd need a different route of breaking into the castle.

I'd burrowed through to get in last time, then picked my way toward the dungeons to save Kane.

I couldn't rely on that method this time.

A bat flew close, whipping its dark wings in a frantic flurry. I winced, ready to blast it with a spray of fire from my hand. Using my magic this close to the castle would be too easy for the dragons to notice.

The corga solved it. Snapping its sharp incisors at the flying pest, it growled a lethal warning.

"Go," I halfheartedly told the bat. But it didn't. It retreated a few feet, then approached closer, hissing as its eyes flared red.

White material showed from its long, finger-like appendages. Talons tipped the curved digits, but within their grasp was a rolled-up parchment.

Instead of birds, they corresponded with messenger bats? I frowned, eager to intercept the communication. One hand on the corga's saddle's pommel, I leaned out to grab the rolled message. The corga lunged its head faster than me, biting the bottom of the wing. My fingers closed on half of the parchment, ripped in two when the bat left us.

It cried as it flapped its wings faster and faster, but its downward spiral had begun. Slanting over the corga, I furrowed my brow and watched it smack into leaves and branches on its way to the ground.

"Hmm." I twisted my lips. "Thanks." I patted the corga's shoulder. *I think.* It might have been handy to know what the entire message said, though. Was Devota back? Had her guards sent word that I'd broken out? Or was that the message that just plummeted to the swamp's fog?

Hanging on to the horn of the saddle, I readjusted in my seat. Under the pressure of my hand, though, the rough leather cracked. Connected with a small hinge, the horn opened like a case.

"What's this?" I wasn't sure why I'd taken to speaking to the corga. It wasn't as though it could reply with anything other than a grunt. Perhaps it could understand me, somehow intuiting I'd wanted a clearer, higher view, but it wouldn't speak.

Between my thumb and forefinger dangled a slim cord. I extracted the length of it from the interior of the saddle horn's small compartment. Strung on the plain leather was a tube marked with strange holes. A whistle? I pressed it to my lips and tried a short puff of a breath.

The corga's boxy ears pointed up, at attention.

"Handy..." It must have been trained to answer to its sound. I slung it over my head, and the whistle piece settled between my breasts. Hidden beneath my shirt. *Very handy.* Once I was through in the castle and had my dagger, I'd have a way to find this corga to take me to Dran.

Because I *would* retrieve my dagger. I stared at the rushing water cascading down the mountainside, the very conduit that expelled me from the Riverfall Chamber and broke Devota's binding spell. I would reclaim my dagger one way or another...and I knew how I'd go about reaching it.

First, I smoothed out the parchment. Scribbles and illegible script spanned the page. I didn't understand it, written in a code like this. Two clues were evident, though. The ink was still smoking, wet with a Somman spell branding the markings to the parchment. It was a new or recent message sent out *from* the castle, not returning to it.

Most importantly, though, it was signed with a clear *X*.

Xandar.

He'd signed this message, recently. So near the castle, it had to mean he was in there again. And where he went, so did my dagger.

"Come on," I murmured to the corga, prodding it to retreat on this branch. I needed to get back on the ground now that I knew what direction to go in. Being up high showed me the lay of the land, and my next leg of the journey would be without this beast.

Once the corga jumped down to reach the muddy soil, I led it toward the river. Bats and dragons made circuits overhead. The closer we came to the fast current cutting into the swamp, the foliage cleared more, showing the beasts of the sky. Inky black wings spanned wide with loud flaps as they patrolled, but this far from the castle's wall, I hoped I would go undetected.

So long as I masked my magic, I should be all right. I'd have no choice but to employ it once I neared it, though.

Water bubbled and churned in front of the corga's feet. It sniffed and jerked its head, then pawed at the sloshy bank.

"You'll stay," I whispered, fearing a Somman guard hiding this close.

The animal snorted. In agreement? Arguing? I couldn't tell. I slipped off the saddle and stepped to the edge of the water, letting the bubbles spray over my new boots. Peering up the stream, I wondered how hard this feat might prove to be.

Because my plan was to sneak in the same way I'd left.

I took one step into the river, balancing on a rock and testing the hydraulic speed dumping from the mountains.

Then I fell.

No.

I was pushed, once again. The corga prodded my back and dipped low, manipulating where I stood until I was on its back—*in* the river completely.

I gasped, swallowing too much water from the spray. Clinging my legs around its waist, I hugged my arms in a tight circle over its head. I blinked, narrowing my eyes to see in this sudden challenge to my vision. Drenched once again, I fought not to lose a grip on the reins to the corga.

Stubborn animal!

I held my breath, braced for a swift sweep further from this spot, but the corga remained steady. Anchored. Its muscled legs stood straight like beams wedged in the current.

How...

I shook my head, then risked removing one hand to wipe back my hair covering my face. Seeing clearer now, I realized the corga wasn't only a creature intended to ride over the terrain—or jump from tree to tree—it was also a swimmer.

Versatile with its powerful and sleek body, it moved its limbs in a sturdy stroking manner. Cutting *against* the river, the corga once again reminded me of an otter, a mustelid creature I'd once read about in Thea's books in our basement home in Dran.

Running, jumping, or swimming, this corga was dependable no matter what.

Head half above and under the violently wavy surface, the corga swam opposite the river's direction.

How it could *know* what way I intended... It merely had to *see* where I wanted to go and assumed? Then took over?

Unlike the royals and humans who tried to dictate my life, I couldn't deny this corga had a better sense of how to take charge. Or to commandeer me to the fastest transportation.

Holding on tight, I rode the corga through the river. Hidden in the water, I relied on the cover of the night and the corga's swift strokes to reach the castle. I'd imagined using my power to make a forcefield and trudge up the river to the moat. That would have been riskier, my expenditure of magic easily detected by the monsters. The corga carried me instead.

Until it could go no more.

Guards and dragons remained ignorant as we slipped along the river, through the constructed moat, and to the point of the fall. Water thundered from above as we waited behind the falls crashing to the moat. Soaked and nervous, I hid with the corga, taking a moment to relax and focus.

"Go on," I urged on a hushed breath. It couldn't possibly hear me under the roar of water splashing down, but I hoped it sensed my hands on its flank, pushing it to go back down the river. I daren't speak any louder. It was deafening here, but I was cautious. Paranoid.

I'd dreamed of escaping for so long that trying to break back in was the antithesis of my soul. I didn't want to see the Riverfall Chamber again. I didn't want to set foot in the dungeons again.

But I had to.

The queen was hunting down my sister. Likely rabid to seek revenge on Kane as well.

I had to be prepared to face her, to stand up to all the perils I was sure to meet on the way home. It was imperative that I collect the dagger that called to my fae blood and charged me to act like the warrioress I was...

No other choice remained. I had to climb up there and get my dagger.

Chin up.

Still, I sat there behind the waterfall and stared at the violent spray.

Chin up!

I drew in a shaky breath and closed my eyes. Behind my lids, the darkness led to my imagination. Replaying the torture. All the brandings. The abuse and neglect. Darker yet, I revisited the image of Kane, beaten and near death in the Somman dungeon.

In phantom memory, my muscles tensed and ached in remembrance, the pain so very real as though Ersilis had never healed me. The whistling crack of a fiery whip sounded in my ears, the droning thunder of the waterfall distant.

Panic.

It settled in so fast that I couldn't breathe. My heart raced, my fingers trembled. But a blossoming throb at the small of my back silenced the sensation before it could overwhelm me.

An absence. A connection that remained severed.

The spot my dagger used to wait in a sheath. The lack of that very weapon punched through me, erasing the grip of panic until I could draw a deeper breath.

"Chin up," I commanded.

My exhale shuddered from me as I lifted my head.

"Face forward." I lowered my shoulders and inhaled a steadier gulp of air.

"And hang on."

Sucking in a deep breath, I dove into the water and lowered my mask. Relying on my Rengae magic, I formed a halo. A bubble-like effort in the fashion of a rain shelter. Domed, so the waterfall pummeled off and aside me, rather than forcing me down. At the same time, I used my Vintar might to spell a hook of ice. Then an axe to pick into the stone.

It didn't work. Water rushed over me, not at me, with my dome of a force manipulating the water falling down.

But I couldn't cut into the stone. Ice was harder than the water, sure, but it wasn't hard enough to pierce into the mountain's stone.

I improvised. I lowered my hand, sending out ice in a tower based beneath me to stand on. Atop it, I could reach the slates of stone polished smooth from the constantly churning water. Laying my fingers flat on the rock, I spread out a sheet of icy frost, forming handholds to grip.

It didn't last, crushed and weathered from the river pounding on it. But I could move. Reach by reach, I forced my way up. As soon as my fingers curled around a protrusion of ice, I hoisted myself that much higher. Once I shifted upright and formed another adhesive icy slab stuck to the rock, the current ice hold would quiver, tremble, then crack apart and shatter down with the river's force.

My power burned through me, lighting me up with a fever to fight, to run, to take on the world itself. And using my magic was the most daring aspect of my plan. Dragons—any monster—could detect me. Other fae could as well. A suctioning pulse would be felt the more I employed my abilities.

Yet, nothing came. No dragons stabbed through the waterfall to bite me. Nothing gave chase. Climbing up the mountainside with the river falling over me rendered me numb. I couldn't hear anything but the roar of water. I could feel nothing but the ice at my hands and the spray drenching my lower half. I saw nothing but the blur of the river.

I was alone, and—I hoped—undetected.

For what felt like an eternity but was likely only hours, I scaled higher. I feared it was an illusion. A ward tricking me to think I was making progress when I hadn't moved an inch. Without the use of any of my senses, I counted on the throbbing burn of the muscles in my arm. I strained my body in a taxing exercise to hold on and climb. I had to be there soon. I refused to consider the alternative, that I'd fallen. That I was merely hanging on at the level of the moat.

At last, the rocks changed.

Smoother, straighter, then curving beneath my fingertips.

The edge! I'd reached the bend, the change in direction where the water fell free from the mountain to plunge below. From the vertical plane of the water streaming with gravity to the land below up to the horizontal flat stretch. I'd crawled and climbed all the way up to the lane of the river that cut through the chamber.

I'd done it! I was there.

Breathing faster, I was riled by the triumph of accomplishing a feat that should have been impossible. I fastened myself to the bottom of the riverbed.

I couldn't jump up. Not yet. I had no clue what waited in this cavernous room. I'd only fled a day ago. That was my best guess. I had no idea how long I'd floated to end up in the swamp. The corga and I rode hard all day and into the night, so for all I knew, I might have broken out of here several days ago. In the aftermath of my escape, all couldn't be "calm" in the castle.

Would Devota be here? Xandar must be. I expected an increase of guards, all Sommans on alert and angry as their queen raged.

I had to lie low. To wait and get a better grasp of what I was sneaking into.

Reducing the effect of my water-repelling dome, I strained to see through the river that hid me. Crawling with only my hands, my belly low to the rocks at the bottom, I edged further into the chamber. Nothing flew overhead. I saw no glowing fire shot around the room. Nothing could be seen looking up from under the surface.

How could no one notice me here? More so, how had no one and nothing detected my use of fae power all this way? Where were they? The guards. The dragons.

Anyone?

I couldn't trust this quiet. Relaxation wasn't possible in this empty riverbed either. Water and rocks. That was all I saw and felt. No sword lying in the turbidity. Perhaps I'd imagined gripping something when I'd escaped—a fever dream. Up ahead, if I continued crawling, I'd run into Devota's blade that she'd wedged into the center of the river when she killed King Vanzed. But if I reached that post, I'd be near the back of the chamber, too far in.

Where was Xandar? I couldn't break in here and fail to find the wretched man who'd last held my dagger. He had to be here. He'd just sent a message that I'd been lucky to intercept in the swamp.

I shook my head, uneasy to leave the security and coverage of the river. But I wouldn't gain anything lurking indefinitely.

Chin up. After I molded a sword of ice, I gripped it in my hand.

Face forward. The blade pointed straight out to my right as I crawled toward the bank.

Hang on. Higher and higher, I snuck out of the shallow yet fast river. Water streamed from me, sending my boots sliding as I tried to gain purchase on the uppermost rocks that would ease onto the dry, hot patio surface.

Flames surrounded the room, dancing and trailing up columns and over the broad walls. Décor lay in ruins, shattered and busted, if not charred to ashes. Destruction was evident in every nook of Devota's stolen throne room.

Lying low, I turned my head toward it. The throne. *Her* throne.

And I readied myself to pounce and kill the malicious fae seated there.

Chapter Eight

"No word?" Xandar gripped the guard by his neck. Devota's favorite servant sat in her regal seat. He looked down his long, bony nose at the Somman. Tiny licks of fire crept down his arm, curled around his knuckles as he fisted the tunic, then petered out with puffs of smoke. "What do you mean there has been no word?"

The guard shook his head. "No word has come from Her Highness, Master Xandar."

He shoved him back, and the guard stumbled, falling to the ground. Xandar draped his arm over the rest, flicking his fingers idly as he scowled. "You must be wrong. She has dispatched all of the dragons except for the castle's perimeter fleet. They cannot fail. They will find her."

Find me. I swallowed and tensed.

The guard rose to one knee, bowing his head low. "Of course, Master."

Xandar tilted his head back, staring at the ceiling. Then he lowered his beady gaze to the ruined chamber. Even from this distance, as I lay on the edge of the riverbank and mostly out of sight unless I climbed to my feet on the stony floor, I saw the wicked glimmer of fury in his eyes. Red flames reflected in his stare, supplementing his mood.

"But... but... until she is found, perhaps we should execute the others." The guard lifted his head a bit, too cautious to look his superior in the eye. "Before they can... escape." Swallowing hard, he paused. "Before they can escape as well."

Xandar shot up, standing as tall as his thin frame could allow. Raising his shoulders only emphasized his disproportional girth at his gut, a bulbous overhang his velvet tunic and sashes could not contain.

"Before the other prisoners can escape?" he bellowed. "You dare to suggest they *will*?"

"No. No, sir."

Xandar kicked out at the guard, nearly falling with the exertion of the action and the over-zealous effort. "Master! I am your Master!"

"Of course, Master. Yes." He dipped his head lower. "Yes, Master."

"You dare to insult me. To imply the prisoners can evade my watchful eye in her absence?" He lowered his hand, and his vermilion sash bearing the Somman crest slid aside. On the upswing, he raised my dagger, the sheath secured below his massive belly.

I licked my lips, locking my eyes on the prize.

There it was. Just spotting it fueled me into action. It called to me in a manner I doubted I'd ever understand. Seeing it in his hand...

It was a travesty I couldn't allow.

"You dare to insult me?" Xandar screamed at the guard, moving his arm as though readying to slice at the submissive guard's neck. Smoke wafted from him, and the barest hint of fire flared along his arm.

"You suggest I will fail to keep the prisoners here until Her Highness returns for their execution?"

The guard's form blocked my exit from the bank. As soon as I stood though, Xandar caught sight of me.

His eyes widened. Mouth hanging open, he lost the scowl.

I shook my head to lose the worst of the water, keeping my glare on him. "Suggest that you'll fail?" I mocked, this bravado to taunt a new thrill I embraced as I faced off with my enemy. "I'll *promise* that you will."

He clamped his mouth shut. A clack came with his gritted teeth bared for me. His scowl returned. Like no time had passed at all, he regarded me with the one staple emotion he saved for me.

Hatred.

On a yell, he raised his hand to shoot fire at me. I ran forward, lifting a shield of ice to deflect the hit. It melted a concave dent in the cold slab, but it held. It remained solid and sharp with crystals of frost shaped into barbs. Without missing a step, I charged at him, knocking him onto the throne.

"Mast—"

I turned back to simultaneously use my Rengae and Vintar powers. First water to douse the Somman guard, then I iced him in place. Saved his neck, really.

Heaving fierce breaths, Xandar boiled with a furious scream. I wouldn't let him expel it. Once I'd smacked him back onto the throne, I jabbed the edge of my shield under his chin, thrusting it up and slamming it down on his throat.

"I'll be taking that," I told him, staring him in the eye as he flailed his arms and attempted to toss me off. I tipped my chin at his right hand, and his fingers tightened on the dagger until his knuckles turned white.

"She'll..." His eyes watered as he strained to breathe, let alone speak. "Kill you."

I smiled, unafraid of this out-of-shape, wicked man. "She can try."

He sparked a flash of live heat at me, and I flinched at the burn. "But first—" I flicked my fingers at him, soaking him entirely. It was becoming a pattern, but what was that saying?

Practice makes perfect.

Just like I'd obliterated the dragon, I locked this evil master under a thick blanket of ice. Framed to his lanky arms, it spread from my ice shield that was choking him off. White, then clear, the glistening surface of my ice caught the shine of the flames flaring within the spacious room.

His shoulders were trapped first. Then his elbow couldn't bend. Further and faster, I spelled the spray of water to harden, cuffing his hand midair.

When he wouldn't release my dagger held aloft in this awkward posture on Devota's throne, I forced the ice to thicken inside. Constricting him. Cinching him.

He closed his eyes, and his head slumped to the side. At last, he loosened his hold on my weapon, and I gripped it.

The moment I held the familiar, comforting weight of my father's treasured possession, my heart sang. My breath came easier. Even my head cleared. I couldn't understand how this simple length of metal could complete me, but it did. Armed with this tool, the missing piece of my strength was secured.

I marveled at this victory, staring at it as it vibrated with a steady, low hum. Then flashed blue.

Twisting off Xandar, I swung my ice shield around as another guard rushed up. He struck with a fire-coated sword and followed with a quick flick of his smoking whip. Above him, a bat flew at me, blood-red eyes blazing with intent, its mouth open and fangs ready to pierce.

I shoved my ice shield up at the bat, sending it reeling into the river. My arm was seared in pain as the whip coiled around me, and I screamed. I'd deflected his sword, and he had yet to gain the return motion of striking at me again. Before he could, I sliced at his shoulder, severing his ability to move that arm.

Xandar gave himself away, standing with a cough. As I pivoted back to him, I faced him just in time to watch him retrieve a flame-tipped staff from a busted chandelier. He might not have the strength and agility to truly fight, but from the step higher on the throne, he had the leverage to thrust it down at me.

I lifted my hand, sending forth a blast of fire and smoke. It ate up and swallowed the staff whole, and he dropped it. A minimal gap was all that lingered. He screamed and dropped the burning staff, staring at me in both shock and fury.

It didn't matter that I'd revealed my Somman ability. He wouldn't live to tell anyone.

I thrust my arm forward and drove my dagger into his chest.

His stunned gaze locked on mine as I held my blade firm. I twisted it, numbing myself from the horror that I'd killed. That I'd taken a life. A healer. I was a *healer*. Yet, I refused to allow any guilt to hit me.

All those days he'd whipped me. Charred my flesh with cymmin brandings as he stood back and snacked like a gluttonous hog. He'd wipe the grease from his mouth with a fine satin cloth, then use the fabric as fuel. Only once it was afire would he fling it at my face, laughing as I screamed beneath his favorite method of torture.

His mouth hung slack as he lowered his arms. With my foot, I shoved his body back as I held firm to my dagger. He slipped off and slumped on Devota's throne. Dying with one hand over the gaping hole in his chest. Blood spread from the opening, running slick crimson over his fingers.

Watching him take his last breaths, I felt a strange euphoria claim me. It wasn't bloodlust, but the primal satisfaction I'd rid Contermerria of his evilness.

"You..." he croaked, snarling at me even on his deathbed.

I swiped my blade clean on the throne's armrest, then sliced at the belt he'd strung the sheath on. Fastening it to mine, I adjusted it so it resided at my back, exactly where it belonged.

"Me," I finally agreed. *I* was the one to kill him. And as soon as he expelled his final breath, I left his body as a gift—a message—to Devota once she returned.

I had my dagger, but I couldn't leave yet. Not in good faith.

Executions? Amaias had to be trapped here, perhaps Heir Prince Isan, too.

While Ersilis had warned me to leave the Rengae princess, suggesting she was fighting a different war, I was *not* a killer. To abandon her was a death sentence. I'd just killed a man—my first human kill—but I couldn't stand back and let another die here. Not while I was able to help.

I licked my lips, rubbing my thumb on the smooth hilt of my dagger.

Then I rotated my wrist, hasty to correct my grip. Just as Kane had taught me. All those lessons and sparring and practicing through the swamp. It stuck. All the tricks and patient corrections...

Kane. I had to go to him, to him and Thea.

But before I fled again...

I ran across the bridge linking the patio. On the other side of the river, I scanned the destruction, hurrying to find the other prisoners to get them out before sure death.

Even if they were fighting the *wrong* war, even if they had secrets upon secrets... she'd helped me too. She'd had my back and helped me to break that binding spell. Countering the black mark on my soul for killing Xandar, I sprinted deeper into the rooms adjacent to the Riverfall Chamber, determined to help before I left for Dran.

Chapter Nine

Shock stunned me.

I'd killed a man.

I'd taken a life.

Xandar deserved it, but the truth of that action dug deep into my psyche as I searched for the redheaded princess. The longer I dashed through here, the more I felt my time was running out. With each hall I ran down, the sinking, clawing guilt of murder ate at me.

I needed fresh air. I needed distance from these flames and heat. Every way I looked, the might of Somman stared back at me in the form of fire.

"Amaias!" I shouted. To hell with the chance of calling guards to find me. Let them swarm for me. I'd stall one and demand to be taken to the prisoners.

"Amaias!" I tried again, running down another fork of stone hallways. Heat sent sweat sliding down my spine, and with it, an irritating desire to run back, give up, and jump into the river.

"Ama—"

Coughs. I heard the faint sounds of respiratory distress, and I skidded to a stop.

That way? I turned my head back to where I'd just run from.

"Amaias?" I said, firmly but not in a shout.

"She—" More hacking coughs sounded. Not hers, but a man's. Behind me, or rather, in the direction I'd been prepared to run in.

I followed the coughing. It brought me to a closed door, and with a blast of bright fire, I broke in. The small room was dark and clouded with excess smoke. My visibility was reduced to no further than I could take a single step.

Waving the dense smoke, I squinted at the sting of it searing my eyes. "Amaias?"

"Here," the man replied, instantly falling back to coughing.

I blinked, turning my free hand in a circle as I relied on my Somman magic. The smoke collected in a similar fashion, a tornado of fumes. It cleared the air from most of the room, showing me the pots in the corner that burned with glowing embers. Propped on the low-burning coals were teeth, the purple venom from a dragon a dark, matte sheen.

I pinched my fingers together, extinguishing the flames.

Smoke faded even more, and with a soft push of snowflakes through the room, I eradicated it.

Isan sat on the stone ground. Amaias's head lay in his lap.

"You're..."

King Vanzed's son met me—informally—in Dran, where I'd served as a healer for his elite troop. But the last time I'd seen this royal, or former royal, was when I'd broken into the castle to save Kane.

"Maren," I reminded, matter-of-fact. It hardly made a difference who I was.

Too many wars. Too many secrets. It wasn't my business, but I could delay finding Kane to help this Vintar fae. I'd accidentally played a part in his father's assassination. The least I could do was help him avoid execution.

"Is she alive?" I asked as I approached. Dropping to my knees, I assessed them. In my left hand, I formed a bouncing orb of blue light, a sphere of spiraling ice. With my right hand, I made contact with Isan's bare, burned arm.

Pale, gaunt, and feverous, he raised bloodshot, weary eyes to meet mine.

"Bare—" Coughs wracked him before he could finish the word. Then he hissed as I sent my healing power into action. As he writhed slightly from my magic, I surveyed the room. Now that the fires had ceased burning and the poison no longer ate away at them inside out, I hoped they could regain their strength to get out.

I tucked my dagger into a slightly awkward hold to press my first two fingers to Amaias's temple. She shuddered as I pushed my magic to her, but with her unconscious state, I feared she'd need more effort to stimulate a recovery than Isan.

"They're going to execute you," I warned.

He frowned, turning toward the window. A fire burned in the opening, and a spell had to have been woven into it to trap the noxious smoke in here as a means of both torturing them and locking them in place.

"Dragon." He shook my hand off and placed his on Amaias's shoulder. "They're coming back."

I frowned, trying to see through the haze. The scent grew, that stink of danger.

"Use the river to escape," I suggested, anxiety tripping my body to prime for a fight.

Closer and closer, the foreboding threat of peril flew at this castle's tower.

"Her sister is eager to find her," I said in a rushed blurt. "Her brother too."

"I don't care," he growled. He flicked his blond hair back and narrowed his eyes at the window pane of red inferno.

"Just leave," I advised. "And—"

He shoved me back, breaking my hold on Amaias's clammy flesh. As I fell back, my ass bruising on the brick floor, Isan arched his free hand, closing himself and the princess in a ward.

No sooner than the pulse of magic rippled into effect, morphing from opaque to invisible, did the wall burst apart.

Larger than the ones I'd killed in the Hunann Swamp, this dragon plowed into the tower. Bricks and stone flew in an explosion, and rocking his head down after busting in, he snapped at me.

Fire plumed, blinding me. All I could do was hold on to my dagger and suck in a sharp breath as it captured me within its talons. Squeezed within its fisted talons, it hoisted me up. Through the falling chunks of the tower, it flew through the space, bashing its head on the ceiling, and shooting up into the sky.

I grunted in pain, shifting in its grip to escape being sliced apart. Expelling roars of fire, it flapped its wings. Up and down, it gained momentum, me as its captive.

Paired with my dagger, I didn't have to think. I didn't even allow panic to enter my frantic mind. Registering the dark formations below, I felt fortunate this monster chose a southward direction to soar.

Closer. A little closer...

Once it swept its wings steadier, bringing us over the swamp, I knocked my shoulder into its scaled palm, using the increased slack in its fist to raise my hand.

Dagger at the ready, I drove it into the top of its foot. It screamed, blasting a stream of maroon fire at me. I met it with ice, diminishing the smoldering strike. I sure got its attention now.

Wedging my other shoulder, I pried my upper body up some more. It clenched its talons in response, but I had the desired freedom for a range of motion to slash my dagger again. This time, I aimed at the back, near the tendons that would connect his clawed foot to his leg.

Blood sprayed out from the deep gouge as I dragged my dagger through.

I dropped, its foot dangling and unable to react to its commands. It'd planned it perfectly, only freefalling for a minute. Blasts of ice allowed for falling slabs. I stepped and fell down them almost like stairs until I smacked into a branch of a tall tree. My ribs took the impact, and my breath shot from my lips. Strapping my arms around the slippery bark, I hung on for dear life.

"Realm above," I muttered on a shaky breath. That was...a sudden fright if I'd ever had one.

I swung my leg up, using all my limbs in a coordinated yet still clumsy reach to lay my stomach on the wood. As I breathed steadier, calming my racing heart, I let go enough to slip my finger under the simple leather cord.

Trembling, I lifted the corga's whistle to my lips and puffed out the deepest exhalation I could manage.

I lay there, still and draped over the branch so up high. Eyes closed, I waited and worried. But panic didn't come. My dagger was tight within my fist. Only when I felt the thump of the corga's paws on the branch did I loosen my fingers. It growled that purring yet demanding sound I'd already grown used to.

"Found me, did you?" I teased weakly as I sheathed my blade.

It leaped over me and then licked at my face, nudging me to rise. Once I managed a shaky stance on my hands and knees, it took over. After it dipped its head beneath my waist, I hugged it instead of the tree branch. My ribs protested and my arms felt like rubber. Yet, I gave in and clung to it as it urged me onto its saddle. I slumped against its back more than sat.

I was secure. As far as the corga was concerned, I was ready to go.

"Dran," I mumbled weakly, exhausted as he moved from branch to branch, lowering to the ground. "Take me to Dran."

I didn't know if it would understand, but with each jarring jolt of him landing on all four feet, I felt rocked and lulled to sleep. Astride the corga, my dagger in my sheath, I breathed easier and placed a protective ward over him.

And casting that one spell was the last thing I could do before I dozed.

Chapter Ten

"Run. And hide." Kane pressed his lips to me. "Please."
Agony filled me as I returned his kiss.
"Don't come for me," he whispered.

A full-body jolt woke me, chasing away the wisps of a dream. I wasn't standing there with Kane in the Somman dungeons. I wasn't dreading a final goodbye with the man I loved.

Figments of the dream—*no, memory*—fell away as I squeezed my closed eyes tighter. Bright, harsh sunlight filtered through my lids. I groaned, lifting my face from the corga's back. Drool had left my lips. Between that and the sweat that the summer seemed to always induce, I'd plastered my cheek to its tawny, stiff yet short fur.

"Oww..." I felt the rumble of a moan as it climbed my dry throat. I lifted myself. Muscles in my arms protested. My neck cramped at the strange, low position I'd slept in as I rode.

Rode where, though?

I'd been vaguely aware in scattered moments of riding. And riding. And yet riding some more. Did the corga ever tire? Ever stop? For all I knew, it might have. I was only grateful I remained in the saddle.

"Where..." I yawned, and even making that facial movement worsened the crick in my neck. I blinked my eyes open, confused. When the corga growled, its hackles raising next to my hand on the pommel horn of the saddle, I realized my dagger was charged. Pulsing at my back.

And no wonder.

Two goblins circled us. The corga spun, never losing direct contact with the beasts.

I snapped to, sending out a spear of ice to pierce through one's neck. While I took care of that one, the other snarled and jumped at me. The corga bit into its leg, pulling in through the air and sending it flying into a smoking pit of a dying fire.

My pulse reached a quick peak at the perilous wake-up call. Sleep to instant danger. As I rubbed my face and held my dagger at the ready, I scanned the remnants of a town. Buildings were half destroyed. What remained standing was charred and splintered. A roof showed parallel scrape marks of talons or claws ripping through. Bodies lay in smoking piles on the rudimentary street. Elkhorns slumped near what looked to be a stable.

Death and destruction. *Devota.* Her dragons had done this. But the sword wedged in a Somman soldier suggested it was a multi-layered attack, not just her monsters running unchecked.

No sounds came forth. Not a single movement could be spotted as the corga strolled through the barren town. Scorched and left to fall to ashes. It was a warzone, empty and slain.

I squinted under the harsh, hot daylight. Lifting my hand to shield my eyes from the brightness proved to be too much. Too taxing. My shoulder ached, and I winced at the pinch in the joint.

I lowered my arm, scowling at the open burns of a cymmin branding. That whip. When I'd retrieved my dagger from Xandar, the guard burned me.

Where are we, though?

Ersilis could heal me, but she'd gone south, to the Poround Coast with Baraan and Sadera. One of their Rengae fae could have healed me too. Other than them, I knew no fae to rely on for healing.

Not true, Maren.

Heir Prince Isan, Devota, Amaias, and her siblings... I knew the royals, not as acquaintances, but I'd met them in varying circumstances. Mostly bad ones. And nothing that could sway me to think they'd want to help me.

They only want to use me. To force me to do their bidding without a care if I lived.

But what was new? My entire life, I'd been manipulated for others' desires.

Despite the discomfort of my aches and wounds from the castle, I felt safe, safer alone with this corga than having to figure out who to trust and what to do. I was on solid ground and could get by for now. But where *was* here?

Wet trees and mud were absent. I couldn't be in the Hunann Swamp. The land bordering this town of devastation showed thin, diseased trees, their trunks like twigs that could be blown over with a hard gust.

The corga hadn't brought me to the hard, barren tundra of Somman. Nor the graffiti-marked and puddled scene of Rengae.

I furrowed my brow, facing north. And sighed in relief.

High mountains stood in the distance. The Northern Peaks. Their caps were faint blue, so unreachable and up high, but they oriented me. This corga had taken me clear across Contermerria. Dran had to be near.

I patted its shoulder, hoping my caress would please it, not annoy it.

Still, no sign or sound came in this deserted area. Alert and suspicious of that quiet though, I tensed and looked around, the same as the corga did walking through. Goblins would have come to scavenge what they could, I imagined. Without anyone scaring them off... Were they *all* dead? Or captured for Devota's camps?

Needing to move, to stretch, I pulled on the reins. The corga didn't stop, perhaps too on edge to be vulnerable in the too-bright wide open of this ghost town. I could relate to its disobedience. It operated on its instincts above what I ordered, relying on its need to move and not be stationary. Staying still wasn't my objective, anyway. I slid off the saddle in motion, testing my legs and taking stock of how badly I was harmed. One foot in front of the other. It was slow going, but the more I walked next to the corga, I broke into the throbbing aches and desensitized to it all.

This was no time to delay or complain.

I was alive. I had my dagger. The corga had brought me on a northern route to Dran—to Kane.

To Thea. How could I ever gripe about my injuries when she was always suffering worse by default?

Maybe she wasn't any longer. With King Vanzed dead, his spell of the longuex would have been broken. A silver lining to the situation. Now knowing that the Vintar king hadn't been the enemy after all, I regretted that he'd been killed. I'd tried to stop it. And failed.

Enough, Maren. I'd escaped Devota, I'd slipped out of her castle not once, but twice. Yet, I still wasn't allowed a reprieve to sit and accept it all.

Later. I'll address it all later. With Thea and Kane. They'll help me make sense of it all. For now, though, my thoughts and emotions had no place in anything but survival.

The corga slowed at a stage-like wooden contraption. Centered in what used to be this town, it resembled a leftover of what had been the platform of "shame" back home. A public speaking area, where announcements, accusations, or charges could be shared with all.

The night my life had changed, I'd been dragged to Dran's.

Here, a man lay with a chest wound. He'd bled out, but none of it touched the flask at his hip. I sniffed it, then unscrewed it to find water. While I drank, I narrowed my eyes at the open flap of his shirt. No cloaks, no gloves, hats, scarves, and boots anymore. From the corpses in this town, it seemed everyone adapted to the sudden thawing and summer by trimming their garments or switching to undergarments.

A historic timepiece remained attached to a chain. I pushed it from his pocket. As the linked chain slithered down his side, the round metallic shape slipped with it. I picked it up, rubbing my thumb over the etching. A landscape and name.

Sannook.

Dran's neighboring village.

I scanned the scene of desolation, and fear seeped in.

If Sannook had met this fate...

Dran wasn't far.

"Let's go."

The corga bunched its shoulders, seeming ready. Bored, even, to go.

I dropped the flask to the former magistrate of Sannook and slipped his timepiece beneath my waistband. Charged with the urgency to go home, I climbed on the saddle. As soon as I picked up the reins and ordered the corga to go, it bounded off at a teeth-chattering, pounding run.

I was wrong. I hadn't woken in Sannook. The further north we went, I realized my error. The Northern Peaks were *too* distant, too hazy, and faint in the light blue of atmospheric perspective. Dran was nestled on the edge of the Sord Forest and right at the base of Contermerria's coastal edge of tall, scraggly mountains.

Town after town, I discovered the same thing. Either empty of life, all people and animals absent, or their slain and burned corpses. I encountered no one to direct me. Not a single person remained to tell me just how badly Devota sought to rule the mainland.

Life had been an oppressive, endless stretch of cold and ice under King Vanzed's fist, but under Devota's it seemed doubly worse.

Did they all relocate and hide? The Rengaens referenced refugees in the south. People had to be on the move—if they were lucky to escape the wrath of dragons and Sommans hunting to bring commoners to the camps. That mayor of Sannook, he, too, must have been on the run, seeking shelter in that nameless town he'd been slain in.

Until those mighty mountains loomed taller, I was still too far from home.

Driving the corga to lope faster, its paws bounding fiercely as it ate up the distance, I dismissed the awe of the landscape. I no longer got stuck in the mind-blowing concept that the snow and ice were gone. Beautiful blooms captured my eye, but I looked deeper. Contermerria wasn't devoid of life. Of people, yes. But vegetation spanned as far as I could see. Carpets of lush grass, clouds of insects, and new sprouts of trees. Plants cut through this once barren plain of the wilds, and with it, the pests.

Flies and stingers. Thick logs of worms and many-legged critters. Strange, winged creatures. Beetles as long as my foot. The corga growled and huffed as it ran, shaking its head when any of the smaller pests flew too close. While I didn't want to use my power, I unmasked it long enough to swipe them away with puffs of smoke.

At long last, we neared Dran. A sense of homecoming didn't stick as the corga brought me near. Worry and curiosity flared stronger in my mind. Sights became clearer, familiar clearings in the Sord. Shade offered a modicum of relief from the burning sunshine, but the canopy of evergreens felt too thick. Covered with vines, choking out the tall spires of pines and spruces.

I slowed the corga, trying to envision what I would find. My failure to find *anyone* in a clear run across the mainland wasn't reassuring. My heart couldn't take it if Dran was empty, if Thea was—

I wouldn't *ever forgive him...* Ersilis was right. If Kane hadn't been able to reach my sister before Devota scorched the land this far north...

Clang. C-c-clang!

I jerked my face up, hearing that distinct tone of the bell. Someone had to live. Unless a goblin lurked close, a person had to have rung that stupid bell.

Hope bloomed, but with it, caution.

Who? Who was there, though? Friend or foe? I had no friends there, none except Thea. While a lack of trust and respect had parted me from my fellow villagers, I had to consider the possibility Sommans might be walking the streets.

"Stay." I slipped off the corga. Feeling the whistle tucked under my shirt, I took faith it would be available once I scouted out Dran. But showing up on the back of an exotic beast might be too much of a shock for the residents of

Dran. I hardly cared what they thought of me or what steed I found. They didn't *know* me. They never had.

The corga grunted, drinking from a stream, and I left. Sticking to the shadows of the trees, I jogged through the thinning reaches of the Sord. Patrollers didn't march at the perimeter posts. But no dead bodies lay strewn either.

On light feet, my heart beating too fast with anticipation and dread, I ran into Dran. Villagers moved in a frenzy. Men shoveled up ashes. Women gathered possessions. Babies wailed. Children were scolded. I took it all in, running down the main path cutting through the village.

"Make haste! Leave what you cannot carry!" A deputy ambled down the street, cupping his hands to yell. "Make haste and pack only what you can carry!"

Everyone was busy, too harried in their tasks of cleaning up—no, packing—to pause and notice me. Horses lugged sleighs of burned wood. It was all torched, yet more stood standing here than in any other ghost town I'd come across on my journey.

Mrs. Gibbon squawked and hollered at her husband, *another* babe in her arms. The jailer ordered a pair of men to roll barrels toward what remained of the blacksmith's building. The market stalls, the post station, the bakery, and the framework of what used to be the stables.

All gone. It didn't take much to imagine a dragon swooping low and breathing out mighty gales of fire.

I spun in my step, taking it all in before sprinting home. *Home*, or the closest thing to it. The basement to the library felt like a prison, a lightless, cold trap to reside in with Thea.

After breaking out of real dungeons, Devota's recesses of hell, I knew better. *That* was a prison.

I skidded to a stop, breathing hard as I stared at the rubble. The library was gone. Piles of smoking ashes and charred wood hung where the outer walls stood. The basement had been caved in. It was *gone.*

If Thea was in there when...

"No."

I'd know it. I'd *feel* it if she was dead.

Shaking my head to dispel the thoughts, I turned and ran toward the magistrate's mansion.

Chapter Eleven

A deputy spotted me first. Before I reached the magistrate's front porch, that wide, once-extravagant entrance to his huge home, Dran's figure of authority frowned, then scowled at me. His shock was apparently weaker than his annoyance.

"Where you've been?" he demanded, setting his hand on his hip. "*Hiding?* Daring to sneak away from your duties while we're sufferin' and strugglin'— Hey! Michael, look who's coming back after all this time. You got a *lot* to answer for you no-good—"

I didn't cease running. Not until I took the steps two at a time, barreling up to the magistrate's home. Not as I passed this deputy, slowing only long enough to punch him square in the face. My knuckles stung, and my biceps burned. I hadn't been healed since the dragon dropped me from the sky into a tree. But I'd be damned if this fool tried to hold me back from answers.

Ignoring the buzz of my dagger activating at the small of my back, I tamped down my anger. That deputy could rot— with his dick. But he wasn't my problem. He wasn't my concern, not now.

I panted, stopping in the foyer as servants bustled and packed. Shoving goods and finery into cases, it seemed the magistrate wanted to move. Following the shouts and rambling orders he issued upstairs, I jogged forward again.

Down the hall, I went. Maids sassed me for stepping on the rug they rolled up, and I jumped over the obstacle, tracking down the magistrate's nasal tone.

The door at the end of the hall was closed. I smacked it open and let it slam against the wall. It bounced back, stopping at my boot as I stood with my feet apart, my arms raised.

On a gasp, the magistrate jerked back. His mouth quivered. Not in fear but indignation. A scroll fell from his hands, and he took a jerky step back.

"M-Maren?"

Lines bunched on his brow, pronouncing his wrinkles as he sneered down at me. Then he reclaimed a step closer.

"You," he hissed. "Get out!"

A deputy raced down the hall. Another joined him. Before they could burst into the room, I slammed the door on them, smacking them in the face. I shoved the panel shut and shoved the lock bar down. As they pounded their fists and yelled for entrance, I strode up to the magistrate.

"Where is my sister?"

He shook his head, in denial or resistance. The cranky scowl tugging his lips down suggested either. "Thea?" A pathetic growl slipped from him as he pointed at the door, walking toward it. "Get out!"

I grabbed his arm as he made to evade me. Spinning him at the same time I kicked at his knees, I dropped him to the ground. He was no true leader of this village. Pomp and title, that was all he had. This was no protector, no fighter. He went down with a struggle, but I soon managed to pin him. I slammed one knee to his crotch, just for making my life hell. Then I pushed him down to his precious ornate rug. One knee pushed into his gut, and I slammed his arm overhead.

It was my dagger at his throat that stilled him with a glare.

"Where is my sister?"

He darted his gaze to my dagger. A frown crossed his face. Blue pulses of illumination glimmered from my blade, and I tried harder to mask my power.

I gripped his hair and twisted tight, picking up his head, and then forced his skull back down. "Where is she!"

He returned his focus to me. "You're not the first one to ask," he spat.

Devota? She was here then?

I lifted and banged his head twice more. I had *no* patience. He had no idea what he was playing with. After facing royals, liars, and betrayals, he had no inkling of the hell I'd put up with. I'd beat the words from his mouth if I had to.

"All this time. All this time you hide out there somewhere while we suffered. You forsook us. Abandoned us in the caverns while the frecens—"

I reared back, kneeing him in the crotch. As he keened a wail, I pressed the tip of my dagger harder against his pale, sweaty neck.

"You locked me out of the caverns!"

"And then never came back?" He choked on his spit for crying. "You never thought to return and help your villagers who'd only offered you protection and—"

Again, I silenced his sputtering with a hard hit of his head to the ground. "Where is she?"

"I don't know!" He cried openly, trying to cross his legs and curl into a ball. "I don't know... As soon as we left the caverns, the seasons. They changed. All the snow and ice gone. We assumed the Vintar King was dead, but we knew it when they came."

"Who?"

"The Sommans." He narrowed his eyes at me, the stern expression a flimsy shot at intimidation when tears still leaked down his cheeks. He was at *my* mercy here, and he didn't have any power over me.

"The prince came. Looking for her."

Fear gripped my heart. I swallowed, my mouth parched. "The prince..."

He grimaced, shaking his head. "Not the heir." He'd assumed I was thinking of the wrong man. "Not Prince Isan."

No. My jaw dropped as realization struck.

Lianen.

I stared over the magistrate's head. Lost as I zoned out, I fell back to the memory of the last time I'd seen Devota's brother. The Somman royal. Prince Lianen, who trained and mastered dragons to use their venom as a weapon. The last time I'd faced him off, he'd tried to stop me from running out of the Somman castle. I'd fought with him—fire versus ice—in that grandiose room Devota had presented to me as she tried to coerce me into serving her.

Lianen.

All this time, throughout my stay in the dungeons and the blur of my escape, I'd forgotten about the other royal. I'd fixated on hating Devota, Xandar, and all the guards of the castle. And as soon as I was free, I was busy deciphering what *more* royals wanted. Baraan and Sadera. Amaias and Isan still as prisoners...

"Them royals. Always got a plan. Then 'nother secret plan." Ersilis's croaky words filtered into my mind.

How could I have dismissed *Lianen*, the first queen's brother? How had it not entered my mind—that Devota would order her brother to carry out her will and capture Thea?

"And right on his heels, that thief showed."

Thief? I blinked, jarred back to the present as the magistrate spoke, snot and tears mixing down his face as he still cried. "Who?"

Kane. He came. He came for Thea.

"That thief. He'd come through the village a few times, always trailing after Isan." He shook his head. "He showed up at the same time the prince took her outta that fine home I gave you both."

I pulled on his hair. "Tell me."

"They fought. He seemed damned bent on getting her from the prince. But then the dragons..." His body shook with shudders and he cried in earnest. "Such...fearsome, wicked beasts. They flew in so suddenly and burned the village as the prince and thief fought. All for your sister. Over *her*, of all people."

"Who took her?" I clenched my fingers tighter on his hair.

He sobbed, perhaps strained from the memories. "The prince."

I shoved his head down and stood to pace.

Lianen has Thea. She was as good as dead. I'd failed her. Kane had too. She didn't deserve a moment spent with any Sommans.

Fury spiraled through me, emphasizing the burn of my aches and wounds. Rubbing my chest, I winced at the sharp stinging pain on the deeper, faster breaths I sought.

And Kane... No. He had to live. Forgiveness or not, I couldn't bear the thought I'd never see him again.

"What of the thief?" I asked.

Was this how it would be? Torn to find Thea *and* Kane? To pick one over the other? I couldn't.

"That man could barely stand after the fight. He took my deputy's axe and held on the best he could as he ran."

I exhaled a heavy sigh of relief. *He lives.* I nodded.

"But then they came. The Sommans. Threatened to end us all. Because of her. Because of you!" He limped to the door, holding his crotch. "The queen wants *you*, and I'll be damned if you dare to endanger us. Leave! Leave us now before they return!"

Lianen had Thea. But Kane...

"Where did the man go? The thief. Where did he go?" I demanded, sheathing my dagger. If I were to return to the castle *again*, I wasn't going alone.

The magistrate scoffed, looking away.

I advanced on him, fist raised to punch. "Where did he go?"

He stepped back, hand up. "What does it matter?" After lifting and dropping a shoulder, he wiped his face and smirked at me. "The thief? A dragon chased him into the mountains three nights ago."

Carrying an axe as he ran from a dragon. Worry climbed, and I turned to leave.

"Don't come back! You hear? We don't need the queen's wrath."

If I'd cared, I could have turned to witness him shaking his hand at me. I did not.

Instead, I ran. I sprinted my way through his large house and pushed through the front door. Deputies shouted at me as my feet slammed onto the dry dirt road. As I hurried on, more villagers turned, pausing long enough to glance at me. Some were likely curious. Others were probably annoyed—either for my absence meaning they couldn't demand tonics and salves or because I was now a target.

A fugitive. Wanted. The second I'd tried to escape the castle, I knew Devota would be on the hunt for me. Just like she'd immediately come for Thea as a means to get me. That had to be it.

If a life on the run was my fate... I was. Pumping my arms, forcing my legs to clear the ground, I hurried out of Dran. Heading north, not east to the thick forest of the Sord, I pushed myself hard.

Kane allegedly left three nights ago. He was taller and stronger than me, able to go far. Most importantly, he was world-wise and more aware of what lie outside the village I'd grown up in. I had no hope to catch up to him quickly. Even worse, I had no clear idea of what direction to run in.

A series of logs posed an obstacle, and my attempt at jumping them failed. Slipping in the moss and mud, I slowed to catch my breath. Panicking and hurrying without care would only earn me an injury. My ribs and side ached from landing on that branch in the Hunann swamp. Caution was necessary.

As was oxygen. I bent over, hands on my knees and I tried to clear my mind and concentrate. Doubling over, the whistle dipped from my sweaty skin. It hung low, pushing against my shirt.

The corga. Reacting rashly to the news, I hadn't even thought to call it. I didn't need to run myself. That beast could carry me better than my own two feet would.

Panting, I swallowed and tried to calm my respiration—just enough that I could have the steam to blow into the slim apparatus. My ribs stung at the deep inhale. I pressed the metal to my lips and exhaled, hoping the corga's auditory abilities were stellar enough that it would hear this call no matter the distance between us.

Again, I blew it, just to be certain I'd tried my best. With or without it, I couldn't linger.

Adopting a milder jog, rather than a full-out run, I resumed my path. No clear line was marked to show where anyone might have traversed recently. Trees, shrubs, and thickets of briars remained thick and dense, not trampled. Before long, though, rocks and boulders covered the way, but still, no signs of the flora being trampled.

Did he even go this way? The magistrate specifically said the mountains. Kane had to have gone north. Unless...

I frowned, slowing my pace more to climb and grip stones rather than run. *Did he lie?* I'd never had a great relationship with the magistrate, and he was known to spread falsehoods if it benefited his image.

Then again, I mused as I grunted and jumped over a deep crevice of the incline, I'd scared him plenty with my dagger. For the sake of avoiding further injuries from me, he might have had an incentive to tell the truth.

So help me... Glaring at the tall rise of stones, I withdrew the whistle from my shirt again. *So help me if he lied and sent me on a wild chase...* I wouldn't hold back the next time I saw him.

I blew the whistle again as I went. Slipping and stubbing my shins, I did the best I could. I was no expert climber. The higher I went, the hotter the sun seemed to beat down on me. Before I grew irritated with my lack of progress, I heard a grunt.

A purring sound.

Finally. I stopped and held my hand on the solid vertical cliff to look back at the way I'd come.

The corga. Hardly out of breath, it ran for me. Gracefully jumping, bounding from one rock to another, it approached with the same speed and drive as it had from the swamp.

"About time," I muttered to myself, bracing for contact.

As I'd expected, it nudged my side. Hissing, I held on to my ribs. "Not so hard..."

It growled lowly, but not in anger or defense. With another low dip and push, it prompted me to reach for the saddle. I held my breath at the jarring aches climbing on produced. Once I was seated on the saddle, I reached for the reins and squeezed my knees. "North," I told him wearily.

His shoulders reared back as he shifted his body. A pounce. A preparation to lunge.

I set my teeth together, praying I'd have the strength to hang on.

And with a heaving rock, he leaped up, carrying me toward Kane.

I hoped.

Chapter Twelve

This pattern couldn't become a habit. I wouldn't survive.

The last time I'd raced after Kane, I knew where he was, the exact location he'd been shipped to.

Now, as I rode on the corga's back and held on the best my aching hands and arms could, I felt lost. Aimed this way on the account of a man who'd mostly been untrustworthy all my life, I battled with impatience and doubts.

Up and up we went, despite my troubled thoughts. I'd told the corga to go north, and it damn well did. Over boulders and along narrow edges of cliffs, we climbed. Heat rose with us, and in intermittent spells, mist clung to the slopes, erasing my vision. How the corga didn't miss a step and tumble down, I didn't know. It was a miracle.

But would this trepidatious climb be worth it? Was I making this journey in vain?

"Easy," I whispered at a challenging series of jumps to reach a level clearance. I spoke it to myself more than the corga. My grip on the reins was slippery, and once again, as I had numerous times on this saddle, I tugged my shirt up to mop up the sweat on my brow, then smoothed my palm over my trousers to dry them too. Without both hands on the leather straps directing this beast, I felt unstable, likely to fall off with his acrobatic fitness.

He skidded upon reaching the wider, horizontal ledge. Rocks scattered down from his paws, and if it weren't for his claws digging into the gravel, I imagined we would have followed the debris.

I stroked my hand over his coarse fur, comforting him with that near-miss.

A low growl came in reply.

"All right." I frowned and removed my hand, surprised he would react to my touch like that when he was at ease to nudge me and make contact when he deemed it necessary.

After I picked up the rein and didn't mistake permission to pet him, he growled again.

And the scent hit me. It wasn't strong, but it was there.

A dragon? The odor was too faint. A hint. When those flying monsters lurked near, they stank with a potency that couldn't be denied.

Growling again, the corga stalked along the ledge. He stopped at a rock and shook his head, sniffing so violently I rose and fell with the heaving motions of his chest.

"What?" I prodded him to walk on. I didn't see anything, and the odor of a monster remained the same. Weak, like an afterthought, not a present full-bodied threat.

As the corga paced ahead, I saw at once why.

It *wasn't* full-bodied. Only a hand. A foot? No. I saw no heel, only the flat shape of a palm.

I grimaced, leaning over the corga's back as we passed the bloody stump. Talons shone, pointing upright like aiming at the harsh sunlight. Each sharp growth was longer than my hand. Stubby fingers lay still, and above the scaled meaty paw and wrist, blood puddled. Darker stains of the liquid had already thickened to dry. Most telling, though, was the ax. Its handle lay stuck out at us, the triangular wedge pinning the side of the amputation to the dirt.

Kane!

He'd run off from Dran with this very tool—weapon—so he had to have come through this way. The odds of two axe-wielding humans crossing this area had to be low. I tore my stare away from the macabre mess as the corga walked away.

That axe proved I was on the right path, after Kane, but another clear detail woke me up and made me more alert from the haze of pain.

Kane had to have been healthy enough with the strength to sever that dragon's foot.

As we moved on, no other scents of dragons hit my nose. I detected nothing in the air. My ears picked up the scratchy scrapes and low thuds of the corga's progress up this incline. My eyes showed nothing but rocky expanses and higher heights to dread. My skin burned and grew taut under the sunshine.

But that dormant instinct inside me cautioned we weren't alone.

Urging the corga to go faster, I considered what seemed like my only two options. I could search for Kane blindly, hoping the corga took the correct path by luck. Calling out for him seemed risky. As weak as I was, I couldn't last in a fight if I invoked danger from anyone or anything else in this vicinity on the mountainside.

The other option posed an identical threat: use my power to attract the dragons to me, and hope I could determine their location and find Kane.

Moments later, my options were nullified. I didn't need a strategy. One came to me.

Deeper and more pungent, I smelled the presence of monsters. Dragons? *No.* It was only at that moment that I realized I was learning the differences among the rank odors. Whatever caused that nasty scent was something new. Something distinct from the freaks I'd encountered in the wilds.

Rumbling a faint growl, the corga reacted to the threat too. *Does he know what it is?* He didn't slow, didn't show a sign of hesitation in carrying me further up the slope. *Is he unafraid because he's met these monsters before?*

I wanted to believe it wouldn't be something fearsome, but annoying.

What I found was more terrifying than the worst twists of my imagination.

Three large forms paced and circled before us. Tucked into the shade of an overhanging cropping of rock, the trio of bodies seemed to guard something at their center.

Similarly sized to the corga I rode, these freaks were squatter, fatter. Bulbous, pear-shaped abdomens lay flat rather than upright, but *their* perspective of what was up or down wouldn't be the same as mine. Nor any other bipedal creatures. On *eight* legs, they skittered back and forth. Thick bristles of hair protruded all over their frames. Such a filthy, thick hide spanned from their heads to the tips of each leg.

Their heads—connected by a strangely long and very flexible neck lined with barbs—roved in a weaving, bobbing sway as they communicated. Either to each other, their prey, or the massive man trying to reach for their prize. Man? I couldn't see the faces of these arachnids, but I got a clear view of this humanlike monster. Coarse, hard skin covered him, his flesh like rocks themselves. Fat trunks of arms waved slowly, like his overwhelming bulk slowed his movements. A troll. It was the only thing my mind could come up with, a faint sketch in one of Thea's books springing forth.

A mountain troll. Taller than three men, with a blocky head sporting snubbed and cracked horns. As I stood so far down below from him, his eyes resembled mere crevices on a weathered, stiff face. His nose was missing, a poorly healed scab hiding the orifice, and his lips lowered and clamped shut—those rhythmic motions rusty and without haste or grace.

He swung his fist into the mountainside, sending an avalanche of rocks and remaining iceberg chunks to rain down on the trio of arachnids. I gripped the reins tighter as the corga lowered its forelegs for balance at the echoing quake of the troll's smack.

Squeaking and hissing, the spiders darted back and forth. But they didn't flee. They remained close but escaped the falling debris, determined not to lose the prey the troll made a grab for.

The longest spider turned its head, spewing a spray of gold webbing onto the troll's hand. He roared, that groan shaking the ground again. Lifting his hand away, the golden threads sizzled and cut into his rocky flesh.

Satisfied they'd wounded him, the trio shifted again, dancing almost, as they surrounded their catch. As the shortest but widest body turned, I caught sight of him.

"Kane." I whispered it. Shock and horror rendered me incapable of another word.

It was enough, though. In sync, the three beasts jerked. Turning their heads, their necks elongated with sessile motions like tentacles.

Facing them was a nightmare I'd never forget. The sight of those feminine faces would forever scar my retinas. Hairy but with clear features that likened them to women in the village. A person, but at the same time, so very *not*. They were monsters of a frightening hybrid.

The biggest tilted her head at me, dark eyes lined with golden light. She peered at me, turning her back to the others as they faced off the troll reaching low again.

I swallowed, readying for the fight. My dagger pulsed at my back, and without any jerky motions, I slowly reached back and grabbed it. The corga remained still, a charged animal eager to unleash its energy.

Behind her, their prey remained bound and gagged. Plain brown threads webbed around and around his body. Not the golden spun length that could sizzle and erode rock. Thick wrappings of their webbing strung him from shoulders to feet. Hanging from rocks, he was suspended above the ground. One eye looked swollen, and blood streaked over his face from what wasn't gagged, but he was awake. Alive. And staring straight at me.

I couldn't be distracted. I couldn't let the joy of finding him fill me.

Because I wouldn't be reuniting with him until I cleared these pests away.

Holding my dagger firmly, I stepped off the corga. It growled, staying in place. While the height I had on his back was an advantage, I wasn't experienced with fighting from the saddle. Close combat was my forte—limited though it was. I needed to be on my feet, letting my dagger guide me.

With the first step I took, aches sliced up my leg. A sprain. A blow from the tree branch. Anything. I wasn't rested and practiced entering this battle.

So I gave in. I surrendered to the thrumming pulse of my magic, elevated by the perceived danger before me. I forfeited all thoughts to the aches and throbs of injuries that would have otherwise broken my concentration. Instead, I retreated and let my fae power consume me. That instinct, that fae energy coursing through my blood. I let it build and fester, amping up my heart rate and tensing my muscles.

The troll stomped, irritated by the two spiders stopping it from reaching for Kane. As soon as the small following avalanche settled, I raised my hand. The spider reared her head back, opening her mouth to reveal long, bloody fangs.

Realm above. The reek of her breath was that odor I couldn't place. It dizzied me, robbing me of the ability to breathe. The sight of Kane jerking in his binding at my coughing, struggled respiration shook me clear of the noxious air.

"Not so fast." I formed a spiraling swirl of water, an open cyclone to spray her poison from this clearing. Her eyes glowed brighter, hotter, and as her mandible shifted, I reacted before those fangs slid back and antennae pushed forward.

Golden streams of webbing were caught in my spray of water. Tunneling in a circuitous force, I sent it at her, skewing the intended projection of her venomous thread. I ducked, glad the corga bounded to the side. Water pushed the spider back. Her threads sizzled and soaked into the dirt, and I stepped over the smoking curves.

And then it became three against one. The spiders teamed up against me, dodging my sprays of water, fire, and ice. In turn, I deflected their webs. My dagger couldn't help. I refused to get close enough to strike their bodies. When I fashioned a sword of ice, the short one was faster, outnumbering me in feet and legs to scurry speedier than I could ever run. I hissed at the slice of its taloned spike of a foot piercing my thigh and its barbed neck scraping against my arm.

Searing pain slowed me, so much that the largest one could lower on its rear legs and use its front two legs to pummel me. I flew up and into the troll's chest, and his rocky, bulges of fingers gripped me to his body.

Heaving up and down, trapped between his hand and his torso, I wriggled and kicked, squirming the best I could to get free. Fortunately, I had help. The corga jumped up, bounding from boulder to boulder to lunge at the troll's face, clawing and swiping at the recesses where its eyes had to reside.

Moaning and thrashing at the attack, the troll stomped and flung his arms—releasing me in the process. I curled into myself, trying to form a defensive stance of a ball as I shot through the clearing.

A piercing arc of golden thread was aimed my way, and I froze it. Encasing it with ice, I turned it into a long shaft that shattered to pieces on the ground. But doing so ruined my focus on how I'd break my fall. For the second time in too few days, I slammed into a tree. A tree trunk halted me. My head jerked at the whiplash, but as I drew in a shaky breath, I realized it was a lucky save too. The coarse bark of the evergreen kept me from hurdling down the mountain.

"Chin up, Maren," I mumbled, rallying myself from such brutal strikes.

A spider dove in, switching its antennae-like appendages for fangs, I rose to my feet, low on my haunches, and thrust my hands up. Ice shielded me from my right, and a geyser of water blasted from my left.

It spun, much like I just had, into a ball as it flew back. As it was pushed away, another jumped at me.

I gritted my teeth, spraying water then freezing it. Shrouding it in ice, just as I'd done to the dragon in the swamp, I squeezed it to death with layers and layers of ice and frosty crystals stacking in. Under pressure, it exploded. Golden threads sprayed out in a firework of glinting shafts, partly hardened by my Vintar spell. I flattened to the ground to evade the burst pieces from stabbing me. My cheek pressed to the gravel and dirt, and with my hard breaths, I coughed and blinked.

Deep thunder rumbled from the surface. The troll groaned and wove his body back and forth. Chunky fingers covered his face as he rocked and roared. Between smacking his free hand on the mountainside and raining down thawing ice and rocks, he stomped and moaned. Like a child, he reacted to the slaps of poisonous golden webbing that had splattered on his face.

I lifted onto one hand, searching for Kane. With all those rocks and ice, the noxious thread from the exploded spider...

There.

He was still bound and alive. His eyes widened at me as he struggled to break free, twisting and wiggling in the cocoon.

I felt it before it could reach me. And rolling on my back, I dodged the next spider from pinning me to the ground. Its pointed feet punched into the dirt where I'd rolled from. Before it could spin to me, I shot it into the air with a burst of snow.

I blinked at the debris as it launched. It shot up, scrambling its legs and hissing, but it didn't fly for long.

Another massive bulk of fur lunged at it. Gray and white, with shaggier locks, unlike these arachnids' brown hide. Large, slick canines shone in the sunlight as the hur-wolf cracked its jaw open. The huge animal lunged through the air and intercepted the spider, biting into two of its legs and snapping them off.

The canine landed atop the spider, and with swift strikes of its paws, it beat it down more.

I couldn't watch the fight, too tied to surviving mine. Between jumps and strikes at the spiders, it was quickly clear this newcomer wasn't an occasion of happenstance. Wolves weren't native to the north. Hur-wolves were endemic to Vintar. With Devota replacing winter with summer, it made sense she would have ousted the great canines. I didn't have time to ponder their migration this far north on Contermerria. Because they hadn't relocated here.

They'd been brought here. Another hur-wolf joined in, helping the corga to keep the troll from stomping toward me and Kane. A third, the largest wolf, bounded into the clearing with a rider.

Isan.

He glared at me but nodded. Acknowledgment? A hello?

I gritted my teeth, my dagger missing a spider's low belly when it lunged forward to sink its fangs into me. Too close to its drugging, noxious breath, clamped my lips shut and refused to inhale until I pummeled an ice-coated fist at its face.

"I saw the explosion," Isan yelled to me amidst slashing his sword at the spiders aiming for him. "I felt your magic and followed it."

Fine. I didn't care. This was a matter of life or death. I could puzzle his appearance out another time—if I lived another moment.

"If I found you—" He growled, waving his arm back and forth as he sliced that blade through the air. Coughing interrupted his words, too. "She will too!"

Devota? Sure. Just what I was missing. More spiders fled the cracks and crevices of the mountain. Either heeding a war cry from the first two of the trio I'd found or fleeing the thunderous hits of the troll's hands and feet on the rock, I was outnumbered.

The corga dove in front of me, saving me from another arachnid getting too close.

No, *I* wasn't outnumbered. *We* were. Wolves and a corga, Isan and me. Our efforts united as we battled back these monsters. Because deep down, I knew he had to be right.

Proof came moments later. After sending a burst of ice at the troll, preventing him from stomping on Kane, I squinted at the bright sky. Dark spots soared, and as they grew in size, more danger was revealed.

Dragons.

Devota.

If not her, other Sommans were here to do her will.

"Help him!" I ordered the former heir prince.

"What?" He grunted, slashing at more spiders, at ease with the balance of fighting from the saddle.

"Kane!" I pointed at him, now fallen from the rocks and struggling to break free of the spider's webbing on the ground. "Help him!"

In eerie unison, the spiders craned their snakish necks, facing in my direction. A deep thud of four feet pounded through the ground. All at once, the spiders hissed, revolving their fangs for the appendages of webbing. It seemed these freaks didn't welcome another to their turf.

Spiders and dragons didn't mix.

I panted, adjusting my dagger as I turned and watched the monster snarl at me. From its back, Queen Devota dismounted, a flurry of carmine robes and ginger tunics. Gold and rubies shone from her jewelry. As she landed in a jump, she grinned and straightened the crown on her black curls. She dragged her hand back to her sheath, locking her malicious glare on me.

Only me.

So long as Isan could help me keep Kane alive, I'd send *this* pest away.

"Maren," she scolded. "How *dare* you—"

I was in no mood for her taunting tone. I'd die a thousand deaths before ever wishing to hear her voice again.

I swung my arm from left to right, sending forth a sheet of crystalized ice. Her countering strike of fire melted it enough that it couldn't hit her.

Her cackling laughter ate at my soul. Wicked, gleeful sounds that assaulted my ears in her dungeons. Over and over and over as she tormented me.

I was no longer her slave.

"Ice?" She flung her arm into the air, grinning that sinister smile. So smug. So cocky. So evil. "I rule these lands now, Maren. With fire." She fisted her hand, erupting a ball of inferno she threw at me. I ducked, letting it spiral into a spider behind me. "With heat." Lifting her hand with her fingers spread wide, she raised a haze of smoke. The dragon swiped its tail, coiling around her as she lifted her blade in a readying stance.

"You dared to defy me. Dared to kill my men. To escape... Now it's time for you to go right back where you belong," she snarled, her anger rising with each word until the last ones trailed in a scream.

I huffed, teasing her with a smile of my own. "Make me."

The dragon roared at me as she ran forward, blade up and blazing with flames.

Chapter Thirteen

A spider lunged at me at the same time, clawing a deep gash on my heel. It helped, though, lowering as Devota charged. On the ground—though sucking in air at the fierce pain—I could shoulder into her legs. Holding up my hand, I formed an ice shield just in time.

"Maren!"

I jerked my head up, scooting back on my butt as I raised my block to the queen. Teeth gritted, lips curled, she hacked at my slab of hard ice, chipping off chunks as I moved with her hits.

I chanced a glance at Kane. He was half out of the webbing. Isan slumped over near him, gasping for air and struggling to breathe. Longuex was a terminal curse of a disease, and the Vintar fae seemed to weaken more and more.

Spiders crawled toward them. Kane had one arm out, reaching for Isan's blade. Unable to run, he'd be covered. The troll still raged too near, and at that moment, he banged his fist onto the mountainside, raining rocks and ice over them.

I flung my hand out while holding up the shield. Flinging out another wave of ice, I constructed a hasty, haphazard shelter over Kane. It adhered to the mountain, but the force I dispatched with it seemed to wane. Was I *that* close to passing out?

Frosty particles floated down, and Isan shivered, jerking up. He made eye contact with me. His face was so pale and tired.

"Isan!" Kane thrust his hand out to the prince. "Give me the sword."

Isan narrowed his eyes, seeming to dig in his reserves of energy. He stood up and attacked when he wasn't cutting at Kane's cocoon to free him then slashing again at the spiders. Hur-wolves stalled the troll and held their own against the arachnids. The corga attacked the three Sommans firing flame-tipped arrows.

It was a losing battle. But it wasn't over yet.

Fatigue and pain tried to claim me, but the burn of magic in my blood would never quit. I was fae—and more than this demonic queen of fire, I wielded the power of all three realms.

"You dare to defy me," the queen snarled, continuing with a rant I'd since tuned out.

Side to side, she tried to impale me with her sword. I pivoted and met her, blocking each strike. Every time her Somman blade swiped near me, breaking off chunks of my ice shield and melting it with lucky pierces, the glow of indigo smears remained.

Dragon's teeth. A venom I didn't want to experience again.

"You dare to—"

I grunted as she hit my shield and knocked my shoulder into a rock. Pain lanced through my arm, and I almost lost grip on my dagger. She was more experienced, trained extensively in fighting.

"*Now,* she *can handle any blade.*"

Kane once spoke of Devota's skill with the sword. I believed him. I'd survived her deft handling of weapons and magic until now. In close combat, my dagger might have matched it, evened out if I wasn't already so beated and wounded. But this woman would never be my true match.

And it was past time to show her how.

"I am your queen. You *will bow to—*"

I slipped my weapon into its sheath. After I rammed my shield up and at her jaw, knocking her chin back, I let the ice slab fall with her. At the same time, I kicked out one foot, ruining her stance.

Standing as tall as I could, I wasted no time ending this. She raised her fiery sword, and I used my Somman magic to flare the flames hotter. Bright red, they spiraled up her arm and into her hair. Eyes wide, she screamed and swiped her sword at me.

The weapon halted in its wide arc, targeted toward my stomach. A wave of water funneled against it, a cyclone I grew larger and larger until it whipped the weapon out of her hand.

Gaping at me, she countered my Somman magic. She put out the flames I'd sent back at her. Hair smoking, skin blistering, she stared at me.

In awe. In shock.

Never before had I used my other powers for her. Her mistake. All this time, she'd thought I was nothing but an inferior Vintar fae. An enemy to crush as Somman took over the land.

Realization hit at once, and she reacted in rage. Scrambling to her feet, she lifted her hands and sent blast after blast of heat at me. Fire and smoke came in a series of tremendous punches.

I brought the water cyclone between us. At her scream, I changed it to ice. It rained down like sleet, revealing a long gash on her cheek where her spinning blade must have caught it. The sword clattered to the ground. She dove for it, flames radiating from her body, roiling and dancing like a morbid outline. As she lowered to reclaim her sword, another avalanche of rocks and ice fell.

She cried out. "*No!*"

Blasting rock after rock apart with bursts of sparks, she sought the sword. Turning her back to me, she alternated her focus to send strikes of fire at me. I met each one with water, the spray putting out her heat. Back and forth, we shared hits of magic. Fire against fire. Then my water and ice against her heat.

She cried out upon finding her blade. Shattered and cracked, it would do her no good. It was ruined, and with one last glower at me, she raised both hands. Heat roared at me, sending me arching backward, but the corga rushed close. Buffering me before I could fall, I locked my elbow and matched her fire.

Water rose in a wave. A tidal force as I strained to keep a hold on my power. Darkness swarmed with the liquid lifting and arching over her wall of flames. It peaked. Crested. And smacked down. Rinsing away the spiders, the Somman archers. One dragon stood firm, and I shot spears of ice to stab him. Another dragon flew up, its wings depressing a hole in the flood, but I whipped at it with sparking lines of smoke. Screaming in retreat, it shot into the air, then swooped down for Devota to climb onto its back.

She clutched the reins, spinning the dragon back at us on the mountainside.

No? She hadn't had enough?

The troll took care of the nuisance of the dragon. Mad—for not getting the spiders' prey, for my explosion of the arachnid's poison that splattered over its face, and for the dragons breathing inferno on its home—it moved faster than I'd witnessed yet.

Roaring, it jumped up and flung its meaty fist at the dragon. Clinging to the corga's saddle as it dug in its claws to avoid being washed down the slope, I squinted and watched the dragon's tail get hit.

Screaming louder, the dragon curled back to spray fire at the troll. It didn't care. That jump was a death move, suicidal as its enormous bulk fell over the mountain, tumbling with earth-juddering shakes.

"Maren!"

I turned at Kane's yell. He clung to the prince, the fae coughing violently again. Caught by a tree, they were safe from being washed away. By the time I looked back into the sky, Devota was but a speck in the distance, retreating quickly on her dragon.

I whooshed out a sigh and closed my eyes.

Exhaustion claimed me, but with a weary lift of my fingers, I ceased the flowing pressure of the Rengae magic, ending the flood, and switched to my ability as a Vintar. Freezing the remnants of water, the rocky slope boosted patches of frost and snow.

Finally. Everything was still. My pulse thundered everywhere in my body, but I could *finally* stop for a moment. I wheezed out another laborious breath and dropped to my hands and knees. Shaking but alert, I wrenched my head up.

Isan staggered to his feet, coughing.

Kane ran to me. His face was no longer as swollen, and the cuts on his cheek were gone. Healthier than he was when I'd spotted him in the spider's cocooned web, he sprinted, eyes on me.

"Maren."

I slumped against him, his hard chest a familiar surface of heat and comfort. His arms wrapped around me, both in an embrace and a supportive hold. At once, my heart raced and calmed.

Kane. I couldn't form the word, too ragged. Surreal relief consumed me.

Effortlessly, he pulled me closer, tugging me off the ground until I grunted in pain at the pressure on my wounds.

"Maren," he repeated, softer with reverence. With awe. With love?

I blinked, not caring to keep my eyes open so long as I could feel his arms around me. His heart racing against mine. That solid wall of his chest was the one place I always wanted to rest my cheek, and I did. My heart was overwhelmed with relief. With joy.

Finally.

His lips pressed against my temple. My hair. My cheek. Cradling my face, he stroked his rough thumbs over my skin. "You're..." He sighed, his breath hot against my skin but the movement of air cooling me. Unable to cease kissing me, he committed me to memory, etching me back in his mind. As though he couldn't believe I was here, that we were together again, he touched me in a thorough reassurance that I was in his hands.

He groaned, brushing his lips against mine. I whined, too weak to hold him to me. It was too sweet of a kiss to miss, too short of a gesture to cling to. It was cruel to break away, but he did, scowling.

"Can't you help her?" he asked before laying his hand on the back of my head and hugging me against his chest once more. "Can't you heal her?"

Isan's hand rested on my shoulder. Though his touch was gentle and his skin was cold, the prick of power from his contact was brief. A miniature pulse of healing—nothing like the powerful force Ersilis gave me in the dungeons.

"No." He removed his hand, staggering aside if the sounds of shuffling feet meant anything. Wracking coughs claimed him again.

"He healed me," Kane said, stroking my hair and kissing my eyes. "As soon as he cut me free, he healed me to help you fight."

"Help?" I retorted, uncaring how wry my tone was. "Me?"

He laughed lightly, maybe incredulous I *could* joke at this moment, so bloody and beaten. I might have liked some assistance, but no. I'd handled it on my own.

"You're tribis," Isan said as Kane held me on his lap, hugging me as though I was a dream and could vanish.

I sighed, clinging to Kane's shirt as I drew in as deep of a breath as I could. His masculine, woodsy scent soothed me, a familiar one I'd fantasized about in my darkest days of torture. How many times I'd tried to remember it, wishing I could be wrapped in his presence instead of the charring, acrid stink of smoke in the dungeons. Tears streaked down my cheeks but I lacked the energy to wipe them away.

I shrugged, opening my eyes the best I could.

"She's a Ranger," Isan accused, returning to us. Kane wouldn't release me as the Vintar fae came close. It wasn't a protective hold. Only a possessive grip I wished I was strong enough to return. If I could hug him back by half as much, I'd never let him go again.

Kane and Isan had been enemies for so long. Also friends—before Kane tried to kill the king? Then enemies again. My thief and the prince weren't strangers, but why and how this Vintar showed here of all times was something I couldn't puzzle out.

Much less why he'd shown up to help me.

Isan shook his head, anger evident in his firm lips. "You knew her from the Rangers and—"

Wincing, I sat up on Kane's lap, grateful for his hand bracing my back. "You knew me first," I corrected him. "You knew *of* me first."

Isan paced, rubbing his chest. "As a healer in the village. My troop consulted you for remedies."

Oh, that was all he remembered? How fitting.

"She was bound here," Kane said. "I found her there after I'd gone looking for you the last time."

The blond prince glared at him. "Yes. All that time you'd tried to track me for that sword." He pointed at me menacingly. "And tasked her to break into my father's palace."

"I didn't know," I said, leveling my tone to suggest he better not think about harassing me. "I didn't know I was fae until Kane got me out of the village. I didn't know what the significance of that sword meant. What any of them mean."

"Do you now?" he shouted. My corga growled at him, and the hur-wolves bared their teeth at him. "Do you understand *now*, after you helped that woman kill him and steal his throne?"

I licked my lips, sensing that his words weren't intended to hurt me, to attack me. Pain—grief—laced his message. I couldn't help but feel sorry for him. Had he accepted his loss yet? All that time in the dungeons he'd been screaming under the weight of the torture, could he have come to terms with his father's death?

Doubt it.

"The same woman I just sent flying away? The one I could have killed if I wasn't so weak I can't stand?"

He gritted his teeth, approaching again. Kane's fingers dug into my hip as he held me, but the fae prince merely set his hand on my shoulder again, trying to push some healing effort into me. Faint, but it was there. He let go, staggering to his knees.

Kane ceased caressing me. We exchanged a glance and I nodded toward the wrecked man.

He kissed my temple once more and gingerly set me aside on the ground. The corga padded over and lay next to me. Panting, it sprawled at my back and I rested against his coarse fur.

"I tried to remove the poison," Isan muttered as Kane helped him to sit. The prince reclined against a rock. "I can't heal you past that." He flapped his hand at Kane, dismissing him weakly. "Wasted it on him."

I sighed, relishing the freedom to simply breathe and be. Relying on fae healing was becoming a crutch I didn't want. All my life I'd made it through scrapes and wounds the old-fashioned way. With rest and ice, perhaps salves.

I never fought dragons and monster spiders and mountain trolls though. Nor a demonic queen bent on making my existence miserable.

"Because she stole the throne. Because she killed my power and ended the Vintar Court. My powers are..." He flipped his hand, palm up, and a tiny line of frost followed up to his pointer finger. "Weak. Especially near her."

"She suctions it from you?" Kane asked, glancing at me.

A bitter laugh left my lips. "If I could have used my power, I wouldn't have stayed in those dungeons for months."

"Bound us both," Isan agreed. Meeting my gaze, he frowned. Not in anger, but confusion. "My power wanes, yet yours does not, *tribis*." He sneered at the end.

"Again," I said, shifting against the corga, "I didn't know. I was bound here. Then when she caught me at Riverfall, she bound me too."

At this rate, I'd spent more time bound than not.

"She's not one of the Rangers?" Isan asked Kane.

Kane crossed his arms. "You *killed* the last Ranger."

"I did not. They fought and froze in the wilds."

"Because Vintar ruled!" Kane lowered his arms, his muscles flexing with the movement. Standing between Isan and me, he was a coiled spring of fury.

Isan nodded. "And that was so bad, wasn't it?" His coughs belied his words.

"Compared to Devota? To Sommans?" I shook my head. "I'm sorry, Isan. For the part I played in it all."

"You didn't know," Kane said, dropping to his haunches and taking my hand.

I slid it back. "Because you wouldn't *tell* me anything."

He pressed his lips together, seeming to bite his words. "I meant you didn't know Devota would use you—and me— to break in and reach Vanzed."

Isan stood. He likely wanted it to be a quick motion with grace, but he staggered, coughing lightly.

"But now she's at the throne."

"For now," I muttered.

Kane shot me a hard look full of confusion.

"Where is Amaias?" the prince asked instead, perhaps done with this discussion about his father and how the Vintar reign had ended. I doubted his anger had dissipated. I gathered that he'd hold a grudge yet. For him to help us though, he had to have reached something of a conclusion that I wasn't the enemy. That Kane hadn't wanted to kill Vanzed. In the end, we'd tried to *save* him. Kane tried to stop Vanzed from going over the waterfall, and I'd intended to heal him.

But Devota was faster to halt that plan.

"A—" I cleared my throat, grateful Kane offered me a flask of water. "Amaias?" I asked after I drank.

Isan pulled his shoulders back, staring me down, waiting.

I opened and closed my mouth, stumped for what answer he was looking for. "Why would I know?" Those words were the first that sprang to mind.

"When you found us," he started.

"You mean when I *returned* to the castle and couldn't leave you there? When I doubled back to find you and the princess and heal you?"

He shook his head. "Don't try to win my praise, Maren."

"You'd rather she left you there then?" Kane snapped.

"Where is she?" Isan demanded.

I rubbed my hand over my face until my fingers touched the bruise near my eye. "In case you've forgotten, the dragon appeared."

"It broke through the wall, yes," Isan retorted. "You escaped, and I fell back within the debris. The ward I set was specific to that room, and when the room was no more, neither was my ward."

"No. I didn't *escape*. A dragon took me out of there and *I* fell."

Kane cursed under his breath, running his hands over my legs and arms, worried anew, it seemed, for how maimed I was.

Isan was reluctant to speak before he eventually asked, "You don't know?"

"Where Amaias is?" I huffed. "*No*. I was flown away. I had no idea what happened to either of you. Ersilis—"

Kane jerked his face up, relief on his face. "She found you then?"

"The first time—"

He gripped my knee. "The *first* time?"

I sighed. Of course, I'd explain. After I rested. My head pounded and my back ached. "Amaias broke me out. I fell in a bubble in the river and my binding spell was broken. I floated for days and the Rengaens tracked me down in the swamp."

"She could *help* you get out, but you couldn't return the favor?" the prince shouted.

"I tried to! I went back to get my dagger. And when I was there, I *did* try to get you both out. The first time, she refused to leave with me."

He looked away, pensive and silent.

"I don't know where she is. I fell and the corga Ersilis gave me came to carry me out of the swamp. She told me you were coming after Thea, but..." I lowered my gaze from Kane.

He took my hand and squeezed it.

"The magistrate told me. They got her..."

Kane slanted his brows down then raised his head, tossing back the hair that had fallen over his face. "They?"

"The Sommans." I looked back up at Isan. "I didn't know where you or the princess went. I assumed the worst when the dragon plowed into the tower."

"I fell back, but managed to get out. Xandar's death had to be why it was so chaotic. I tried to find her, but I had to slip away before they caught me again." He ran his hand over a wolf's back as it paced next to him. "They hadn't killed *every*thing. And this one found me to take me away."

"To chase after me?" I asked.

Isan nodded. "You were the last to have seen Amaias—other than me. I guessed you'd head home to hide up north."

I shook my head. "I was alone. Asleep and wounded for most of the ride."

Isan dipped his chin. "Then I will find her myself." Wheezing tiny coughs, he climbed onto the hur-wolf's carrier. Before he gripped the reins, he tossed a small sachet to Kane.

He caught it, sniffing it.

"For messages," the prince replied as a black bird perched on his shoulder. "For the trouble you went to see to my father's death, I expect you to apply the same dedication to killing the queen."

Kane nodded, slipping the packet into his pocket.

The prince's brows raised at the sight of my corga. "Keep one," the prince added dryly, tipping his chin at the other surviving hur-wolf. He cast a doubtful look around the rocky ground as though he expected more trouble, perhaps more than my steed could handle.

Before the Vintar fae turned and left, he winced and bent forward from his saddle, waving his arm in a wide arc and placing a wide ward over the clearing.

Heavy feet pounded down the mountain, his wolf running fast. In their wake, as the protective dome settled over us, a shelter of opaque magic formed and rippled into place once it touched the ground.

I had no idea what could come next, but for now, we would be safe.

Chapter Fourteen

I closed my eyes and drew in as deep of a breath as my aching ribs would allow. A wheezing grunt accompanied the effort, and Kane knelt next to me.

"Maren." If he could say it with less pity, less heartache, I'd fare better. I appreciated Isan's effort to heal me—especially at the cost of his own energy. And even more so because he hated me. His attempt at *helping* the woman who'd accidentally participated in his father's death showed just how decent of a man he was.

I frowned anew as Kane framed my face.

Decency?

I opened my eyes and regretted it. Fading sunlight burned too bright, but Kane shifted, blocking it out as he hunched over me.

"Why did he heal me at all?" I asked.

Kane hesitated on whatever ready answer he'd been about to say. Rethinking it, likely for the same reason I was.

I didn't know the former heir prince personally. I couldn't claim any connection that would merit him *caring* about me. But to help me along from death and suffering...

He wants something. Just like everyone else in the world. Prince Isan expected something from me. Beyond saving him from that poisonous cell and indirectly playing a role in freeing him from the castle, he couldn't possibly feel like he owed me anything.

He only wanted me to live long enough to find Amaias.

"Maren," Kane repeated, seemingly unable to help himself from repeating my name like a mantra. I, too, warred with the disbelief that we were alive and together again, but the pain wracking my body diffused my enthusiasm. I gripped his hand when he cupped the back of my head. "I'm sorry."

"You'll never forgive him."

His apology cut me to the core. He didn't need to ask for my forgiveness, but the stark reminder that Thea was in the enemy's hands sent despair through me.

"What happened?" I tried to sit up, but my back was throbbing. Too many tree hits. Too much freefalling from monsters' grips.

"Shh... I will explain it all. But first—" His rough hands slid over me until he could scoop me off the ground. "Do you have any power left?"

"Why?" I frowned, safe in his strong arms but so confused. We were safe in this ward, an afterthought of consideration from Isan. Where did he want to go?

"Let me clean off your wounds. I can't imagine when we'll find another fae to heal you, and the last thing you need is an infection."

Water. I sighed in understanding and if I had the strength, I would have smiled at his consideration. I lifted my hand and issued a spark of an ember to a chunk of ice the mountain troll had dislodged. A gentle stream of water gushed from the block, creating a simple tributary. Kane brought me there, laying me on gravel at the lip of the waves.

Wincing with each movement, I braced myself for the sting of liquid on my cuts. Isan had eliminated the magical residue of the spider's poison from its barbs and legs. Some of the golden web must have smeared against me, though, because blisters showed as Kane eased my shirt off.

Careful and slow, he removed my clothes. Half sodden with fresh water but already damp and rank from sweat, the garments clung to me, delaying the process.

I cried out when he tried to get the sleeve off my arm. My shoulder radiated in white-hot aches, and he cursed. Opening my eyes, I stared up at him. Brow furrowed and lips firm, his expression wasn't a happy one. I didn't doubt that he was angry I was hurt, but I suspected he might have been more irritated with himself that he couldn't do more.

I laid my hand on his, and he paused. Deep pools of blue shone back at me, and his scowl softened to a miserable frown. "Tell me," I repeated. Perhaps it would serve as a distraction for us both. To prevent him from wallowing in misery and hating that I was wounded, and to keep me from passing out to the pain.

Still, he didn't speak, swallowing hard.

"I thought you were dead until I heard you call out for me at the edge of the waterfall." Tears leaked from my eyes at the memory. "Every day she tortured me, I prayed you made it. And it was the idea of finding you again that made me want to live. To escape and run—to you."

His eyes were glossier as he drew in a hard breath and lowered to kiss me. I clung to him, dismissing the agony my muscles seemed locked in. His mouth was hard and insistent against mine, a commanding pressure I'd never tire of giving in to.

Parting my lips, I strained to rise up to him, to taste him, to savor him. My heart cried out in celebration, so grateful we hadn't lost each other against all odds.

Only him. Only Kane could render me soft and needy like this. Only this strong, stubborn thief could remind me of love and passion. As he angled his head, cupping the back of mine to secure me in a deeper kiss, I felt certain I needed this moment to reconnect with him more than I wanted any wounds cleaned and bandaged.

His mouth against mine was the salve my soul needed to beat steady again.

He groaned, slipping his tongue in to thrust alongside mine. Joy and relief complemented his hard kiss, grounding me. Until I arched up, moving my arm toward his neck to truly cling to him.

I hissed and flinched back, pain once again claiming my consciousness. Black dots threatened my peripheral vision, and he swore, cursing himself. As he gingerly lowered me to the gravel, he slipped off that sleeve. Ever the clever man—sneaky too.

"I knew you would live," he promised. "I never doubted it for a moment."

"Because I'm a tribis fae?" I huffed a dark laugh as cool water trickled over my bare arms. "She bound me. I couldn't do anything."

"Because I'd been there before."

Twice. He'd been imprisoned at Vintar and Somman. I frowned harder, and he smoothed his hand over my cheek. "I'd nearly given up many times. I didn't have anything to live for. But you did. You do. I helped you leave your village for the purpose of finding a kalmere plant to help your sister."

I grunted as he eased my pants down. Modesty couldn't bother me. We'd already seen each other practically bare. My muscles and bones were too weary to consider the idea of covering up an inch. Limp as a rag, I gave in to gravity and the feel of his strong, hard hands so gentle on me.

"And to find that sword," I reminded him wryly.

He tilted his head to the side, a silent admission of acknowledgment when he was too stubborn to admit it. "You had your sister to live for."

"And you. Even though you're an insufferable idiot to keep secrets from me."

"I never doubted you'd endure the hell she ordered. My fierce fae." He almost smiled, wetting a section of my shirt in the water before he pressed it to the cut on my arm.

"I went over with the king. He was almost dead, but as we fell, he formed a sleigh. An ice sled. Something solid that we wouldn't die upon impact."

"Did he—"

He shook his head. "He was with me. I held on to him, and sank, safe within that ice. But he was too far gone. Before his last breath, he forgave me. He said he understood."

"Understood what?" I asked. His stern expression of concentration returned, but I didn't miss the pain behind his words.

"I think for my grandfather's death. He understood that when I'd tried to attack him, I'd wanted revenge."

"But he didn't kill him."

He scoffed. "Sure. Even if Isan hadn't killed him, the cold did." Conflicting stories debated the last Ranger's death—his adoptive grandfather.

"He said they shouldn't have wasted time." Frowning again, absentminded in his focus as he wetted the fabric and dabbed at another wound, he said, "The last time they spoke, that meeting before my grandfather succumbed to death..."

"What were they talking about?"

His hair covered his eyes as he shook his head, hunched over me like he was. "I... I don't know. And I'm not sure who to believe. Baraan suggested something that warrants more thought. Though I haven't had time to apply to anything beyond you and your sister."

With that deep, throaty tone, he explained as he so delicately rinsed my wounds. On my arms, my sides, my face. My injuries were far more extensive than I'd thought. Even if they weren't that bad superficially, I relished the feel of his sure hands on my flesh too much to tell him to stop.

"I floated through the swamp. In a flash, the seasons changed. The first month was hard. Ice melted so fast, the flash floods carried larger chunks of it. Goblins and lerneps were washed away with me. I had no idea of how long had passed, carried with the water through the swamp, until Baraan and Amaias found me."

I raised my brows, regretting it when it worsened the sting of a cut near my temple. "Amaias?"

He frowned, nodding.

"Not Sadera?"

"No." His smirk suggested I'd said something stupid. "She never leaves her fortress on the coast."

Want to bet? "Why were the royals in the swamp then?" The Hunann was otherwise known as a no man's land.

"It was a mass escape from the coast. Sommans went south to capture able-bodied citizens for encampment. Fae were killed on the spot. Rengae was always a conflicted realm with too many small powers in the place of any proper leader. Corrupt magistrates and deputies at war with gangs. And more war. As soon as she took that throne, it was war. Rengaens were fleeing north as the Sommans swept along the coast. Vintar tried to escape the palace and hide in the swamp. Baraan and Amaias were helping their people against flooding and the increase of monsters, because as the ice thawed, so many more beasts thrived. Overnight, it was chaos—all over the mainland.

"Ersilis found me among the troops and groups of refugees. She healed me, and Amaias clung to the idea of freeing Isan."

"Her rival fae?" I shook my head. He spoke with accuracy though. Ersilis sought *me* out in the dungeons, while Amaias had gone to Isan.

"Her *lover*, you mean?"

I opened my eyes wide. "No."

"Yes."

"No..."

"Yes..."

"But...he's Vintar and she's Rengae."

He shrugged, wetting my shirt again to clean the long, deep gash on my right leg. "You're a tribis and I'm a human."

"But we're not—"

He arched a brow at me, a suggestive smirk tugging at his lips. Heat blossomed on my cheeks, and I couldn't find the words to finish that argument.

We hadn't— We *weren't* lovers. But...

He wiped too quickly, pressing debris into the cut, and I grimaced.

His wince followed the slip. "Sorry."

The reminder of my injuries cooled his teasing tone. I would've preferred more of it, and even acting on this simmering chemistry even a war couldn't erase.

"She wanted to get him out, but I refused to help her unless they understood *you* were priority. While we argued, we found the Somman guards. Baraan..." He struggled, reluctant to continue.

"Tortured him to speak." I nodded. No point sparing me any atrocities now. Now a surviving victim of torture at the hands of a sadistic queen, I was sure that deceivingly quiet water prince wasn't as cruel to that guard.

"We learned of interest in Thea. They spoke about it with the guards, the handlers for the dragons sharing plans. So, we improvised. Amaias wanted to free Isan. And I asked Ersilis to get you out and heal you while I rushed north to protect Thea for you."

"Thank you."

He scowled, not facing me as he wetted the cloth again. "I wasn't fast enough. I arrived in Dran at the same time Lianen did. I'd been watching the skies for dragons, certain he'd ride one of them to cross the mainland now that summer cleared the air."

"He didn't?"

Kane shook his head. "No. On an elkhorn. He had just captured her. I reached your home as he dragged her away. We fought, but he refused to release her."

"Was she...harmed?"

"No. Coughing. Weak. But unharmed. He didn't treat her like the guards had been, with fire and whips. I gave chase, I tried, Maren. I tried to get her away, but more troops showed. *Then* the dragons came. I couldn't fight them all and he got away. When the Sommans arrived, I hid in your basement—" He grunted and left me.

I rolled my head to the side, shivering at the pleasant trickle of water along my spine. Across the clearing, still within the warded dome, he grabbed something from where he'd been trapped in the spiders' web. Running back, he returned with a brown bag.

I couldn't help a faint laugh. My bag. In his hands, it seemed like a relic of a lifetime ago. After so much danger, startling changes to my identity, and too much heartache, it was difficult to reconcile with the idea I was once nothing more than a healer everyone took for granted.

"I grabbed this and a few things I thought we might need." He dropped to his knees and rummaged through. Producing clothes, salves, food, and water, he presented a quality stash of essentials.

"I only got out by luck. Everyone was running and trying to hide. The dragons showed no mercy. As soon as I grabbed this, I ran out. A guard challenged me near the blacksmith, and I picked up the axe for defense. When a dragon targeted me, I ran in the direction Lianen had taken off."

I sat up at his direction, his rough hands carefully supporting me to sit as he dried me off. Picking through the collection of jars and tubes of ointment he'd swiped, I selected the painkillers.

"He took Thea north?" I asked skeptically. "On an elkhorn?"

He nodded, drying me with an extra shirt from the bag. "As far as I could tell. With the dragon after me, I knew I had to hide. Live to fight another day."

"Where you managed to hack off its hand and then get snared by spiders," I finished for him.

He huffed. "And then enticed a mountain troll to try to steal their dinner."

"Good thing I showed up, huh?"

Standing now, with one of his hands at my hip and his other arm wrapped around my back, he changed tactic again, kissing me hard. Instant desire hit me. I sucked on his tongue, wanting more than this quick and short affection. I wanted to steal his breath and savor in his hold. I wanted—

He reared back, breathing hard. Dammit, he was *still* a tease.

"I fear the day you *won't* run to me."

AMABEL DANIELS

Chapter Fifteen

I framed his face and kissed him slower. Sweeter. Tenderly. *I will always run to you.* When I raised my other arm, I again fell back. When would I remember that the joint was too inflamed for movement?

"Easy," he soothed, holding on to me as he reached for the clothes he'd set on a boulder. Dressing me with care, he didn't let me fall. Winded from the exertion of standing, I teetered on my feet. He caught me in his arms and carried me toward a tree. Beneath the shade of its dense leaves, he lowered me to rest on the pine needles. A couple more back-and-forth trips had me settled. I sipped water and managed a few bites of dried meat while he bandaged my cuts under my supervision. After I pointed out which salve was to prevent infections and which cream could numb the inflammation, he hurried to tend to me the best he could.

I fell under a drowsier state of mind. The cream comforted me, and his hands calmed me. Knowing Thea had been alive and unharmed thus far gave me the peace of mind to tell him all that happened since we'd reunited in the Riverfall Chamber.

Devota stabbing me in the back, then healing me to torture as her slave. The dungeons and masses of prisoners within the castle's underground colosseum. Ersilis and

Amaias arriving and how I'd broken out. The swamp. My *return* to reclaim my dagger and help the royals—kind of. Then my trip up here, running into him. So much action, too much danger, and for me, too many conflicting thoughts and questions that lingered.

"Why did Isan's Vintar power fade when mine didn't?"

Kane bundled up the last of the bandages and stowed everything in the bag again. "He's too weak. I asked when he was trying to free me from the spiders. Since Devota took the throne, his powers faded. Which makes sense. Somman—even Rengae—magic was weaker when King Vanzed ruled. Now that Devota's in charge, Somman power triumphs over the other two."

"Mine hasn't changed."

He smiled, a wickedly smug grin I wished I was awake enough to respond to. With it, he crept closer until we lay together. Spooned against him, I sighed and closed my eyes. His hard warmth, his sure arms around me... I felt safe in a way I hadn't since I warmed him up in that igloo.

"Because you're tribis," he reminded me unnecessarily with a kiss on the back of my head. "Are you comfortable?"

Pulses of soothing coldness had yet to cease on my wounds. My recipe for that antihistamine cream wasn't the same as a touch of healing from a fae, but in these circumstances, it would do.

"As much as I can be," I admitted before a yawn.

He stroked his large hand over my arm, careful of the bandage he'd wrapped there. "Rest, Maren. We'll figure it out tomorrow."

"Figure it out?" I turned to face him, but the strain that accompanied twisting my back and neck hurt too much to make eye contact. "We'll go after Thea."

He didn't reply. His silence unnerved me. The idea that he *wouldn't* continue to be on my side and want to protect her... No. It was impossible. I didn't for one second think I knew this secretive man who didn't want to be anyone's hero. But I couldn't possibly be so wrong to err in assuming his motivation or misjudge where his loyalty lay.

"We'll go after Thea," he finally replied. The guarded, pensive tone of his words sounded off. Alarm tried to rise within me, but with his comforting hold and the opportunity to rest, I couldn't fight back. Drowsiness snuck in faster and heavier, and before long, my body declared it was time to recover as I slept.

Since I'd escaped the castle, my sleep had been forced on me. Recovering from the binding spell being broken, exhausted from fighting and soaring through the air, and now this night, within Kane's arms, my body simply surrendered. Too defeated to stay awake, I had no control, but high up here in the Northern Peaks, a *restful* slumber was impossible.

Nightmares took me at once. First, I was in the colosseum, moving pieces of ice that were impossibly coated with flames. As I carried one after the other, a sick spin of illusion made the next piece larger and denser. When I set one chunk into the cart, it reappeared as a bigger duplicate.

The corga nudged me, licking my face when I whimpered awake. After a moment of my eyes adjusting to the darkness and not-so-debilitating heat under the tree's shade, I clutched Kane's arm, reassuring myself he was here and we were alive. He slept on, ragged from his own fights and trauma despite Isan's healing force.

Next, I was in the river. Dragons swam with me and after me, spewing golden fire as spiders sprouted from their nostrils. Wicked and confusing, these evil dreams captured me in agony until they shifted again. Devota—times ten. She stalked around Thea trapped in muddy ice, each replica laughing and cackling, that nefarious sound I never wanted to hear again.

"Don't you dare," the images of the queen threatened in a repeating taunt, her crown catching fire until it turned the ice to molten lava inching closer and closer to Thea as she pleaded for help.

Don't you dare.

Don't you dare.

Don't you—

I screamed, breathing hard as the vision of Thea blistering from the heat diminished.

Kane covered me. On one elbow, he hovered over me. Staring at me with concern blazing in his dark eyes, he swallowed. "Maren."

I choked on my breath, struggling to dismiss the peril of that dream. Thea's cries echoed in my mind, chased out only by the jeering, insistent taunts from the queen.

"Maren," he soothed again, framing my face. "Come back. I'm here. Come back to me."

I sobbed, clinging to his presence and his order to leave the grotesque horror of my dreams. It was all in my head. Thea wasn't locked in ice. The spiders were gone. Kane was alive. But still, my heart raced at the imminent suggestion of danger lurking anywhere I went.

On a cry, I reached up to him. Raising my good arm, I slid my hand around the back of his neck and pulled him down to me. Against his taut, firm skin, my fingertips trembled, pushing in as I threaded them through his hair and held tight.

"It's all right," he whispered, lowering to hug me while careful not to crush me and worsen my injuries. "It's all right."

I shook my head, our brows pressed together. "Not even close." Nothing was all right and I couldn't see how it would be.

"I've got you," he promised, kissing my cheeks. With his thumbs, he wiped away the tears wetting my cheeks. All the while, he murmured soothing words of nonsense. It was all nonsense. He—no one—could stand by a falsity like vowing all would be well in the world again. It was impossible.

My heart raced despite his crooning tone. Gentle words couldn't eliminate the fear that gripped me in sleep. His hands never ceased. Holding me to him and stroking my hair back, he at least stayed true to his word.

He had me. For now, I was all right—as much as I could be.

Eventually, my pulse slowed. My breaths came easier as the panic attack lost its clutch over me. Pressed against him, I reveled in his warm body and the familiar ridges of his muscles. Slower now, he continued with reverent caresses. But when he shifted, adjusting his position on his arm, I gasped, agonized that he would move apart when he'd brought me to this state of calm and security.

"I've got you," he promised again, pressing his lips to me. A delicate brush. This kiss lacked the urgent demand he usually bestowed upon me. And I reacted.

I curled my fingers against his scalp, his long hair so soft beneath my touch. Keeping his head where I wanted him, I pressed harder, fusing my lips to his. A grunt left him. When he eased back, worry in his eyes, I whined and tugged him close again.

In that instant, desire rescued me. A hot, flaring thrill filled me, tingling inside out. As I answered in kind, brushing my lips against his, the last tendrils of fear from nightmares slipped away.

No more thoughts. Fears and anxiety had no claim on me.

Right now, kissing Kane, I surrendered to the magnetic power of lust. Of attraction. Of need. It could have been my body. A purely physical reaction of biological basis. My hormones could have taken the helm now, just as I'd been so fatigued to forfeit to sleep.

"I've got you," he murmured between sharp pants when he broke the kiss for air.

At his throaty rasp of a vow, I knew it was more. This stubborn attraction between us was deeper than physical needs.

"I've got you, Maren," he repeated, staring me deep in the eyes.

I stared right back, getting lost in his gaze. I licked my lips, momentarily unable to vocalize how thoroughly I understood the wrenching rawness of his promise. Smoothing my fingers over the back of his neck, I nodded.

He slammed his mouth to mine again. I parted my lips, welcoming his tongue as he focused on tasting me. I explored in kind, moaning at the heady thread of desire that tightened down to my core. His fingers gripped my flesh, his digits curling into my side as he growled into our kiss.

He consumed me, his wicked mouth insistent. He stole my breath, his tongue a tease as he pistoned it in my mouth. He lay over me, pinning me with his welcome weight.

My world narrowed to him and the intoxicating pleasure he drew from me.

All I could feel was him. I opened my eyes, lidded in a drugged gaze, as he broke the kiss. He stared down at me and licked his lips. His unreadable expression sobered me. What was it? I was confused, but more so, frustrated.

Already breathing hard, he opened and closed his lips. Then he dove back in for another punishing kiss, seeming to have swallowed whatever he was going to say.

Each kiss grew demanding, his mouth locked against mine as he stole my breath. His hands roved along my side, ever careful of my bandages. My heart raced faster, harder, and I submitted to the rush of it all. As long as he had me, as long as I gave myself up to him, the demons of my nightmares couldn't touch me.

Safe.

I was safe from the world with him here, but I wasn't at all protected from the charging need burning me up.

I needed *more*. I showed him by kissing him harder. When he retreated, trailing hot, wet kisses along my jaw, I showed him again by pulling him back to my face and nipping at his lip.

He started and stopped a curse mid-sentence, gritting his teeth. Reaching down, he unbuttoned my shirt, shoving the fabric aside. My simple brassiere hadn't been removed when he'd rinsed out my wounds, but it had been wet enough that it gave to his greedy mouth and impatient fingers.

"I've got you," he promised again, and only now did I suspect what he really meant.

He'd tend to my wounds, he'd bandage my cuts. He'd see to my nourishment and rest.

Now I understood that feral look in his eyes when he'd paused earlier.

He'd only begun taking care of me.

I closed my eyes at the first touch of his mouth on my breast. A soft, delicate kiss. So tender as though he worshipped my flesh. Goosebumps spread across my skin as he brushed his lips over my racing heart. His fingers weren't idle, continuing lower to push down my trousers. He had yet to remove my underwear. As he laved one nipple and pinched the other, he shoved my undergarment toward my knees.

I uttered a deep sough of an exhale, painting his name with it. A plea. A damnation. He was too slow! Edging me further in this aching buildup, I spread my legs, grimacing only slightly at moving my most injured leg.

He made up for the discomfort, distracting me with his fingers tracing my slit. Back and forth, he teased me.

"Kane." I gasped his name that time, threading my fingers through his hair and holding him close. Pushing that sinful mouth to my breast. He bit, nipping to the point of pain that I groaned. Low and long, I moaned out my opinion of his teeth scraping me there.

Chuckling a dark, gritty laugh, he doubled down, sucking my other nipple into his mouth and letting it go with another bite.

"Oh—" I couldn't speak. I could only hold on and hope to ease this growing tension low in my stomach. And the throbbing tenderness further down. He stroked his fingers, not rough, but not quite gentle either.

I swallowed, my mouth dry as I tried to accept this need. This pull to— "I've never..." I didn't know what I wanted. For him to stop? That would be a crime. For him to... I whimpered, the needy sound something I'd never issued before.

"Oh, I know. I've got you." He dragged that low rasp over my sensitive flesh, trailing his mouth across my stomach. His hands, so large and rough, braced my sides. Holding me like a treasure, he retreated even more, replacing the finger he'd stroked over my slit with his mouth.

Friction burned against my thighs as he brushed his lips over me. From my entrance up to my clit, I was spread wide for him. With that hungry gaze locked on my eyes, he'd shifted his shoulders, pushing my legs apart. He wasted not a second to smash his face to me, using his tongue to lick me.

Long, lazy licks. He stroked his tongue all the way up, circling at that throbbing bundle of nerves until he closed his mouth and sucked.

Gasping at the exquisite pressure of pleasure beyond my reach, I felt my stomach clench. Unable to resist, I arched my back, mindlessly straining to deliver myself to him.

He lowered his hands, smoothing them along my sides until he scooped them under me, lifting my butt. One cheek in each hand as he lifted me to his face. His fingers bit into the globes of my flesh, and I shook as he repeated it all over again.

Hard, steady licks. Sucking at my clit. His teeth. Realm above. He scraped them and nipped, and with a jerked pinch of discomfort, my desire spiraled higher and higher.

Nothing I'd ever experienced prepared me for this. Threats and warnings of rape littered my childhood and youth. As an adult, I'd learned to kick hard and run fast.

FIRST QUEEN

Never, not once, had I given consideration to this all-encompassing pressure. A tension. A band of building aches that felt unbearable before it could snap.

I heard him, the sounds only fueling me, pushing me closer to an orgasm.

The slippery suction of his mouth, his tongue tormenting me with his steady attention. My juices, the cream dripping from me and chilling as it dribbled down to my butt that he still gripped hard.

His grunts and moans. Like a wild animal feasting on me.

He was. Famished for me and determined to show no mercy. Just when I thought I couldn't take another moment. When I feared I'd go insane at the teasing edge he urged me to. My breasts felt so heavy, my nipples beaded to the brink of pain. My pussy throbbed and my clit begged for him more friction.

Then, only then, did he insert his fingers into my sopping entrance. He stroked and stretched, curling his digit to that spot that had me wrenching on his hair. Pushing his head down as I lifted my hips, I sought the bliss that had to be waiting. I had to have relief. I had to snap.

Explode. I was going to come apart for him.

But he still was nowhere near done with me. Thrusting his tongue into my opening, he teased me closer yet. Cries and moans alternated from my mouth. I squeezed my thighs together, trapping him to me.

When he licked up from my hole to my clit, nipping me there, I broke. I cried, real tears slipping from my eyes as I sobbed at the crushing relief. Wave upon wave of ecstasy thrummed through me as I welcomed this release. He gentled his mouth on me as I rode out the overwhelming sensations. As my legs quivered and trembled, he rested his head against my lower stomach, breathing hard, quick breaths against my skin.

Realm above...

My limbs shook. Goosebumps spread over my flesh, every nerve ending sensitized to euphoria. Still, he stayed with me, prolonging the sweet torture with following pulses of another, smaller orgasm. Cupping his hand over me, he ground his palm against me, the hard rub more than enough to induce another cry from my lips.

Lying with me, over me, he waited for me to come down from the high. The first and only time I'd ever flown to that primal height. An orgasm so strong, so long, so heady that I relaxed and succumbed quickly to sleep.

And *then* I dozed peacefully, not a trace of a nightmare haunting my mind.

Chapter Sixteen

When I next woke, my body seemed tighter. Stiffer. Not only from the injuries as they tried to heal, but also—or more so—from the use of muscles I'd never used quite so thoroughly before. With the first traces of sunlight forming me to rouse, I sighed. I could have slept for hours more, but the heat climbed to a state of annoyance that I felt too sticky, too hot.

At the idea of something clinging to my skin, my cheeks warmed even more. A blush? Now? After what he'd done to me in the middle of the night? I lifted my hand to rub at my face, feeling the heated skin. I wasn't sure what expectations followed a woman's first orgasm, but a sense of shyness pricked at me nonetheless.

Would he think—

"I didn't mean to wake you."

I started at Kane's voice. He was no longer next to me, lying on the ground. As I turned to find him across the clearing, shifting my legs, I realized there was no stickiness of my cream glued to me.

He must have cleaned me up after I passed out.

"You—" I cleared my throat. "You didn't."

He remained there, not making eye contact. Shirtless and barefoot, he sat on a boulder. Holding his hand out, he offered food to the corga. And for the panting hur-wolf Isan left us, he tossed a strip of meat.

Then he faced me. Muscles bunched as he shifted, and I wasn't strong enough not to stare at his golden, firm skin.

"Hard to get used to, isn't it?"

I blinked, stunned at his crude words.

A sexy grin lifted his lips. "The heat."

The heat.

He twirled his finger in the air. "Summer."

I dumbly nodded as that blush reignited fiercer than before.

The heat because it was summer. Not what he'd—

"It's odd to lose the cloaks and boots and scarves." Dusting his hands off, he pushed to his feet and strolled toward me.

"Uh-huh." I swallowed hard, reaching for the flask of water to rinse out this dry awkwardness choking me.

"What'd you think I meant?"

Blinking fast again, I strained to think of something—anything—to say.

He licked his lips, *enjoying* this. Teasing me about something so simple. So natural. Not a topic of life or death. My shoulders slumped as I gave in to the humiliation, this weird shyness I couldn't turn off.

"What were you thinking?" He crouched down, sitting back on his haunches a foot away from me.

"I..."

He reached out to tuck my hair behind my ear. *Did I just lean in to his hand?* His smile was playful and soft as he rubbed his thumb over my cheek. "You..."

By the crick in my neck at this slanted angle, I had my answer. I *had* leaned in to his touch, needy for his hands on me.

"I was wondering what you would think." I cleared my throat again, determined not to break eye contact with him and to be blunt. "What you would think when you looked at me after what you...did. Last night."

"I can only think..." His lips twitched to the side. I knew that tell. He was hiding a smile, but perhaps not at my expense this time. "That I can't wait to taste you again—"

Twin thuds banged against the ward. I flinched, dropping the flask and spilling water on my trousers. Kane pivoted onto one knee in front of me, putting himself between me and whatever had made those noises so suddenly.

He reached for my dagger lying next to me and thrust it at me. I grabbed it, eyes on the ward as it rippled. Outside the mostly transparent dome, hazily diluting the rocky forest beyond since something impacted it, two shapes scrambled together. No, three. Four? Gangly arms and legs mixed in such a rush, I couldn't make out how many goblins wrestled with each other. Grayish, gnarly skin identified their kind, but as I breathed easier that it wasn't a dragon or Sommans lurking near, I realized they weren't fighting.

To get upright, yes. The four freaks fought to stand after tumbling into each other, unsuspected the invisible forcefield of a ward set in the middle of this clearing. But they weren't squabbling with each other. As a group, they stood. From this distance, their fright was clear. Trembling limbs. Whining whimpers. Hissing urges as they pushed each other to run. To hurry away.

"What are they running from?" I whispered to Kane.

He watched them with me, tense and cautious but unmoving. They could see us in here, but they couldn't trespass Isan's magic in the ward.

Hunched over, cowering from a threat we couldn't see or guess at, the goblins scurried away in another direction. In a blind run, they fled whatever chased them.

I blew out a deep breath. They'd startled me enough that my muscles tightened and my heart raced. Calming down, I drew in air steadily and willed my fight-or-flight response to ease up. I gripped my dagger, but I waited for it to relax as well and tone down its vibrating warm glow.

"We're safe." Kane stood then, glancing at me. He wasn't frowning but so serious as he walked outward until he pressed a hand against the ward midair. Light waves showed at the contact, then smoothed into clear transparency again.

"We're safe in here." But he pushed his fingers to the ward once more, as though reassuring himself Isan's ward was intact.

"*We* are," I agreed, not afraid to let my annoyance bleed into my reply.

All those months I'd faced hell in the dungeons, war had raged outside the castle. Devota's flair for destruction had riddled Contermerria with encampments and imprisonment. Her court of magic further disturbed the land with intense heat and flash floods of the ice thaws.

I'd ridden past evidence of the war. I saw the destruction in the brief times since my escape.

But I had yet to witness the war in action. What could have been pursuing those goblins? This far north, too?

Kane frowned at me, returning to where I sat under the tree.

"Thea isn't. She won't be safe until I find her."

She was out there, in the war somewhere, in Lianen's hands. Indirectly—in Devota's.

He hung his head, breathing in deeply.

I hadn't said it as an insult, a reminder that he'd failed me there.

"You need to rest, Maren. To recover first before..." He trailed off, leaving this assumption of guilt hanging between us. At least he understood without words that as soon as I was able-bodied, we'd go after her.

I nodded, setting my dagger down. The corga lay near the boulder where Kane had fed him, but he remained alert. Curved, stout ears twitched, and his gleaming silver eyes never blinked in the roving scrutiny he cast on the forest.

Lifting the flask, I tapped into my power to refill it with water. Then I waved my hand at my lap to remove the moisture dampening the fabric.

Kane grunted, perhaps amused at my parlor tricks. "Here." He carried my bag to me and opened it. After he reached in, he showed me an option of dried meat strips or a stick of nuts glued with molasses. I chose the meat. It'd go bad first.

He must have already eaten because as I chewed the thick strip, he sat and idly traced his finger in the dirt.

"What?" I asked a moment later, tired of trying to guess what had made him so pensive and quiet. Was it my words? How I'd reminded him that Thea wasn't safe? He still thought I'd blame him for not being able to protect her on my behalf?

"Baraan," he started hesitantly. "What did he want?"

Huh. He wasn't wallowing in guilt but thinking back to what I'd explained yesterday. Before I fell asleep and he—

That damn blush. My cheeks warmed again and I shut down that line of thought.

"To find the sword. To help you find your grandfather's sword—the Ranger's sword." I licked my lips, holding back on continuing. The blip of memory taunted me. So unsure of my mind, I couldn't decide if I'd truly felt that hilt under the water in the Riverfall Chamber or if it had been my imagination.

"He said that? Those were his exact words?"

I frowned at him. Why did it matter? "Yes."

"He asked you to find me, to help me recover that sword," he clarified.

A sword I may or may not have seen...

"Yes. But..." I closed the cap to the flask and set it aside, not wanting to face him the more I spoke.

"But what?"

But I can't. I shook my head. "They want the sword to end Devota's reign. Just like everyone had schemed to kill Vanzed and end the winter of the Vintar reign."

He scoffed. "You object to that plan?"

"I can't. Not until I know Thea is safe."

"Did you see the sword in the Riverfall Chamber?"

Of all things he had to ask. If I told him I might have, I'd have to fight harder to go after Thea first. Or I could go alone. So soon after reuniting with him, I wanted to *stay* together.

I lied, hating the taste of it. "No. I can't go searching for that sword again, Kane. Not yet."

Rubbing his hand over his mouth, he held in a reply and looked away. "Then who will?"

"Why *should* it be me? Or you? Devota's determined to hunt me down, so much so that she'll take my sister to further punish me. She will hate me—until the end of her days."

"Which can't come soon enough!" He stood, pacing.

I gritted my teeth, eager to challenge him again. Fighting with him was nothing we hadn't done before, but I wasn't well enough to stand up to him—physically.

"But why should *I* be the one to do the royals' dirty work? I am no one. Nothing. A common healer—"

"You're a tribis fae!" He gripped his hair and growled, pacing back away. "Didn't you see? Didn't you see how she reacted when you revealed it? When you showed her that you master all three powers—didn't you see?"

"All I saw was a deranged woman who wants to kill me. Powers or not, that's the crucial fact I will heed."

He glowered at me, almost mockingly.

"They can look for that damn sword," I reasoned. "If Baraan wants, he can find the Ranger sword and kill the queen. Or Sadera. Or use theirs. Where are *their* swords?"

Shaking his head, he continued to stalk in a furious gait. Like running in place but from his anger. "Their blades won't work."

"Not the ones they carry. Sadera didn't even have one on her in the swamp." The corga sensed my mood and came close. With it as a support, I painfully climbed to my feet to face off with this man. Sitting wouldn't do. "Don't treat me like I can't understand. I do. Only a fae blade can kill a ruler. Only a fae blade can end a reign. Right? So where are the Rengae blades?"

He didn't reply, refusing to make eye contact as he paced.

"Devota took Vanzed's sword and killed him with it." I pointed at the ground. "I just blasted that blade yesterday. It's gone."

Still, he didn't look at me. The corga sat, and I leaned against him.

"Isan last had Lienan's Somman blade—"

"It wasn't on him." Now, he glanced up at me. "When he took Thea, he didn't have his sword."

I shrugged. "Then his sister probably has it at the palace. If a fae blade can end a ruler, why not the Rengaens? Why can't they step up?"

"Because their reigning blade is lost too."

I looked up at the tree's canopy and shook my head. "Of course. How convenient."

"Amaias has hers, I would assume, but she's missing now. Sadera never wore one. The hilt of Baraan's sword was found in a piece of ice years ago."

Crossing my arms, I watched him pace. All that energy wasted. "So there's, what, the Ranger sword—"

He tipped his chin at me. "And your dagger. They are spelled as tribis blades. Forged by fae long ago."

My heart thudded a deep bass. Time seemed to hang so heavy, trapping me until panic neared. "Are you asking me to kill the queen?"

Do you think you need to ask?

He shook his head. "No. We'll go out to find my grandfather's sword. Baraan can kill her with it. Isan. Amaias. Any of them."

I furrowed my brow, not missing the other Rengae sister. He wouldn't include Sadera? Why?

"Absolutely not." I sat, tired of this argument and weak from the effort of standing. It wouldn't matter if I stood or sat. No one and nothing could budge me.

"What are—"

"As soon as I'm better, I'm going after Thea."

"And then what, Maren? What would you do when you find her?" he shouted.

I scowled. "I would keep her safe."

"Where?" He stopped over me, his hard face stern. "How?"

No reply came to my lips. It wasn't that I hadn't thought that far ahead, but, well, I hadn't. I hadn't had time to yet.

"The queen will hunt you down. You said it yourself. She'll be more invested in eliminating you now because she knows you're tribis." He raised his brows, and I wished I could punch that cocky expression right off his face. "Where would Thea be safe with you? Hiding?"

"I'd—"

"Where would you hide that she couldn't find you? You would hide Thea to keep her safe? Trap her from a life? Just like you had been. Your village healer bound you to keep you protected and conceal the fact you were a tribis fae. Trapped, Maren. You wish the same for her?"

"Trapped and hiding alive is better than dead."

He clenched his teeth. "Wouldn't it be better yet to kill her? And remove the threat to Thea's life? And yours?"

Of course that was preferred. But to kill the queen, I'd need to get involved with this damn search all over again. For a sword.

"Kane is fighting the right war." Ersilis had whispered it to me. A common fae. Not a royal. Of all the pressure and demands that fell upon my shoulders, of all of them, I felt most inclined to listen to her. Not a royal, but a commoner. Like I had been.

But which is *the right war?*

"Are you suggesting that I give up on my sister? And instead continue this wild chase for a sword?" I leveled my glare at him, unflinching and deadly serious.

He pulled in a deep breath and stared right back, just as sober. "Yes."

AMABEL DANIELS

Chapter Seventeen

Disbelief.

I choked on it. Swallowing back a scream, I tried to rationalize what he admitted. Anger bubbled and I fisted my hands until the scrapes on my knuckles bled again.

The corga purred, nudging against me.

"What did you say?" I bit out.

Still, he stared me down. Serious. He'd meant it. Kane actually thought the best course of action would be to abandon Thea in the hands of the enemy to look for a stupid sword.

How could he, though? Why? He'd risked himself this far. He raced across the mainland to reach Thea before Devota could. He'd understood the urgency to save her in my stead. How could he change directions like this?

"You don't think she deserves to be saved from the same hell and fate I just barely survived?"

He sighed, lowering his shoulders but maintaining a firm tone. "I don't think she's in danger of it."

I gaped at him, stunned. "They have her already! They took her, before you could—"

"*Lianen* got her. He took from the village."

I slammed my fist to the ground, ignoring the pain. "Yes! The queen's brother, acting on her orders."

He shook his head, confusing me even more. "Lianen got her just when I reached the village. He didn't want to surrender her to me. And when the Somman troops arrived with dragons, he didn't surrender her to them, either."

Sweat trickled down my spine as I sat there and tried to make sense of it. I couldn't look at him, too enraged at the suggestion he wouldn't agree with me about my sister's fate. But could he be right?

"I think Lianen might have been operating on his own."

I agreed with that statement even more. The little I knew of the Somman royalty—before Devota became queen—supported that disconnect. She was bold and took charge. He was submissive and tried to find his place.

She'd bound him, too. In my brief stay at the Somman realm, I'd discovered the memory loss and hesitance that came with a binding spell. Xandar had to have cast it, or maybe Devota had. I had no problem believing Lianen endured a rocky relationship with his sister. I *knew* how manipulative she was.

But it was another thing altogether to think I could *trust* Lianen with my sister's life.

"He didn't harm her," Kane continued to say. "He wasn't rough with her when he captured her."

I huffed. "He wouldn't have needed to exercise excessive force. She can't run. She's too weak to fight back."

Kane shook his head, and I glared at his stubborn hold on this ridiculous idea. That, what, Thea was safe with the queen's brother?

"He was gentle with her. But fierce to fight me back from her. And the Sommans he should ally with. *His* people. Unless they are not his. If he's deviated from what the queen wants."

"That's all speculation. You can't know any of that. For all we can assume, he took Thea straight to Devota."

Leaning against the biggest boulder in the clearing, he crossed his arms. Settling in, it seemed. "I've known Lianen for years."

"By fighting him? When you were in the Somman dungeons? When Devota asked him to kill you as practice of 'hardening up' as a prince?"

"He—"

"Or when you schemed with him to go through the Hunann swamp and break into the Vintar castle to assassinate the king? Where you only succeeded to *lose* his sword?"

He clamped his lips together. "Regardless. I've known him for years. I know how deeply he loathes his sister. He spoke to me before I was extradited to the king. He visited me in the dungeons."

In my mind's eye, I was transported back to the Riverfall Chamber when I broke Kane out of that fiery cell. Moments after Kane had shared that news with me, that Lianen snuck to speak with him, Devota and her dragons burst in to kill the king.

"Lianen visited me in the dungeons and shared some...news. Some suspicions. She controls him too, but he's traveled and learned of withheld facts."

"And what did he say?" I couldn't help but assume—and hope—this would explain that cryptic comment Ersilis told me. That Kane fought the *right* war.

"That he didn't back Devota's plan to rule. He had no say in it, but he feared worse threats would follow if she stole the throne."

Which had come true. Encampments, war, floods.

"He wasn't in any position to change her mind. But he advised to keep the king on the throne for the sake of all of us."

Lofty words. A brother not agreeing with his sister was too vague of a conviction for me to agree with giving up on going after Thea. It wasn't enough to make me believe that Thea would be safe with this supposedly rebellious Somman prince.

"And what convinced *him*? What withheld information did Lianen learn of that makes him so sure Somman shouldn't rule?" As I asked it, I wanted to laugh. A Somman prince suggesting a rival Vintar should *remain* in power?

"It's—" He sighed, looking at the ground before facing me. "Old lore. Rumors. Partial ideas of the paranoid."

"And *that's* supposed to be the basis for me to trust in the Somman prince? That he bought some half-cocked stories and I should now take faith he's going to protect my sister?"

"No. But it proves—"

"Nothing!"

He sighed hotly. "It proves he might not be the puppet he seems to be. That while he will likely keep Thea safe and away from his sister, we can go find my grandfather's sword and end the queen!"

I bit my lips, lest I scream in frustration. "All because the prince believes lore about more fictional threats."

"To kill her, so she doesn't destroy the continent. Regardless of any stories or lore. I would think you, of all people, would be lining up first to take her life."

He was wrong. He didn't know me half as well as I thought he did. I wouldn't deny some of his knowledge. He sure knew how to deliver me to ecstasy with his mouth and hands.

But he was a damned fool if he thought I would give up on my sister.

Chapter Eighteen

Hurt and furious that Kane could change his mind about something—someone—with such significance, I closed my eyes. I refused to look at him. The less I filled my vision with the source of my frustration, the better I could breathe. Each time I let our argument play in my mind, my heart raced and my head ached. I wasn't fit for this. Still recovering from so many hits, I couldn't stomach *more* stress. And stuck to the safety of this ward until I could walk out and go find Thea on my own, I had to be near him.

How quickly we'd shifted apart. I'd been so eager to find him alive. I'd been cherished and felt so special under his care to clean my wounds. To give me that orgasm too. Reconciling that caring, giving man with this person who wanted to give up on my sister...

Enough.

With my eyes closed in defiance, the best method I had of ignoring him after our heated words, I fell in and out of sleep most of the day. Kane was there. Pacing often, although with a slower gait. He never left me, perhaps so stupid to think I would somehow come around to the way he thought we should proceed.

I woke at random spells, dehydrated and aching. Refusing to acknowledge Kane, I took care of myself. A lifetime of it was one heck of a preparation for it. I sipped water, perhaps took too many painkillers but not a lethal dose, and reapplied the numbing salve on the worst of my injuries.

Resting was both what my body needed and the perfect excuse not to interact with the man I would split from.

Whatever this soul-deep connection was that pulled me to him, I couldn't sacrifice my sister. Love. Was it love that I felt for Kane? I couldn't know. But my loyalty to my only relative had to be stronger, especially when his only reasoning was based on supposition.

Into the evening, I slept. Apart from Kane as he seemed to intuit my anger with him. Silence was boring, but it made it easier to sleep. And within those unconscious hours, I fell into another world. Of dreams. Nightmares. Stranger visions I couldn't decipher—though those seemed to come after the liberal doses of painkillers I helped myself to.

When my mind replayed the dungeons, I was again stuck in that inferno. Flames surrounded me. Whips cracked. The Riverfall Chamber claimed the scenery, and over and over again, screams reverberated. From me. From other prisoners. Cries and moans of misery coalesced in my mind. My ears felt like they were bleeding, the agonizing pressure within my skull crushing my soul. Louder and louder, those screams and cries squeezed me.

Until I jolted awake.

Breathing fast and sweating through my shirt, I gasped. Upon the first breath of consciousness, I schooled myself to settle. If Kane dared to approach me, to comfort me now,

I'd kick him away no matter my wounds preventing the logic of such a movement.

He slept. I panted, glancing across the darkness of the clearing we were warded in. Sitting against the boulders, he dozed. Much like the first night I'd met him—another time when I wasn't able to trust him and what he planned—he rested in a most uncomfortable position. Head tilted to his shoulder, his long legs slapped out in front of him.

He hadn't woken to my gasp and fitful sounds.

Past him, though, another sight caught my attention.

Back and forth, the corga and hur-wolf stalked. The tawny mustelid to the north as the lupine strode south. At the edge of the ward, they remained alert. Growling and breathing hard.

I stood, confused. What was their problem? I smelled no threat. I—

A scream. It cut through the air, pulling at my heartstrings.

The corga bared its teeth.

Kane didn't move. I stared at him, certain I was loopy and disoriented from too much sleep. Imagining things that weren't there. It had sounded too similar. Just like the vocalization of begging sobs in my dreams. But that was in the dungeons. I was clear across the mainland from—

Another. Plus a wail.

Someone was hurt out there.

I stood, collecting my dagger, and breathed in deeply.

I detected no odor, no sense of a monster lurking out there.

Tongue lolling, the hur-wolf paced to me, then doubled back to the corga at the ward's wall.

Again, I glanced at Kane. Asleep. He didn't react.

"What is it?" I wondered it aloud to myself. The beasts couldn't reply. The corga seemed to though, noticing me and running up close. He remained at my side as I approached the ward. Limping and clinging to the saddle's horn, I focused.

With each step, more screams came. Faint, then louder. Such cutting, terrifying sounds of pain. I lifted my dagger, wincing at the assault on my ears. Outside the ward, a large shape crept close. Tall and wide, it resembled a massive man. A long length of an arm raised, and the animals reacted.

The corga pushed into me, and familiar with its actions now, I obeyed. I fell into him and slid atop the saddle. Isan's wolf pawed at the ward, snarling with saliva dripping from its maw.

Instinct guided me despite my sluggish speed from my injured state. I lifted my dagger and cut through the ward. As soon as I managed that slit of an opening, the wolf burst out, chasing at the dark formation. I followed. The corga did, and I clung to his reins the best I could.

Air hung hotter out here, thick and stifling. But the wind chilled me as we raced through the trees and up the stones.

Faster than he had previously, the corga scaled higher. Right behind the growling hur-wolf as it raced up the slope, I rode the corga.

Screams ceased, but that dark, misty shape hurried away. Fleeing. Upward and over the rocky terrain.

We pursued it to an angled cropping of stone carved from the earth. Weathered and beaten from the winds at the coast, the jagged edge seemed to lean toward nothing. Leading to a view of the seas.

With one mighty lunge, the hur-wolf roared and pounced. It smacked into another rock, a force of wind smacking it back. The corga jumped too, somehow sensing this monster was about to shoot into the air.

A dragon? Was it so dark, I couldn't distinguish this rapidly fleeing form as a fire-breathing monstrosity?

I would've smelled it. I would have felt its smoke trailing after it.

I would've—

The corga twisted at another hard push of air. Spinning over the cliff's edge, it rose high. Midair as I flew off the corga's saddle, I lost track. Details blurred. It was already hard to see in the darkness of this moonless night. With a hard smack, I landed on the stone. The hur-wolf whined, rising to its feet, shaken from its violent impact. My corga closed its teeth on my ankle, stopping me from falling over the mountain.

Toward the sea.

Hanging upside down, I peered out at the vast blue. Dark and endless, the seas spanned the horizon. Never before had I viewed the seas surrounding Contermerria. Traveling the Northern Peaks had always been an impossibility. With ice, avalanches, and the threat of frecens, no one ever dared to climb these slopes.

But here I was. Stunned. In awe of the serene surface, like a smooth blanket of water so far away and down below. And in fear, I considered the deadly drop it would be to plummet to its waves.

Blinking at the surreal vista, I struggled not to resist. Any movement I'd make would challenge the corga's grip on me. Blood trickled down where its incisor cut in. As I grew dizzy from the upside-down hang, I spotted dark shapes.

Unlike the ambiguous entity these animals chased, clearly formed objects appeared. Flying. Soaring. Inky figures hailing from above.

Dragons.

I had to run. Back to the ward until I was able to stand against those fearsome monsters.

Tapping my magic was a risk. How easily I would be detected lying against the rocks so near the seas. No other ideas came forth. And carefully, I formed a slab of ice against the rock. A ledge to lean against. Then another chunk adhered higher up. A handhold. Straining and grinding my teeth to hold back a cry at the pain in my sides, I curled upward until I could grip the rein dangling down from the corga.

I sucked in a breath and gave it one last try, reaching up. Falling against the corga, I landed back on more level ground. Remaining there in a heap, I waited for a moment.

The screams and wails didn't return, and I had no idea what to make of this.

A dream? A nightmare? Reality seemed like such a joke since I'd left the swamp. I hardly knew what to make of these strange new details of the world.

A dragon. It had to have been a dragon, sneaky and manipulative, luring me out of the ward. At the corga's purrs, I acquiesced and crawled back onto its saddle. New burns of aches robbed me of any more sanity. Riding wasn't part of relaxing. Chasing down a monster didn't fall under the concept of recovering. As we returned to the ward, I chastised myself for taking such an impulsive risk.

I wouldn't be any good wounded. Thea couldn't count on my rescue if I wasn't one hundred percent.

When we reached the ward, I was relieved the cut I'd made appeared untouched. Nothing else seemed to have found it. In my haste to chase, I hadn't considered sealing it to keep Kane safe inside as he slept.

Although he angered me and I intended to do the hard thing of splitting from him, I didn't wish him harm.

The hur-wolf entered first, then abruptly stopped. Sniffing and raising its head, it turned toward me on the corga's back. We had yet to enter the ward, and as I wondered at the Vintar beast's pause, I heard it again.

Again.

Wails. Sobbing cries of suffering.

Not again.

I hadn't taken *that* many painkillers, and they were products of my own creation, not drugged with too many narcotics. Fear sliced at me. Not for the cries but my sanity.

Was I going insane? Was it a spell? I didn't know how to trust myself and what I sensed.

Kane woke then, as I sat on the corga halfway into the ward and halfway out. He stood, opening his eyes quickly, alarm immediately setting across his face.

"Maren?" He frowned, hands lowering as he noticed me at the opening I'd cut. "Where are—"

Louder and longer, the sobs increased.

"Who is that?"

I jerked my face toward him. "You— You can hear that?"

His brows shot down. "Why wouldn't I?" He hurried toward me. "Where were you?"

I couldn't ignore the sobs. I wasn't going crazy. He heard them too.

"I—" Shaking my head, I turned the corga around to seek out the source of those sobs.

"Maren!" Kane ran after me.

"Find it," I told the corga, hoping it could understand my flimsy order. It seemed so smart, so clued in to what I expected, I wanted to hope it would deliver.

Hot air stung my eyes at the burn of the wind. The corga didn't run as fast as it had after the hur-wolf, but it was another hard pursuit my body wasn't healed enough to handle.

Kane matched me, atop the hur-wolf as it raced through the woods.

A fat tree stood ahead, and while the corga sprinted and veered to the left, Kane went to the right.

Rounding the large trunk, we happened upon the same scene. The source of those heart-wrenching sobs, and the cause of the misery as well.

AMABEL DANIELS

Chapter Nineteen

A woman leaned her back against the tree. Soot covered her face, smeared in black lines from the streaks of her tears. Her eyes were closed tightly shut, lines of wrinkles fanning out and breaking up the filth that covered her skin. Singed tips hung at the ends of wiry hair. In ragged clothes, torn and burned, she resembled any one of the prisoners I'd slaved beside in the colosseum. Faint though it was, the emblem of the Somman crest lingered on a tattered scrap of her sleeve.

A Somman. Yet, my dagger didn't react. Because I didn't. I couldn't even think of attacking this weary woman. No need for defense rose.

Instead, my heart ached at what she held.

A slender boy, similarly dressed in what was once likely a stunning, expertly tailored outfit of red and purple garments, lay still in her arms. One eye remained squinted open. The blank stare of the dead explained enough.

Kane swallowed hard, and I drew in a deep breath. Sorrow hung in the hot air, so suffocating my eyes welled with tears.

Too empathetic, Thea used to lovingly tease me. I was, perhaps. At heart, I was a healer first. I still was, or I wanted to believe I was despite killing Xandar and wishing the queen the same grisly end.

This stranger's pain spoke to me on an elemental level deep in my soul. No words came. Offering my condolences seemed trite, and speaking up at all felt intrusive.

My corga huffed a hot breath. The woman flinched. Her shoulders tensed as she clung to the boy, her arms in a secure hold. But she didn't open her eyes, resigned to whatever awaited.

Kane turned to me, and I met and held his gaze for a moment. He wasn't sure how to handle this either.

"Get it over with," she uttered in a cracked plea a moment later. "Go on. I have nothing left to live for." Her thin frame shuddered as she inhaled. "Nothing else to fight for."

Those same bold words. I faced Kane, staring at him with meaning. He'd referenced that very thing—having someone to live and fight for—when he'd explained why he went after Thea for me. The declaration he'd seemed to have changed his mind about overnight.

This woman wished for death, pushed too far in this existence.

No one moved. The woman cried silently, tears sliding over her cheek. A squat scorpion sped down the tree trunk for her, and I lifted my head.

A simple blast of ice stopped it.

She sucked in a breath, opening bloodshot eyes at me. Had she sensed my use of power? Wide with shock, her blue orbs told a sad story as she stared at me. "Vintar," she breathed.

Close enough.

"You escaped the camps." She licked her lips, her voice so hoarse. "But how?"

I shook my head. "I..." I shrugged. "Yes." She didn't need to know my history.

A croaked grunt was her reply to my excuse for an answer. "Good. Good on you."

"Did you come from the camps?" Kane asked.

She gazed at the boy, nodding. "I was a cook. For the soldiers there. *Before* the summer came."

"What happened?" I gingerly dismounted and limped closer, checking that the boy was in fact dead. He didn't breathe, and I guessed he'd passed hours ago, but at the sight of a maroon bruise along her shin, I pressed my fingertips to her ankle. As soon as I used my magic to heal her, she dragged her leg away.

"Don't. I told you. I have nothing to live for."

I winced as I shifted on my haunches, giving her more space. Remaining low to the ground, I wished to show her respect, not intimidate her from a higher stance.

"You left Somman?" Kane guessed, rigid and guarded on the hur-wolf's saddle.

I turned to deadpan at him. *Clearly. She's right here in front of us now, is she not?*

"Before the summer came, I was a member of the staff to serve *her*. I began at the palace as a girl, working my way to the kitchens. Long before I reached womanhood, at the first sign of my Somman power, I became a servant under *Master Xandar.*" She spat the name, a snarl twisting her face.

I raised my dagger, interrupting her. She tracked the low pendulum swing of it as I held it loosely before her. "I killed him with this blade."

Narrowing her eyes at me, she released one hand from the child and gripped my wrist. *Her* healing power coursed through me. She was fae, sending her magic to me and erasing all signs of my injuries.

Fire glinted in her eyes. She didn't smile, but she drew in a deeper breath and nodded. "Good."

"What happened?" Kane asked.

"I worked there until she took the throne. Camps were transferred to the Vintar castle. She captured all. She—" She sucked in a deep breath, steady in her healing despite her emotions. "She took our children. Any child, every child. She forced those with Somman power—even mild folk like me—into camps. Rengaens... they fought the hardest. You, the Vintar, all slaughtered. My husband was a troop leader, but when he spoke against the cruelty, he was ordered to execution." Sniffling, she refused to stop. "I took my sons and we fled. My firstborn..." Her lips quivered as she stared at the boy on her lap.

Fully healed, I turned my wrist to hold her hand now.

She squeezed tight. "He died that first day that we fled. A beetle got him, and longuex took him before nightfall."

I frowned. It *killed* him? That made no sense. Many were afflicted with longuex. But it was a long-standing, slowly debilitating, and chronic disease.

"That quickly?" Kane asked.

She nodded, her lower lip pouting as it trembled. "Yes. Within the day."

"But..." I shook my head.

"Since summer began—" She pointed up at the scorpion I'd frozen to the tree. Water dripped down from the shape now. "So many more bite now. All with the longuex hex within them. I've passed others as we escaped. Some speak of witnessing folk drinking from pools and falling ill with it hours after."

"It's more potent? Acute?" I asked.

"Longuex is *everywhere*. And deadlier than ever before. Everything bears it as they rise from the soil, a gray ashen powder flaking off them. That residue is the only clue they're coming as infectious parasites." She shook her head. "There is no escaping it. After my firstborn passed, we ran from goblins. I couldn't even say goodbye to him before they—" She tugged her hand free to wipe at her face. "They chased us north, and..." Stroking the boy's hair back, she finished. "Petre was bitten too. He passed at dusk."

Silence hung between us, no sounds save for the corga and hur-wolf panting. Kane dismounted to stand to the side.

"At the first news of the princess taking the throne, we celebrated. Cheered her on for finally killing the king. We all thought it was his spell. That with the fall of the Vintar Court, longuex would be a myth. A thing of the past."

Instead, it grows worse?

"Those already infected, their health declined rapidly. So quickly, they struggled to even breathe."

Isan. Amaias. I hadn't seen Thea, but by Kane's account, she was weak, too. The royals had coughed and wheezed. So weak that I couldn't help but notice.

"Kalmere grows all over. It flourishes with this heat. But it does nothing. These new cases of longuex are not slowed, no matter how much of the plant is ingested."

Disappointment hit me. I'd left Dran just to find that specific plant to help Thea. But due to my actions, my mistakes that indirectly altered the law of the land, I'd orchestrated an unforgivable *opposite* reaction. If kalmere couldn't help this uptick in longuex infections and couldn't prevent deaths, what else was there to hope for?

"You truly killed that Master?" she asked, jarring me from trying to understand why the longuex was worse now.

"I did."

She tilted her head. "And you journey south now?"

I opened and closed my mouth, unsure what to tell her. She couldn't be a spy. I refused to think it. It simply didn't ring true. Yet, speaking of my plans was tricky. I didn't want to tip off Kane that I planned to split.

"Wherever you go, they're watching," she warned. "Hunting. She wants to control all of Contermerria."

"What's watching?" Kane asked.

"The dragons?" I guessed.

"More so the bats," she replied sagely. "They breed them at Somman. They took the dragons to the main castle and use the Somman grounds to raise fleets of flying menaces to report to her."

I acknowledged her with a nod.

"If you must go south, avoid the west. Somman is unpassable. *She* is watching there. I know because I killed a messenger of that filth. When Petre passed out and I had to carry him, the pest dared to bother me. Pecking and hissing like a foul bully. I blasted it." She gave a stiff-lipped nod. "The least I could do in retaliation."

"Good," I praised, borrowing her word.

"The message was clear despite the burn I shot at him," she said, gritty satisfaction in her admission.

"The bat carried a scroll?" Kane asked.

"Yes. She is eager to find her brother. An ambush to stop him is planned. They suspect he is headed toward Somman, and she's rallying forces to intercept him there. I never minded him. Kinder. Calmer. But even he won't survive this hell she wishes upon all of our land."

Kane's stare burned on my back. I ignored it as what this poor woman said sank in.

Lianen and Devota *weren't* working together, then. This more or less confirmed it. But I wouldn't back down and give Kane the satisfaction of telling me *I told you so*.

All I could focus on was the fact Lianen might be en route with Thea. Devota setting up an ambush wouldn't bode well. Not at all.

I stood, refusing to look at Kane.

"Maren..."

No. His low, careful utterance of my name in that warning tone wouldn't change my mind either.

"Wherever you go, steer clear of the prince—" She curled her lip in disgust. "Of the *queen*. I heard of some seeking out caverns up north here, and if Petre hadn't been bitten..."

"Go. You can seek shelter there," I advised. Pointing in the direction of Dran, I watched as she shrugged.

"There is no point now. No hope." She tipped her chin up at us. Without making eye contact, she dismissed us, her loving, sad gaze on her dead son. "Goblins will come. They'll scent his blood and they can finish me, too."

"There is hope," Kane argued, firmly yet not unkind.

She shook her head. "Not for me. Not for this land."

I backed away, swallowing hard to withhold a goodbye—for good. "Thank you. For healing me." If she wished to be ended, I wouldn't stop her. In the throes of grief, she was untouchable. I had no right to tell her what to do.

Still refusing to look up, concentrated on her son, she sniffed. "Thank *you*," she insisted. "Vintar or not, anyone who killed that horrible master is a friend indeed."

I couldn't look back. I climbed onto the corga's saddle and gripped the reins. My muscles braced at the jolt of the ride as he turned and ran under my direction.

"Maren!" Kane raced after me, the hur-wolf huffing in chase.

South. To Somman.

"Maren!" he yelled, charging through the woods after me. Down the mountain we went. Gravity aided the corga to hurtle down the rocks and steep cuts of land. Healed and rested, I could brace and buoy myself with the teeth-rattling run.

"Mar—" I tuned him out, in no mood to hear him. He could argue until he was blue. I would not give up on my sister.

A thick pile of broken trees and boulders was jumbled in an impenetrable pile ahead. The corga seemed game, his legs eating up the distance and seeming prepared to jump onto and over this obstacle. Not far behind, Kane chased me on the hur-wolf.

I heard his grunt just before I felt the impact. His ride had adapted to the same goal. Climb and leap off the pile. Too close together though, Kane left his seat and flew toward me.

Caught in his arms, he took the brunt of the fall and rolled. I remained trapped within his embrace as he tugged me tight against him. Boiling with fury, I waited until he'd stopped to force my way free.

Punching, twisting, wrestling, I resisted his hold.

But he was bigger. Taller and stronger, and dammit, more experienced at fighting. Never mind the fact he'd taught *me* how to fight. This student couldn't beat the teacher.

"Stop!"

He pinned me to the ground, and I did the opposite. Straining against him, I tried to buck him off. If I tapped into my power, I'd have him retreating in no time. But this was Kane. This was—us. Never agreeing. And because of that tenet to this bond between us, I gave up. The physical resistance at least. No matter what he said, I was firm. He wouldn't change my mind—and he had to let me up sooner or later.

Breathing hard, he scowled down at me. He hovered too close, his long hair draping down like a curtain. Shielding him in more darkness and amplifying his ominous mood.

"You cannot. You cannot go charging to Somman."

I slid my jaw to the side, trying and failing to find a sliver of patience to be diplomatic. "And I obey *you*?"

He pounded his fist to the ground. Dust flew up and floated near my eyes.

"Didn't you hear her? That poor widow?"

I slitted my eyes. "Didn't *you*? She lost her entire family, and I risk that same fate. Thea is all I have."

His hand was so swift I could barely track it. He cupped my chin in a possessive grip. "Not me?"

I trapped my lower lip between my teeth until I tasted blood. I thought I had him. These unexplainable emotions I felt for him. A contradiction of passionate concern—a force that made me rush after him into Vintar and save him—and insidious mistrust.

"Don't do this to me," I threatened. "Do not think to test me, to expect me to choose. I fight for her."

"And I live for you!" Again, he smashed his fist into the dirt, venting his furious energy. "I went after her to keep her safe *for* you. Because I live—I fight—for you, Maren."

I swallowed hard, my mouth dry. Seeing him explode like this was too raw. Naked and...honest. I felt the truth in his words, but that sentiment didn't match his actions.

"Then fight *with* me, Kane. Come with me to make sure she's safe."

He shook his head, rearing back to straddle me. Running his hand through his hair, he growled.

He rose to stand, gripping my hand and bringing me up with him. "I know she's safe. That woman confirmed it. Lianen isn't working with Devota."

"That doesn't mean I can trust him though." When he opened his mouth, I walked right into his space. Hating how tall he was, I felt robbed of any power having to crane my neck and look up to him. "I have given all my life. Since I was a child, I have given. I never took for myself. I was forced to heed what others wanted. Others' needs. Never mine." I stabbed my finger at my chest. "I have spent the last several months giving *more* of myself. I have helped, even unwillingly as a pawn, in the machinations and games others wanted to enact. I cannot be selfless with this. I will not be able to live with myself if I fail Thea."

His nostrils flared as he glared at me. Dark and foreboding, his eyes drew me in.

"I refuse. If you want to go look for that sword—*again*—right now, then go. Do what you need to do."

He gripped my shirt and pulled me close. "What I need is *you*."

I licked my lips, undeterred by the insistent lust that spiked through me when he tracked that movement with his hooded gaze. "Then come with me. See to Thea's safety with me. That is all I need to do before I can help you with this damn search again." I tipped my chin up more, defiant though he held me in place. "You cannot expect me to trust him this easily."

We stared each other down, cloaked by the darkness of the night. Secluded in this moment in the warm forest, we waited for the other to speak. For him to back down. Or maybe he was hanging on to the hope I'd lighten up and bend to his will.

Chapter Twenty

After too many moments of tension crackling between us, he relented. With a heave of his chest, he sighed and shook his head. "Fine."

I ran my tongue over my lower lip, relieved he could be accommodating after all. *Because he cares.* Deep down, I knew it, even if I wasn't prepared to announce my vulnerability out loud. Was he mine? To live and fight for? Of course. Yet admitting that felt like too large of a grievance that he could hold against me.

"We'll head to Somman to find Lianen and Thea—if he's there."

I should have known something would be contingent on his agreement. "You doubt that woman? The message she read?"

He gazed at me steadily, but his demeanor softened. His arm went around me, and despite the anger I held as I fought with him mere moments ago, I was too attuned to this pull between us. Stepping closer, I rested my hand on his chest. After months apart, wanting to be close to him, I couldn't resist soaking him in.

"I'll believe a message I can hold and see myself. I do believe what she said, but Lianen might change his course, too."

I hope he can improvise however he needs to so long as Thea is protected.

"We'll go to Somman and look. I doubt he would go to Somman to stay there if he went to the trouble to reach Thea before Devota could. He'll have somewhere else in mind, I'm sure of it. But if he has already gone through there, or changed their path elsewhere, we go to find the sword."

Find *the sword? Find?* That hazy memory in the water pricked at my conscience. I already had found it in the Riverfall Chamber, maybe.

"Agreed?" He lowered his head, canceling out any chance I could look anywhere but at him lording over me. "We'll do as you think is right and go to Somman to check on Lianen's intentions with Thea. But after, we'll seek the sword."

I licked my lips, looking down. I couldn't face him, knowing I was likely the last to have seen that specific weapon. He growled, pulling me so close our bodies were flush.

"Maren..." he rasped. His fingers pressed my chin up, and I faced him.

"Agreed."

I expected a cocky smile. I hadn't counted on a hard kiss, instead. Too soon, he pulled back. "*Together*," he reiterated, stepping back. *Now* he gave me that smug grin. Unfinished with that kiss, needing more, so much more to sate this desire he sparked to life, I leaned forward. Off balance as I followed the absence of him pressed against me.

I drew in a breath, reining in this ridiculous magnetism I was locked in with him.

"Together," I muttered, praying this wouldn't be a regret.

"Because that corga would outrun a wolf any day," he said wryly, approaching the animals.

For two days, we did just that. Remained together. Side by side, we headed toward the Court of Somman. Riding, arguing if we were lost, then riding some more. The last time I journeyed from the Sord Forest toward the realm of summer, I was unconscious from breaking the binding spell that had kept me ignorant and trapped in Dran all my life. We'd been under attack in those woods, then captured. Prince Lianen had found us there, and on the way, looters showed up to complicate the situation even more. Awake and impatient for *this* trip, I felt like this dense forest would never end.

Wildfires spread in staggered patches, requiring rerouting through the labyrinth of trees, shrubs, and darker ravines. Insects trailed us, but the corga seemed to scare them off with a growl. Worst of all were the goblins and rabid no-longer-shaggy saberhorns. I didn't want to use my power on them. Kane didn't want to expend the energy fighting. Fortunately, the corga and hur-wolf ran faster than those lowly monsters.

We stopped briefly to eat and move around. Their stamina seemed to know no bounds, but our steeds needed to rest. Alternating in shifts, Kane and I took turns sleeping on the saddles.

"What happened to the frecens?" I wondered aloud the first day, surprised we hadn't run into any.

"Likely hiding. They hate the sun. I think they are mostly blind, so summer can be friendly to their kind." He shrugged. "Maybe they died off."

If only we could be so lucky.

While we'd created a compromise, going to Somman first, then for that sword, it seemed our argument installed a gap between us. Words didn't come easily. On my part, I was hesitant to speak up. I felt certain he'd want to launch into the how and where of looking for the long-lost Ranger blade. The longer I didn't mention it, the bigger the hole became.

Though, it wasn't my fault. When I fell into the river at the Chamber, I'd been operating on survival instinct. A woman—anyone—could only flail and flounder with too much chaos. From the idea of Ersilis breaking me out, to being healed, then tasked to help Amaias... I'd been tossed from one stunning moment to the next. Had I known it *was* that special blade, yes, I would have grabbed it.

Likely would have saved a lot of trouble, too, already possessing the one thing that might save this continent from Devota.

Particularly as the stink of dragons grew with every stride we rode. Dragons, so many of them streaked ahead. Not close enough to gauge them as a danger to us in here, but coming and going. Fainter at first, but increasing with our journey, pulses of magic hit me. Those sonic pressure waves indicated fae further ahead, and it could only mean the Sommans. The enemy.

"I think we've rounded it now."

I frowned at Kane's words. Out of the blue, it seemed. For hours, we rode with masks fashioned over our mouths. Scarves protected us, wetted with water from flasks we'd scavenged from corpses goblins had already reached. They must have been fleeing the Somman camps like that woman had. Small bags of preserved food and flasks of water helped us. With the heat, traveling light was wise.

Smoke blanketed the land. So thick we couldn't see ahead, we had no choice but to slow the animals. Hurtling through an impenetrable nothingness would be lethal. Our pace was slower, but with the wildfires claiming the forest that had to be the northern border of the Somman realm, we were redirected. Still south, but more to the western coast. Mountains were singular here, spaced up yet still posing a challenging path.

Kane raised his hand to his face, rubbing at his raw, dry eyes from the air. He pointed, and I squinted to follow the direction he aimed.

"That's Mount Crexen, the highest peak that landmarks the southern edge of Somman." His arm arched toward his left. "If we continue this way, we'll reach Rengae."

We were forced to travel along the coast, it seemed. I nodded. While this man played games with the concept of trust, I had full faith in his knowledge of the land.

"This way then?" I tilted my head toward the east. We'd need to cut a sharp turn to get back to where we'd planned to go—or where I'd planned to go and he'd reluctantly agreed.

He nodded. Brows creased, he frowned at the thick cover of smoke. We'd be charging in blind.

"I can—"

"No. They'll detect you."

I huffed a laugh. "We have to be near their land. I've smelled dragons circling since yesterday."

His frown slid into a harsh scowl. "You have?"

I shrugged. "Yes. It grows stronger now. We have to be close."

"Which is all the more reason why you shouldn't risk being detected using your power."

I blinked, wishing I could cry. Any tears would do. Something—anything with moisture—to wet my aching, dry eyes. Instead, I dragged my wetted cloth up and pressed it to my face. "I don't think the dragons could determine who is using it with so many around."

He grunted. "So many around?"

I nodded, lowering my cloth to cover my nose and mouth again.

"What else aren't you telling me?"

I barely caught myself from flinching, feeling caught red-handed. "I've sensed fae magic. It comes in pulses, or suctions of air." He wasn't interested in *how* I could tell power was being used nearby. Just if it was. "Something is going on to warrant so many strikes of magic. I can't imagine my one use would be anything different from what the dragons are already picking up on."

To demonstrate, I lifted my hand and cleared the smoke. With Somman abilities, I could manipulate even that state of heat. Visibility returned. A clear path showed as I parted the smoke like a river split in two.

Kane was a man of action, not words. He charged down the lane I'd opened, taking advantage.

"As long as I don't use Vintar force," I added, riding hard next to him. "I shouldn't stand out using Somman magic."

"That's what you detect over there?"

"Somman and something else. Rengae, but not as much."

I'd only just discovered the distinctions of my perception. How I'd known that dragon foot he axed off was just a trace of the monster's stench. Then the newness of the spiders and mountain troll. As I rode, with too much time to think, I realized they were all unique. With each mile we covered through these woods, I registered the notes of the fae too. Somman was so spicy, cloyingly thick in this smoke. Vintar was crisp, almost minty. And Rengae called to mind a salty trace.

We drove the corga and hur-wolf hard, and as they labored to bring us closer to the heart of Somman, I worried for them. Respiring that quickly and harshly with the exercise of running, and in this poor air quality. My concern for them wasn't all I could focus on for long, though.

The nearer we came, the louder the war sounded. Dragons screamed and roared overhead. Cries and shouts lifted like a din, coasting toward us. Flames rose high in the distance, but until we cleared this forest, we couldn't *see* anything.

"Stay low," Kane shouted needlessly. I'd already dropped, crouching so low I almost hugged the corga's neck. I'd parted the smoke from our way, but overhead, as charred remnants of tree trunks were thinned from the fires, the sky showed.

Bats. So many winged pests. Smaller than the dragons, their bodies swarmed in a frenzied mass spanning the sky. Above them, the larger bulks of dragons soared past, but closer to us, the bats dipped and swooped. Cried and hissed.

What is this madness?

My first fear was that we were too late. Devota planned to ambush Lianen here. That was what the message said. But would she do so at the risk of burning her homeplace down to ashes?

Because that was what we found. Skidding to a stop at a clearing, a platform that seemed to have once been carved as a decoration, we reached the palatial grounds.

I'd run from that castle—Devota and Lianen's home before she killed King Vanzed. Kane had been imprisoned in the deep-down dungeons within the stone structure. I'd been a "guest" in a lavish, opulent suite. Now, it was cloaked with smoke and flames, nestled within an inferno.

"The camps." Kane coughed, pointing to the low-lying buildings I'd never received an explanation for. From here, at this slightly higher vantage point, we could see down into the arenas. Men and women fought. Somman guards tried to tamp down the violence. It was nothing but death. *Every*one struck out. Fists, swords, clubs, and even hammers. The encampments were full of killers.

Dragons dove down, blasting fire at them all, the guards and prisoners alike. Children, too. A group of youths tackled a woman, stabbing and striking at her.

"I don't—" Kane cleared his throat. "I don't understand."

I tunneled my vision on the mass violence. A mob, where they were all fighting to the death. But there, in the middle of the chaos, I spotted something I at least recognized. As clueless as I was to *what* that thing was, I'd seen it before.

A darkness. Forming from a shadow, it moved like a large predator. Humanlike, but otherworldly.

"I—"

A larger dragon screamed, fire trailing from its snout as it torpedoed into the castle. Similar to the one that plowed into the tower at the main castle, when I'd gone looking for Isan and Amaias, this one knocked into stone as though it was merely shoving down a stack of twigs.

It turned, rocks, shingles, and dust flying out at its impact. Up into the dark red sky, it gained speed. Perhaps to do it again. In the brief moment of it slowing to pivot, though, I spotted the dangling angle of its ankle.

It was the one I'd cut. The one that dropped me into the swamp. This dragon was one of the queen's fleet.

"To the castle. Come on."

I didn't wait for Kane to agree or object. I went. The corga heeded the urgency in my commands. I couldn't explain it, but that dragon being there had to mean the queen had arrived. And if she was only supposed to be here to ambush her brother, that meant he—and Thea—had to be at the slowly crumbling and smoking Somman castle.

The pounding footfalls of the hur-wolf followed close. Kane soon passed me, charging faster toward the first double doors to the once-mighty palace.

Bounding up the carved stone steps, the corga cleared the polished patio. Then it leaped into the doors after Kane on the hur-wolf.

Chapter Twenty-One

"Where should—" My question was interrupted and answered.

A dragon growled heaving breaths as it squeezed into the hall and tried to run. Scraping the ceiling, its wings knocked down more sconces and bowls of oil with lights. The fallen decorations added to the flames blazing along the plush rugs. Paintings slanted lopsided as the dragon tunneled through, its legs smashing into the walls so hard it dented and cracked the stone surface.

"Get out!" I yelled it at the corga as I dismounted. Kane left the hur-wolf's saddle in the same moment, smacking its flank to send it running. With no time to prepare an alternative, no chance to devise a block, I knew this monster would trample us. A wall of ice, a fire, a geyser of water. No element could stop this beast from smashing through such a confined space at that speed.

The corga and hur-wolf turned and raced back outside. As I lifted my dagger, bracing for impact, Kane barreled into me, rolling us together until we slipped under the void of space. Allowed only by it lifting its feet and moving its fat thigh, we could shove under it unscathed. Kane grunted, pushing off his shoulder to roll us again, missing the footfall of the dragon's rear leg.

We clambered to stand, on our feet long enough to see the queen. She sprinted down the hallway that intersected what was once the apex of double-winding staircases. Voluminous space filled this wing of her former home. Beyond this grand foyer space, the museum galleries depicting Somman history waited.

Witnessing the queen running *from* a threat was so odd, I couldn't make sense of it. She was fearless, sadistic, and lived to cause suffering. What could—

Kane sucked in a breath, gripping my arm and pulling me back with him. He swore, breathy rasps of fear. *This* man was afraid.

Devota screamed, strange instructions that must have been codes to her staff or dragons. Her red cloak billowed. Her flowing orange and purple tunics and trousers whipped with her fast stride. So determined she was to escape, she didn't look back. Didn't slow enough to notice me there in the perpendicular hall, either. She dashed away with another, smaller dragon catching up to her inside this once-grand building. The beast leaped into the air, smashing through stained glass windows, and with a rope of fire, she lassoed it just in time to escape on its back through the window.

And there it was.

The darkness. A shadow that slithered into a form. Then back into the inky swirling nothingness. Filtering back and forth, that *thing*, that shadowy shape, stopped midstride. It pivoted on one stick of wood. The prosthetic spun him to face me. Kane tugged me back, but I dug in to wait and *see*. To know what this damn thing was.

For Queen Devota to fear it...

What is it?

Shifting from swirling shadows to increasingly clearer forms, it filled in. Then receded to the darkness again. Either was terrifying. In its shadowy mist, it emitted a gripping, choking pull on my mind. As a slowly transforming human, he was a hulking, horrendous species. Muscles stacked upon muscles revealed his brute strength. Hardened lines cut into his face spoke of scars and weathered flesh. Sinister, vacant eyes of pure obsidian stared with gruesome threats.

Tall and wide, he was a bulwark of promised pain and torture.

Dragons. Trolls. Goblins. That lernep. Mutant hurwolves...

My heart thundered as I panted faster. Adrenaline filled me, but that was nothing compared to the striking burn of my magic filling my veins.

What's one more freak?

"Maren, no," Kane warned, pulling me back.

The thing cocked its head to the side. I braced, fisting my dagger that glowed a fierce cyan glow.

"No," Kane urged, trying to pull me back.

Laughter and screams swirled together. The sea-weary man grinned, his stringy beard dropping lower. As his mouth opened, the shadow within that orifice pulled out and reverted. It enveloped him, swirling until he'd phased into that dark shape again. Before I could draw another breath, the inky smears of his shadow shot forward, spiraling around Kane and dropping him to the ground.

"Kane?" I lowered to one knee. "Kane!"

He groaned, shifting slightly. When he opened his eyes, blinking, relief hit me. I panicked, registering the heavy stride of my large opponent approaching me. Back to a hideous human, reeking of decay and sweat, he stalked closer.

"Kane—"

A scream strangled my voice. He knocked me down, lunging into me. I braced my arms against him, eyes wide and frozen in shock, as he reared back to drive his sword down.

Into me

To kill *me*.

"Kane!" I kicked and bucked, twisting out of his approach.

Baring his teeth, he turned and flipped to advance again. Used to the way he fought—he'd taught me how—I anticipated his strikes and hits. I formed a shield of ice to counter him, but with a feral ferocity, he attacked.

"*Kane!*" I screamed his name, clueless about what came over him. He'd never— He wouldn't do this. This wasn't him. It couldn't be. I loved him. He lived for me. Wanted to fight with me.

Not attack me himself!

He slammed me against the wall, pinning me there. He grunted like a beast, and as he stared down at me, I saw not him. I didn't gaze into the smoldering, intense stare he usually bestowed on me.

I saw nothing. Pure darkness—just like this stalking behemoth that still approached.

It was him. That thing. Its shadow. This wasn't Kane attacking me, but that *thing*.

"Maren!"

I turned toward the source of that shout. Lianen skidded to a stop at the intersection of the massive foyer. He'd sprinted from the galleries, and staring at me wide-eyed, he slung his bow over his shoulder.

The prince aimed at Kane, but the man didn't flinch. Didn't register the flaming arrow embedded into his shoulder. All he did was lift his free hand to remove the fiery tip and reach around to stab it into my face.

Tears blurred my vision. I feared he was gone. Lost to that shadow. But the pulsing heat of my dagger overruled my instinct to panic.

I wrenched my arm free from my ice shield, driving my dagger to the side to thrust it into Kane's stomach. He stilled.

The behemoth growled a thunderous rumble. Energy clouded around him as he lumbered toward us faster.

A gilded frame fell from above, smacking into my shoulder as the walls shook from this thing's gait.

"Kane!"

He'd frozen the moment I impaled him. His lids lowered, then lifted. Revealing that darkness spiraling in his eyes until it faded. As his face relaxed into a frown, then a grimace, my hand trembled.

The ice shield fell to the floor, sizzling upon contact with the licks of flames lining the rug. Stepping back, he looked down at my dagger in him. He covered my hand with his, pushing, trying to free the blade from his abdomen.

I couldn't have yanked it free if I wanted. At the contact of my dagger with his body, a tugging mechanism of force volleyed. A darkness locked my dagger inside. A countering push resisted, the force causing my hand to quiver as I held steady. Blue fanned out in a blinding sphere, and black streaks of shadow circled the illumination. Faster and faster. The inky smears were extracted at the site of my dagger piercing my man. Until they intensified, blanketing the bright hue.

Then it burst, the cyan brilliance radiating out in an explosion of might. Green and red shone, interspersed until each color glittered through the remnants of the black.

Kane staggered back, breathing hard. He slapped his hand to his side, the wound *I* gave him with this blue dagger. Opening his eyes, clear with that dark-blue gaze that captivated me so often, he stared at me.

Shock. Confusion. Agony and pain. They all flittered across his face until he tripped on his foot. Drunkenly, he fell back to the carpet, rolling from a stubborn trail of fire on the rug.

I licked my lips, stunned. He was...cured? Would he fight me? I'd pulled the darkness from him. Somehow, I'd returned him to the living as he was normally.

But the source of that darkness was nearly here. Growling and running, he charged at me.

"Maren, no!"

Lianen ran closer, firing arrow after arrow at the thing. The man. The shadow. None of the fiery arrows distracted this shadow man from running for me. Curling hands of talons and stretching arms rose from the fire—signifying Lianen's use of Somman spells to deter this freak. Still, he couldn't be slowed.

If this weathered mutant's darkness reacted to my dagger, I had something to work with here. So long as I lived to fight.

The man sprinted, his wooden leg stabbing into the floor without a misstep. His wrinkled, filthy clothes clung to his bulk, and algae swayed as he lifted his arm. Again, he opened his mouth. Inkiness built and grew from that opening, readying to launch out with another nightmarish roar. Before the darkness within him could ease out and be shot at me—at Lianen or even Kane again—I beat him to it, striking first.

Chapter Twenty-Two

I thrust my hand up, spraying a jet of sleet at his face. The shadows rolled back with the hit, but it hardly stalled the monster. At the impact of my ice, he phased into a shadow and appeared behind me, snaking out a beefy arm for my neck.

"Get down!" Lianen's shout sounded a second before his burst of flames came flying toward me. I slipped down, sliding, but the fire didn't affect this freak. He shook his head, the shadows creeping from over his shoulders to smother the flames.

"What *is* this thing?" I screamed, running from him chasing me again.

"A Wetherone!" the prince launched over a wave of darkness roiling over the carpet to claim him. He spread his hand out, fanning his fingers to buffer himself from the darkness's reach.

I shook my head. A Wetherone? A fabled boogeyman? I refused to believe. But I had to.

My naivety was a weakness I could no longer excuse.

If I was a tribis fae, why couldn't those fantastical frights exist?

"A *what?*" I yelled back.

He'd reached Kane, and from the push of magic through the air, I took faith that he was healing Kane. I backpedaled, forming shields of ice to block the dark streaks this thing shot at me. When I wasn't deflecting the snaking reaches of darkness, I struck back with long staffs of ice.

I couldn't stop it from prowling close.

"A Wetherone!" Kane replied. His voice was strong and clear as he and Lianen joined the fight. "Defeat it!"

Trying to...

The Wetherone didn't pay attention to Kane swiping a long busted candlestick of gold at the tendrils of shadows slithering toward him. It didn't care about Lianen's repeated shots of fiery arrows.

It wanted *me*.

I drew in a deep breath, thinking fast. Plotting on the spot. If my dagger could draw out and crush its shadows... Hissing, I jumped back at a near-miss. Each time I was close enough to stab it, the darkness jumped at me.

If I could keep it still, though...

I flooded the hall. Torrents of water filled in, waves rushing down the battered building space. The thing cackled, buoyant and at ease as I lifted us off the ground. Before it could swim and use the water to its advantage, I ended my Rengae spell and froze him in place.

Or I tried to. Evading me, slipping from one side of the room to another, it transported as shadows. I tried fire, next, to blast it with heat. Then ice.

When it sent out a cloak of shadows, I iced my hand and gripped the tangible yet abstract darkness. Using it as a rope, counting on my ice to protect me, I wrenched it close.

A flick of my hand evaporated all the water. Flames spiraled down my arm as I clung to the branch of shadow. It squeezed in on itself, reducing to slip free. The Wetherone roared, mouth wide to send out more shadows. I encased him in ice, agape and trembling with fury.

Another hard pull on the rope of shadow, and it dragged toward me. The momentum of his resistance snapping propelled him toward me. I jumped, not losing hold with my ice-covered hand on him. As I landed on top of him, I drove my arm down and stabbed my dagger into his chest.

Shadows flickered, chasing back and forth in a skittering pulse. Finally pinned as a man, the Wetherone snarled at me, eyes obsidian and mouth open in a soundless roar. All his darkness swarmed. Sucked into the magic in my blade. Just as it did with Kane, the shadows merged into a suffocating blur over the light beaming from my dagger.

Then, they burst.

A relieving pop of pressure skated through the hallway. Sound ceased as the Wetherone's screams of fury reverberated within my skull.

He lay there. Dead as a human corpse, and I stumbled, falling over him to rest on my knees. Drawing in lungfuls of air, I came down from the rush of the fight. A battle like no other I'd faced. And one I never wished to experience again.

Being even that close to his darkness was a sickening spell that breached my hold on my sanity.

"Maren." Kane ran up to me, catching me in his arms. I breathed him in, my cheek smashed against his chest as his heart raced within. His hands lifted to stroke back my hair from my face, and I closed my eyes, relishing his comfort. I pushed down, my fingertips trembling but determined. Pushing up his shirt, I felt for the wound. My dagger's scar. There was none.

"I healed him," Lianen promised.

Lianen.

I shot out of Kane's embrace. "Where is my sister?" I demanded.

"Safe."

I tilted my head to the side, advancing on him.

"I placed her in a ward. Somewhere safe."

I narrowed my eyes on him. "Why?"

"Why?" He scoffed. "Because the queen wanted to bring her to the prison. When she couldn't break you. When you wouldn't bow to her willingly, even as a slave, she thought using your sister as torture would achieve your fealty."

I shook my head. The extremes that lunatic would go to. I noticed how he'd called her *the queen*. Not *my sister* or *Devota*. According to him, she was worthy of no name or family relation. His scathing tone matched that Somman woman in the forest we'd found.

He'd cut ties with her, indeed.

"I went to get Thea and keep her out of the war before *she* could."

I crossed my arms. "Out of the goodness of your heart?" I taunted.

"To fight back," he snapped, getting in my face. "You wouldn't understand. All my life she's controlled me. Ordered me. Manipulated me." He punched the wall. "Bound me here, her and Xandar always trying to hide me in lies."

"Not anymore. Not Xandar."

He stilled, seeming to accept the truth I shared. "He's dead?"

I nodded.

"When you escaped that night, the dragons fled. I hadn't known she was storming the castle to kill the king. I hadn't known. If I had..." He shook his head. "I was never part of her dreams. I never wanted a part of her genocide and power. And taking your sister out of her reach was the first way I thought of doing that. What little good it could have done—" He shook his head, huffing. Incredulous, it seemed, at his own words. "Little good. She can save us. She can help us all."

I furrowed my brow. "*Thea?*"

"She can read." Lianen pierced me with his solemn stare. "Read, Maren. She can *read*."

I flapped my arms up. Literacy. That was her power? "I— *Read?* So can I!"

Lianen licked his lips, still out of breath. "She can read the Ranger's words."

I blinked, not following. The Ranger's word of what? Of course, my sister could *read*. She was literate. In Dran, she taught the children how to follow letters and work toward phonetics to better their chances of being an elite soldier.

"The Rangers, Kane," he said, turning toward the man. He'd quietly stepped aside, staring down at the Wetherone I'd defeated. Kane wasn't fae, but he had the closest tie to the last leader of the Rangers—nomadic tribis fae. He'd traveled with them, the leader of the scattered minority adopting him as his grandson to train for a hard life on Contermerria.

"When the queen's troops showed in Dran, I took off to the north. We camped up high, as far as my elkhorn could carry us on the northern trail. At that peak, we saw them. We saw them coming." He looked from Kane to me. "Thea could read their banners through my scope. Because winter is no longer, because summer rules and all the ice melts—"

I drew in a fortifying breath. "The ice that once surrounded the mainland."

"Yes." Lianen nodded. "Because she took the throne, all that ice—that was protecting us from invasion—is gone. The Wetherones will come." He pointed at the one I'd killed. "They are already coming as the bergs break up at the shore."

Kane finally looked up then, frowning at us both. He came closer and took my hand. For his own sense of support? To connect with me? He seemed so grave, I didn't have the heart to protest. Instead, I curled my fingers with his and squeezed.

"Thea can read the Ranger's word?" he asked me.

I shrugged. I didn't know what this language was. "She reads all the time. She... I guess?"

"She could read the Wetherone's banners from their ships as they neared," Lianen said.

Ships. Not dragons. That night I chased the dark form—a Wetherone, I now knew—I'd hung over the edge. Upside down, I thought I saw dragons in the distance, but from that inverted angle, I'd been looking at shapes in the water, not the air. Ships.

"Myth and lore. We'd all been told they were stories. Pretend dangers." Lianen shook his head. "And no one knows how to handle them, how to defend against them." He narrowed his eyes on me. "Except, according to what your sister claims she read before, the Rangers. The tribis."

"Don't look at me."

"I *am* looking at you. Neither Somman nor Rengae, nor Vintar alone can defeat their shadows. But a tribis can."

I opened and closed my mouth. "All right, but—"

"*You* can counter their magic." He pointed at me, and Kane smacked his hand down out of my face.

"She cannot singlehandedly defeat an entire army of them," he challenged.

"But there must be a way. The Rangers recorded it. Thea's certain more literature can explain. That's why I came here. I warded her in the center of the continent and rode here. The libraries are extensive with old tomes, but I found nothing of the Ranger's texts. Then..." He shook his head, bitterness heavy in his absent stare. "Then *they* came. The Wetherones climbed over the coastal peaks. Only a few, I think, slipping in from the western coast."

Pointing in the direction of the internment camps, he explained. "One got in there and turned them all against each other. Devota showed up, likely on my tail for stealing Thea out from her clutches. But when she saw the Wetherone, she ran."

I snorted. *At least she's afraid of* something. A threat to her reign, apparently.

"Where is Isan?" Lianen demanded. "Help him kill her. Restore winter. The Wetherones are near, but if we can block the mainland and render it safe from invasion—"

Kane rubbed his jaw. "Isan is out looking for Amaias."

Lianen frowned, his features scrunching in confusion. "Amaias? Where was she?"

"Imprisoned at the castle with Isan," I replied. "She's...out there somewhere. But Vintar can't rule again. Isan's too weak to fight, much less drive his Vintar blade through your sister—if he had it."

He scowled. "She's not my sister. Not my blood. She's a monster. I've disowned her."

"And his fae blade is..."

"Is in the queen's hands." He gripped his hair and pulled. "Get it from her," he insisted. "You're tribis. You can override her power."

I shook my head. "That Vintar blade is..." I cringed.

Lianen tilted his head to the side as he glared at Kane. "Don't tell me you lost *that* too."

"I, uh." I winced. "Broke it."

"A troll did," Kane corrected.

Lianen spun back, muttering and swearing. "Then find something!" He pointed at my dagger. "Use that. Find any fae blade and kill the queen. Because if she refuses to cease this war on the people, we won't have any survivors to defend our land from the Wetherones."

I gritted my teeth and gripped his shirt. He slitted his eyes at me as I pulled him close. Nose to nose, we stared each other down.

"I don't bow to you, either, *prince*."

His jaw slid. Fire curled up between us, and I fanned it hotter until he surrendered his magic.

"We'll look for a blade. So long as *you* keep my sister safe." I released him with a shove.

He glared at me, not in antagonism, but somber seriousness. With one curt nod, he turned and ran off.

Chapter Twenty-Three

Sounds of battles had faded outside. It wasn't still and quiet, but fewer screams and wails came from the direction of the camps on the edge of the Somman royal grounds. Of what was left of the palace. Walls bore large holes where dragons burst into or out of the building. Why and how the monsters *entered* was an oddity I didn't have time to puzzle. I guessed Devota ordered them to follow her once she spotted the Wetherone on land.

After Lianen ran away, Kane pulled me by the hand and rushed out the way we'd come.

The corga and hur-wolf were nowhere to be seen. I must have lost the whistle pairing me to the corga because no string hung from my neck. During that strange and morbid fight with the Wetherone, it must have broken off.

"There." Kane pointed to an elkhorn. Many antlers rose from his head although it seemed like most had broken them off with the coming of summer. Lean and muscled, it was a mighty, majestic creature pawing its hoof at a broken ruin of a gate. Trapped in there, it was clearly frantic to escape.

Barren grounds housed charred remains of the castle. I feared the other animals in the stables were gone as well.

Overhead, bats circled, but not in the layered masses of wings as there had been when we arrived.

Kane released my hand. Speaking to calm the panicking animal, I used a blast of water to shove the metal and wood blocks apart.

"Can he carry us both?" I asked.

His reply was to climb up onto its saddle and reach down for me. I rose on my tiptoes, sliding my forearm up to rest my fingers around his. Linked to his strong arm, I jumped, and he hauled me up with him. I sat in the scant space in front of him, at once missing the freedom of the corga's more flexible saddle. I'd grown used to its longer, lower gait, too. Atop this tall steed, even braced with my back flush to Kane's chest, I had to reacclimate to the juddering jolts of its hooves.

We hurried away, leaving the destruction beyond. Smoke cloaked the skies, but as we angled away from Somman, heading toward the vast plains of the wilds that made up the center of the continent, the sting of the heat lessened.

"Do you believe me now?" he asked.

I cringed inside, hating the accusation in his tone.

"Do you believe me now? That Lianen will keep her safe?"

He had a point, but it still felt so small against the heavy burden of skepticism rooted deep within me. I wouldn't apologize for doubting. I wouldn't regret my instinct to keep Thea safe.

Only, now...guilt came. It didn't drown me, but it pricked at me, an insistent bother I couldn't dismiss. Yes, I now understood Lianen wasn't working for or with his sister. He'd denounced her and her reign. Thea would be protected with the Somman fae as much as she could be with me. Perhaps more so, if he could find any dragons used to his command that Devota hadn't taken.

And since Kane had stood by his promise, to deviate from our plans to ensure my sister wasn't within the enemy's reach, I had to fulfill my half of our agreement.

Find the blade.

He sighed, shaking his head behind me. I couldn't see him to know it, but the scruff growing along his jaw caught my hair and tugged it. His arm did too. With that aggrieved exhale, he banded his arm around my waist and pulled me closer in a hug.

"I won't lie to you, Maren," he said, his lips lower to my ear. "I learned my lesson."

He hadn't spoken false truths, but he had omitted too many details. Lie by omission. That he could own up to it so bluntly was a big step forward in our partnership.

But I have. I swallowed hard, emotions warring in my mind.

"Now that you know he's with her and he'll protect her, we can focus on finding that sword. If it wasn't in the Riverfall Chamber, then it must have fallen to the moat. Carried away. We can go to the swamp, or Rengae. It might not be a bad idea to check in with Baraan since he is eager to end her too."

I gripped the reins and pulled back hard to reduce the elkhorn to a meandering walk instead of a gallop. I couldn't listen to him carry on like this. Every word cut me, harsh reminders that he was clueless about where that sword was. That I thought I had seen it but said otherwise as I prioritized my sister over the fate of the mainland.

"What—" He reared back, allowing me space to rise to my knees and spin. Facing him. It would be hard enough to own up to *my* fault, to my lie to him. If I was going to come clean, I wanted him to be able to look into my eyes and see the honesty behind my words. To know I regretted it.

"I—" I paused, worried when he cringed at this unconventional movement on the saddle. Such a small space to be forced together. Uncomfortable, but in other circumstances, perhaps intimate. I pressed my hand to his side, worried a residue of pain lingered. "I'm sorry."

He grated a hard laugh, covering my hand with his and lifting them. Reaching back, he placed my hand behind his neck at the same time he gripped my thigh with his free hand. Hugging me to him, as I slotted onto his lap with my legs draped over his, he shook his head. "No, you're not."

He kissed me, hard and urgent, then rested his brow against mine.

I closed my eyes, savoring his touch. "No. I'm not."

"It would've consumed me." His breath shuddered out of him as he held me closer. I wrapped both arms around him, clinging to his neck. "It takes over your mind. With screams and wails. With no control over your thoughts. It overpowered me, and had you not removed its spell, I would have killed *you*."

The agony in his tone wounded me. Desperate to remove the idea of such an atrocity, I kissed him. Air ceased to matter. Only his mouth on mine. That was all I needed. This reassurance of *us*. That we lived and survived, and burned for each other despite the grievance of my secret I had to share.

"I cannot—" He growled the words against my throat, lifting me with his hands. I rose, dropping my head back to give him better access. "I cannot bear the thought of losing you."

The wicked heat of desire consumed me. Faster, now, perhaps because he'd already shown me a taste of what he wanted. Of what I wanted but didn't know how to explain. Desire. It was a needy demon that came alive within me. My stomach ached, and I grew wetter, my legs spread apart in such a wanton position over him.

"I will not." He rasped, his breaths hot against my fingers at my chest. I trembled, forcing my fingers to open my shirt. Buttons slipped and ties tore, but the fabric parted. He lowered his mouth to my breasts. Over the material of my brassiere then tugging it aside with his teeth to suck on my heated bare skin.

The elkhorn grunted, still walking aimlessly with the reins hanging loose. Uneven and almost off balance, I gripped Kane's hair, holding his face to me.

"I will not lose you," he promised.

Fired by his words, I gave in to this need. I was consumed with wanting him, and he matched my urgency. He held me on his lap, adjusting as I lifted to my knees. His hand lifted, rubbing against me, cupping his palm to my clit where I needed that friction. Throbbing and dripping wet for him, I strained to turn. To reach for the reins and stop the animal.

No one was around. In these plains, it was just us on the saddle, the clearing smoke hiding the stars above.

"I need—"

He caught me, his hand rough as he gripped my chin. I kissed him hard, ravenous for his lips on me again. Clinging to him, I let him lower me back. Arching toward the elkhorn's mane, I felt him lifting my leg. My pants slid down. He shifted some more, rising up himself. Feet in the stirrups, he slanted over me. Through harsh breaths and groaning rumbles, he didn't let up. He leaned over me, deepening his kiss. I sucked on his tongue. My fingers tugged on his hair. As he swallowed my whimpers, another thrill shot through me. I was wet, dripping with my cream. But I felt the air against that slickness, realizing I was bare, I ached even more.

As I slung my leg around his waist, holding on as the elkhorn walked, I felt him too. His solid thigh, his taut skin against mine. Bracing his arms around me, one hand on my ass and the other cupping the back of my head, he lifted me with him. He straightened to sit, bringing me upright with him. Over him. On him.

I gasped, shocked at the feel of his erection against my core.

After the shock of more danger awaiting us. Facing the dangerous fights expected of us. And so close to the idea of losing each other in death. We were lost to desire, making up the worst possible what-if.

"I need you, Maren," he muttered against my lips.

I lifted, his hand on my ass cheek guiding me. "I need you too. Now." Then I lowered my hand to grip his length, lining it up with my soaking hole. Staring into his eyes, feeling the depth of his love with his tortured gaze, I slid down. Taking him inch by hard inch.

I cried out at the stretch, a fullness I'd never experienced. In pain, yet not, I hesitated. He kissed me, muffling my reaction to losing myself to him. Gentle and tender, he nipped at my lips and traced me with his tongue. Waiting to adjust to him filling me, I sat on his lap. Rocking from the elkhorn's walk, swaying against Kane on this saddle, I returned. I answered in kind, kissing him back.

He lifted his hand to frame my face. Smoothing his thumb along my cheek, he forced me to meet his gaze. "I will always need you. Now and forever, Maren." He thrust his hips up, and I moaned. "You are *mine.*"

Gazing at him, my lids half-closed as I surrendered to this lust burning me alive, I lifted. His hard, thick length stroked deep inside me, and I relished the burn of him stretching me in a way I never had experienced before.

Over and over, I rocked on him. His dick pounding into me. Claiming me.

I lowered once more, steadier in my dip down on him. Riding him. Faster, but jerkier, I dragged myself up his long erection, then slammed back.

He breathed faster, his pants mixing with mine. Uttering curses and swearing strings of filthy nonsense, he maintained eye contact. I focused on looking him in the eye and chased after my release. An orgasm built, and I ground against him with wild urgency.

"That's it," he crooned, his gravely tone turning me on even more. "Come for me. With me." He widened his legs, forcing mine apart too, and I sank lower on him. He leaned me back, staring at my breasts with a hungry look as I bounced on him. His hands held my back as I rode him, working up and down. Frustrated at the tension, about to scream, I dropped my head back.

He jerked back, pulling out of me completely.

"No!" My breath left me as I dropped onto the elkhorn. Slanting up over its neck, I was laid out for Kane. My legs hung over the saddle, bouncing with the ride. Scooting back, he helped me turn. Facing forward, I followed his lead. Cream dripped down my legs as I spun around.

I braced my hands on the edge of the saddle. His hands smoothed up over my ass and along my thighs as he pulled me back onto his lap. Groaning at the tight shove of his dick deep inside me again, I let my head hang low. My breasts swayed, so heavy and aching.

Keeping his hands on my hips, he held me in place. On my hands and knees, I kneeled there while he stood on the stirrups and pounded into me. Closer. I was so damn close to coming. Tears spilled as I strained to get there. To give in and let him take me.

"Please," I begged.

He sat down again, groaning in pleasure, and he pulled me onto the saddle again. Harder onto him. Hugged to him, I let my head roll back against his shoulder. He cupped my breast with one hand and kissed my neck. Sucking hard, he jerked his hips. Prompting me to move. I jolted at the deeper thrust. As I raised my arms to loop them back over his head, he slid his other hand down to where we were joined. Seated on him, I let the rocking motion of the elkhorn's pace torture me. With each push back on him, he thrust his hips up.

I gripped his hair, turning his head so I could kiss him.

His lips sealed against mine. His tongue thrust into my mouth. His hand gripped my breast. His fingers rubbed my clit. His dick anchored my pussy as I slammed down.

And I came. I cried out wordlessly as he kissed me so roughly. Before I could relax, my limbs quivering as he held me on the saddle with him, he tensed. Then with the pulsing jerk of him deep inside me, he joined me.

Together. We'd come together in a blissful combustion of tension we'd dragged out for too long. I slumped against him, pliant to his hard, solid frame. He dropped his chin on my shoulder, catching his breath, and I rolled my head toward his, too spent to move further. His calloused fingers caressed my thigh, smooth, steady rubs that helped to calm me, to catch me in the aftermath of such an intense orgasm.

Committed and connected. After the fear of losing him to the Wetherone's spell, and following the horror he'd faced at trying to kill me, we grounded ourselves with each other. Making love to contradict the close call of death.

"Forever, Maren." He whispered the promise with a kiss to my jaw. "You're mine forever. No matter what comes next."

What would come next was that sword. We were in agreement now that this was our next step—together. I wouldn't renege. I would help him find the lost Ranger blade.

But I'd have to tell him the truth, first.

And sooner than later because he seemed to be directing this elkhorn south to Rengae, as he'd rambled about. When, in fact, I knew he needed to steer us toward the Riverfall.

I reached for the reins again, and as I leaned forward, he slipped out of me.

Hating the way I'd ruin the peace between us so soon after that bliss, I pulled on the reins, stopping the elkhorn—as I'd intended to before we lost ourselves to the feverous lust that couldn't be ignored. "About that..."

Chapter Twenty-Four

Shame made my cheeks burn hot. Not because I'd given in to my desire for Kane, but because I'd done so before speaking up. Though, I was glad, too. Had I confessed my lie a moment sooner, I never would have had a chance to experience him deep inside me. That was a gift I'd cherish and take to my grave.

Knowing he'd never want to repeat that mistake with me hurt more than I could have imagined.

"What?" he asked. His tone was already hard. He wasn't stupid. He'd likely already gathered that whatever I was about to say wouldn't be good news because of my timid, uneasy tone.

Guarded. He was more than guarded. Leery of me.

"I lied to you." May as well come out firm and clear from the start, matter of fact about it. Still, I looked down, pulling my clothes back on as he dribbled out of me. A stark reminder of how quickly things had changed between us. A physical reminder of what we *could* have if we were two ordinary people without lies marring the future.

He shifted on the saddle behind me, adjusting himself into his clothes too.

Already, a gap of distance was wedged between us after we'd come together so intimately. So...lovingly. I doubted this man would love a liar.

I felt his sigh and hated the push of his chest against my back. That I was the cause for that troubled sound and deep breath.

"I did see the sword."

A swift curse left his lips. He reached past me, taking the reins. As though he no longer trusted me to call the shots.

"I saw the Ranger sword," I clarified without reason. "And it *wasn't* in Rengae."

His arm flexed at my side, and I watched his fist form over the leather straps.

"Where?" Such a low, dark tone. Aimed at me, like I was the enemy.

"In the Riverfall Chamber—in the river."

He pushed his knees into the elkhorn's sides, prompting it to gallop so suddenly I reached for the saddle horn for balance.

"I think I gripped it," I added. "Underwater."

"And you didn't consider holding on to it?" His shout wounded me, but I wouldn't cower at his anger.

I elbowed him hard. "Don't judge me."

"You knew—" He groaned, venting his fury as the hot air whipped past us. Galloping due east, he steered the elkhorn toward the main castle where the river rushed through the Riverfall Chamber. Where I was mostly sure I saw the blade we sought.

"You knew all this time. You know where it is, but—"

"I *think*. I *think* it was the Ranger blade."

"Tell me."

Never before had I heard such a furious edge from him, directed toward me. So soon after his seductive promises, it jarred me. "When Ersilis freed me, she healed me. A dragon came, woken by Amaias fighting the guards to get Isan out. I tripped and fell into the river. Dragons tried to get at me, even underwater. During the seconds that I fell in, my hand brushed against it. I think."

His chest beat against my back as we raced across the plains. "You *think*? I doubt you'll ever master a proper grip on your own dagger, but—"

"Don't be an asshole!" Again, I elbowed him from the opposite side, but he thought quicker, blocking my jab.

"You either felt it or not. Tell me!"

"It wasn't a rock. I opened my eyes, but it was so hard to see. I think it was the sword."

"How sure are you?"

I opened and closed my mouth, hesitant to claim anything with accuracy. Telling him something not entirely true would only worsen my predicament with him. I'd dreamed of the weapon. Was it a memory, or the constant, questioning presence of it on my mind as I debated what I felt and saw at such a rushed, blurry moment of life or death?

I couldn't lie to him again. Cringing, I replied what I ultimately believed deep down. "Very. I'm very sure I felt it at the bottom of the river."

"Why did you lie!" He shook the rein, not changing his instruction to the elkhorn but moving his hand to vent.

"Because you wouldn't listen to me. I wanted to make sure Thea was safe first. Not go rushing after a sword since the last time I did caused war!"

"How's that working for you now, huh?" He grunted. "Thea *is* protected, just like I told you she would be."

"You didn't *know* that. When it comes to my sister, I need to know for myself."

"Because you can't trust me? And what I say?"

I hardened my resolve, stubbornly firming my lips into a thin line. "After the games you played with me when we first left Dran, are you surprised?"

He didn't reply.

"I've been thrust into this life of dangers, and royals, and secrets, and tricks. You didn't help *any* of that. You could have told me the truth from the first day I met you."

His chuckle was dark and threatening. "I *did*. I told you that you were fae. That first night. And you didn't believe me."

Fine. He had a point there. I hadn't believed him because it was just so ludicrous at the moment. "I was bound. I was under a spell to *be* ignorant."

"You're trying to say you had no control over what you felt?" He tapped a finger to my temple and I dodged his touch. "That *you* couldn't trust me regardless of the details?"

"Why would I? We'd just met. In the jail! You were a stranger."

"Doesn't seem like anything's changed." He grunted in dark amusement. "You *still* won't trust me and what I say."

"Everything—" I caught myself from spilling more truths. To me, *everything* had changed on that journey. I'd learned I was fae. And along the way, I'd fallen in love with him. *My mistake.*

Fuming, I relied on silence to control my temper. He didn't have to be so cold. So inflexible. If he could view it from my perspective, he'd understand. That he couldn't, stung. With that disappointment, in myself and him, I sank into a bitter quiet, refusing to listen to my heart. I'd never obey this stupid, damnable attraction between us ever again.

After a lengthy silence, he spoke up. I listened, instead of tuning him out in defiance, sure that I'd locked down all my emotions and iced my feelings for him.

Lust, love, and lies aside, this was no time for wallowing in past mistakes. No matter how much it broke my heart.

With the Wetherones invading from the sea, and Devota stimulating war on the land and its people, I'd dismiss this turmoil in my head and my heart until it didn't cut so deep. Until his words couldn't wound me.

"How can you not be certain?" he asked hotly. "Did you see the Ranger blade or not?"

I licked my lips, my anger rising regardless of my efforts to calm down and numb myself to him. *I told you!*

"I only saw the Ranger blade for maybe a few seconds. I spotted it, or what I assumed was it, in the middle of trying to save King Vanzed. I wasn't paying attention to details then. I wasn't aware of what it looked like. I was focused on keeping him alive—because without any explanation at all, *you* told me he needed to remain on the throne. I wasn't looking for any weapons, too busy trying to keep a 'proper' grip on my dagger and save the day. To make sure *you* didn't die, either. All I knew was that I spotted *a* blade near the river. A sword that seemed forgotten. And I assumed it was your grandfather's sword that you'd been looking for."

"I'll draw you a picture for future reference," he said dryly. "So you won't miss it again."

I deadpanned at the horizon. His sarcasm wasn't necessary.

"Did you see the sword in the chamber while you were there? At all?"

I hesitated to reply, my temper flaring too hot and provoking an uncensored retort. "All I saw was misery and pain. I was a *slave*, Kane. Not just a prisoner, like you'd been. Not just an object of torture. I was a *slave*. Manual labor until, if I hadn't had a reason to live—for *you*, for Thea—I would have begged for death."

His silence was hard to read. Did he pity me? Loathe me? I didn't care. I'd be a fool to care. It seemed I'd finally grasped the lesson of shutting down my heart.

"I didn't see anything but the colosseum and my cell. Until Ersilis broke in to free me, I wasn't allowed a glance at the river or what might have been in it."

In the distance, jagged peaks of mountains cut into the sky.

Vintar—or what was left of it.

One place I sure as hell never wanted to return to for a third time.

"My guess is—if that blade is the Ranger's—it fell into the river when Vanzed was killed. I brushed against it in the river. Then when I climbed back up the waterfall to sneak in and retrieve my dagger, it was no longer there at the bottom."

"Then it was carried away in the river," he concluded.

"Which is why I say it is at Riverfall. It likely went over the falls and sank into the moat. Near the castle. *Not* in Rengae. I floated into the swamp near Rengae because I was in a bubble. The sword weighed down by its dense metal."

With each word, we agreed on one thing. No more emotion. Just sticking to the facts. Business only. I wouldn't challenge him with that tactic. As short as the connection had been between us—on a saddle, no less—it was over.

Why *would* anyone have time for a stupid and vulnerable thing like love in the middle of a war? Of multiple wars?

Kane stiffened. I was alarmed at the tension in his body and hated how easily I was attuned to him. I glanced up at his scowling face, following the line of his sight for what had snagged his attention. For what had distracted him from his anger with me.

Wings flapped. Black, but not of a bat or dragon. Smaller than both and sleeker. A messenger bird was aimed at us. It circled. Once, twice, then it called out in a creepy caw.

Clearly, we were its designated target. Yet, how could it reach us and land while we galloped? "Maybe—"

Kane shot a stern look at me, his face unforgiving as he stopped the elkhorn.

I turned my face away, in no mood for his attitude.

The bird lowered, landing on Kane's outstretched arm. The talons pressed into his taut, tan skin, and at a trickle of blood, I immediately wanted to heal him. Whether I was mad at him or not, I hated the idea of him in pain. The hard glare he sent me suggested I *not* mention that offer and touch him any more than necessary.

Asshole.

He opened the scroll, and taller than me, he held it out of my sight at first. I gripped his wrist, bringing his arm toward me, and siccing a shot of healing magic anyway.

K

Bring the tribis to Poround. Wetherones have invaded.
E

I frowned. Was I some functional, dispatchable tool now? I'd just survived my first encounter with that pirate freak, and I wasn't eager to rush into another. Couldn't I have a day to simply breathe? Recharge?

Kane scoffed. "Ersilis?"

I'd noticed that too. Prince Isan was the one who'd given Kane that scented packet. He must have it in his pocket yet for this messenger to have found him with this missive. Why did Ersilis pen it, not Isan?

Kane stared at the scroll for a moment longer. I didn't need to look at it again to absorb this news. Short and to the point. Nothing there to misinterpret.

I crossed my arms and looked away. Sour irritation ate at me.

Would I die serving everyone else? When could I expect a break from doing what others wanted?

I hadn't asked to be a tribis fae. But now that I knew I was, was I supposed to have obtained a sense of servitude? To accept that others would use me?

I didn't wish anyone to die, especially within the warfare the Wetherones used. As Kane had pointed out to Lianen, though, I was only one person. Sending an individual out to battle an entire fleet was suicide.

But they won't care. Knowing I was expendable hurt as much as Kane's coldness.

"What—" Kane caught himself, then exhaled a harsh breath. "What do you make of it?"

I frowned at him. "Huh?"

He lifted the scroll, emphasizing it. "This message. What do you make of it?"

I raised one brow. "You *care* what I think?"

"Seeing as they're asking for you, yes."

"Asking? They're telling me to go. No. Not even that. Ordering you to just deliver me there."

He rolled his eyes. "Fine. Not asking. Requesting."

That doesn't make it much better. "I think they want me to come die for them. Because they have no other options to defend themselves." I shrugged, belying the pain of that admission.

"No." He shook his head, again staring at the few words delivered to him.

"No, what?" He didn't want me to die? Or that I was the last resort?

"Not that," he said, rubbing his face. "Why'd *she* send it? Ersilis."

I'd wondered about that too, but it hardly mattered. "Isan probably asked her to. Maybe he's too weak to do anything."

"Or it's not a message to be trusted."

And here I thought *I* was supposed to be the skeptical doubter.

I shrugged.

"Should we go?"

Again, I stared him down. "You're asking *me*?" I repeated dully.

"You're the one they've as—requested."

"Don't bother asking me if I feel special."

"Unless..." He shook his head and rolled the scroll back up. Instead of pocketing it, he attached it to the bird and it flew off again. "Unless it's a diversion."

"How?"

The elkhorn huffed and pawed at the ground, and Kane prompted it to walk out its restlessness.

"If someone didn't want us to go to the castle. To get the Ranger's sword."

If it's there.

I shook my head, picking at his logic and trying to guess what he was thinking. "Who would know that we're headed there to begin with?"

He twirled his finger at the sky. "I assume something's always watching. Dragons, birds."

And we'd just... My cheeks heated. Right out in the open. To know someone—especially an enemy—could have watched... *Nothing I can do about it now.*

"The Wetherones pose the bigger threat."

I raised my brows, not chiming in about that.

"Don't you think?"

I bristled at his words. "Don't trick me into thinking you value my opinion."

"Get over yourself, Maren. Whether you want to or not, you *do* play a role in all of this."

"Only because I ever met you."

"Fine. Hate me. I don't care. What do you think is the bigger risk?"

"Between Devota on the throne or the Wetherones invading?" I considered it, but I must have taken too long because he spoke up.

"Devota is ruining Contermerria. But if the Wetherones can invade so far that they reach her and tap into her sadistic mind?"

Two evils in one.

"The Wetherones," I answered. A chill snaked up my spine at the idea of what kind of life we'd have. Without our minds and subject to a malicious woman.

"Then we'll go to Rengae." He said it with a command shouted at the elkhorn, which turned and galloped faster.

To my death. If they summoned me to face these pirate beasts for them, I'd have no backup. No resistance to rely on.

Alone, and sacrificing myself for others. Again.

Chapter Twenty-Five

Riding with Kane was a slow, endless torture. To be so near him, pressed flush to his back, but feeling so far apart at the same time made me hold back tears. The longer we rode, the more my heart broke.

From one miscommunication, one source of a disconnect, we'd ruined the camaraderie we once shared. Trust, as simple as it should be, would never be reached between us. After he'd brought me to such heights of pleasure, of feeling so complete with him inside me, I felt broken. One half of who I should have been.

Together on this saddle, I didn't have a chance to escape the despair. I could only hope to mask it as I had to do with my powers. Just like the need to conceal my identity as a fae, I couldn't let Kane see how badly this argument hurt me. Being vulnerable with my heart felt like too big of an error to make.

The ride to the Rengaen shore, the southern edge of Contermerria, should have taken us five days. For the first two, we stewed in silence, riding through the heat. More obstacles delayed us. Goblins herding after us. Some refugees trying to take the elkhorn. Simple fights that we paired up for and tackled well without a single word spoken.

Despite how much we couldn't see eye to eye, we did have each other's backs.

On the third day, we passed an abandoned village, and I secured an elkhorn of my own to ride. It had to be easier, a reduced burden of weight for the Somman's elkhorn to carry. Once I sat astride it, though, a pang of loss hit me. The saddle was slimmer. Harder. Not broken in like the one Kane rode. Also not the same as when we'd—

Stop, Maren. Chin up. And just forget about it.

Romance wasn't on the agenda. Not for me. The sooner I came to terms with that, the better.

Camping in brief intervals, we both sought rest only enough to recharge our bodies to continue. Food and water were found from the remnants of war everywhere, and we ate and drank in small, rationed amounts while we rode. I used my power only to set wards while we took turns sleeping in those brief periods.

On the fifth day, well into Rengae territory, our steadfast but otherwise smooth trip changed. Gangs fought us, not as clumsy and quickly deterred as the goblins. We both killed several, escaping with wounds I healed.

After a particularly hairy moment, when we'd gotten lost in a ramshackle fort—accidentally offending the members who claimed that land—the pale redheaded fighters came too close for comfort.

I'd warded the elkhorns. No one could steal them.

Kane fought off three. He'd taken a sword off a corpse and nabbed a cutlass from another. With both hands, he battled the Rengaens determined to hold their ground. We were only passing through! But they didn't care.

I faced a pair of filthy, grim-faced strangers. One woman and a man, doubling up with linked chains, clubs at the ends. She also taunted me with a pickaxe while he whipped the linked weapon at me.

It was with an unspoken understanding that I shouldn't use my power. Unless it was a case of survival, of absolute necessity, I couldn't risk being detected. Too many larger, deadlier threats could pinpoint the use of magic, and I knew better than to consider it. Relying on the fighter's intuition my dagger gave me, I resisted this duo.

Until they removed that advantage. I gripped my dagger, but I sank into unconsciousness. My fae blade could guide me—so long as I was awake. And now, with my next breath, I was almost falling asleep, disoriented. After a puff of lavender dust was blown into my face, the woman cackled.

My vision blurred. My legs went numb. Paralyzed. She'd drugged me, and the man tackled me to the ground before the sensation fully claimed me. Watching through blurry eyes, I panicked. I couldn't react. I couldn't speak. As I lay there, the man gripping my ankles to drag me into their stained and ruined shack, I willed my dagger to do *something*.

I sought my power. Of winter, summer, rain. Any of them. But nothing registered, I was truly locked within this numbed stasis of no control. Lucid, but motionless.

Kane! I screamed his name in my mind, desperate for him to notice me being carried away.

I was a tribis fae. I'd killed a Wetherone. Royals had asked me to come rescue them.

How could I be deemed such a powerful person, but still so weak as a human, too?

How could I spend so much time focusing on the big wars but dismiss the simple perils that could find me no matter where I was?

Once inside the one-room shack, the woman slammed the door shut. Lying on my side, I could see her giggling, then drinking from a dark-brown jug. She burped, giggling louder. "Poor lil poot," she cooed at me.

"Shut yer mouth," the man ordered.

She rolled her eyes, lazily dropping the lock bar on the door.

"You keep talking, and I won't have my fun," he warned.

"Pretty little poot," she crooned again. "We'll get lots of coin for her."

The man grunted an ugly chuckle. "Not 'til I have a taste first."

I recoiled, my gut tightening and my lungs seizing. Breathing and seeing, that was all I could do. It wouldn't help if I ceased respiration. But then again, as the man pulled me further into the room and hurriedly dragged my pants down, I wondered if I *should* wish I were dead.

So soon after giving myself to Kane and sharing our bodies in a rushed but no less intimate way, I would be defiled. Raped. Taken and sold. The horror that awaited me locked me tight. Into a numb, cold space of fury. Until my power could save me...

I closed my eyes, forfeiting the only other thing I was in control of in this room—my sight.

It would be too late. My power wouldn't save me. I couldn't save myself, and what a cruel fate that was. A tribis fae, heralded as the apex user of magic, and I was reduced to nothing but a victim in the most horrendous way possible.

I heard him grunting as his garments rustled. Any second now, it'd be too late. I'd be—

The ground shook as the door slammed into the wall.

Kane. I cried in relief. A sweeping, battered hope swept through me, and I wrenched my eyes open.

Then slammed them shut. Blood. I smelled it, the bitter scent too strong in here. The woman screamed, begging for mercy as Kane killed her. If I could have moved a muscle, I would have cringed at the deadly, gruesome sounds.

I'd killed Xandar and slain countless monsters. I'd exploded a dragon and destroyed a Wetherone, but this gory situation sickened me more than all the others.

Then Kane turned his vengeance on the man. The Rengaen tried to run but tripped over my unmovable leg. With swift *swish*es through the air, the blade Kane had picked up slayed the man, too.

"Maren."

His voice was a hard, gravelly plea.

I blinked my eyes open, and his tortured face filled my vision. He exhaled at once, almost closing his eyes. Swearing dark promises and mumbling incoherent curses, he pulled my pants back on. Gently, yet quickly, as though even seeing a hint of what had almost happened destroyed him.

His fingers trembled. His hands were firm but tense. Like he was handling an explosion ready to blow, he picked me up into his arms.

At the first touch of his hard chest bracketing me to him, I relaxed even more. How many times he'd held me now. Since he'd met me, he'd taken care of me. Holding me, carrying me, bringing me to safety.

While his face didn't relax, his lips tight in a grim line and his eyes focused with a lethal glare, he paused to glance down at me.

"Heffen..." His curses came harsher now, renewed as he spotted the drug that had rendered me helpless prey. Lowering to one knee, he reached for a rag in a dish wash bin. After he wetted it carefully, he dabbed the fabric over my face. Delicately. With each rinse, he cleared the drug from my skin.

A flashback to the last time he'd done this hit me hard. Just days ago. He'd cleaned my wounds and cuts. Studious and careful. All to make sure I was all right.

Tears clung to my lids, and I struggled to swallow past the lump in my throat. Choking on emotions, I shoved down the immediate trauma. I recognized, accepted, and erased the fear and anxiousness that barreled through me after so nearly being taken advantage of.

He'd saved me. I would be all right.

And holding tight to other thoughts anchored me to him.

The loving, tender ways he treated me. The consideration, although sometimes seeming like an afterthought. His staunch belief in me, convinced I was somehow braver and stronger than I often felt.

Most of all, that he was *mine*. The rock I could lean on. The gentle giant who would see to my needs. The fierce protector who would kill for me.

He was that one person—and mine. Lies and mistrust couldn't break that. We couldn't unravel so far that who he really was to me would change. Yes, we would always have our differences. He came on too strong, trying to make decisions for me. I fought back twice as much, stubborn and skeptical. Our tempers would never align in a synchronized peace. That was part of what made the most sense between us, two opposites, against all odds, remained magnetized to the other.

So long as I held on to those truths and remembered how he would always be my rock, my protector, I could let go of the headaches of figuring out lies and secrets.

So long as he would always be the one to pick me up and save me...I had to feel hope.

Even after such a low moment of trepidation that could strike anyone—fae or not.

We spent so much time concentrating on the big battles. The war claiming our mainland. We strategized with royals about such overreaching problems, that for a moment of stunning terror, it had been easy—foolish—for me to forget these other perils existed. The hardships of the common life that just because I was on a larger mission, applied to me.

I was humbled by the reminder that people, no matter if they were a sadistic queen or a lowlife rapist, could *all* pose a threat.

But as long as I have Kane...

I'd survive.

Chapter Twenty-Six

Kane hoisted me into his arms, and so lifeless and limp, I sank into the cradle of his hold. He hurried out of the shack so fast, he almost clipped my head on the doorframe. With a sharp breath, he realized his error just in time and shifted. The quick sidestep had me plopping too far to the left, though, and he hurried to balance me again.

The dark sky filled my vision. My head lay propped against his arm, tipping back slightly. No stars shone. No precipitation, either, which was such an odd detail to clue in on.

This was Rengae, the realm of water and rain. I hadn't been here much, but I'd already come to associate this southern, rebellious land with rain *all* the time. Under King Vanzed's reign, it was icy sleet and rain, never dry. Now, I stared up at not even a cloud in the sky. It had to be because Somman reigned.

Summer. Heat. It dried it up and removed all the moisture.

Kane growled, faltering in his hurried departure from that shack.

What happened? What now?

He glared at our surroundings and paused to wipe my cheeks.

Tears? That was what had startled him? I hadn't known I was crying. They fell without thought, my body reacting while I stubbornly insisted in my mind that we'd pass this. We'd deal with it and move on—now.

Frowning fiercely, he practically scowled at me. But his fingers contradicted him. So gentle. Soft and slow as he rubbed my tears away. Calling attention to the fact I'd been weeping, I realized they'd streaked to his arm, and that was how he'd noticed.

While my mind reverted to a numbed state from the trauma of what I almost suffered, my body reacted as expected. Tears of fright, shock. But mostly, as I inhaled the air clear of smoke, seasoned with brine, I cried in gratitude. In thankfulness that I had escaped. That although Kane and I hadn't been on the most peaceful terms just before that scrimmage with the gang, he'd saved me.

As long as I have Kane...

A funky stink hit me before I could think about anything more.

Danger.

I couldn't sniff or twitch. I was too paralyzed to signal to Kane that a monster neared.

My limited experiences with the lavender heffen dust included treating and healing the women who left Sannook's gritty brothels. A powerful narcotic collected from the purple and orange flowers high up in the trees. Risking a climb to get the flowers was a fool's errand. But the pollen was so coveted because it sure made a woman docile and submissive.

Hydration was key. That and rest. Since Kane rinsed off the excess dust the Rengae woman had blown into my face, the pollen granules wouldn't seep into my skin for long. Waiting out the paralysis was my only option, for perhaps a couple of hours. But right now, I had to tell Kane a monster lurked.

I swallowed, trying to force a sound, but that basic action was too much to hope for. I couldn't move anything.

Yet, he looked down at me in his arms. His frown had phased into a sterner expression of confusion. He was alert regardless of my inability to convey the urgency to him. Adjusting me in his hold, his fingers smoothed lower on my back. Down my spine and toward—

Yes!

I couldn't react, couldn't move, but that didn't mean my dagger would go inert. As he covered his hand over the small blade, it pushed against me. Within its sheath, the pulsing charge was more noticeable. He'd felt it too.

I stared at him, trying to express the urgency with my eyes. My brows wouldn't move. But my lids might have lifted higher.

He swallowed, the muscles in his neck flexing as he slid his jaw. Clenching his teeth, he raised me higher. Then onto one shoulder as he retrieved the cutlass. As he shifted me, I glanced at the carnage he strode away from. No one lived. The gangsters who'd arrested us, offended that we'd dared to pass through their turf, were all slain. Dead or bleeding out. The scene was only clear to me for a moment before my face was pressed against Kane's back.

But it was gruesome. Wickedly sickening. I hadn't been duped. Kane hadn't tricked me into thinking he was a saint. He'd been trained to kill, to fight. The Rangers had raised him with a lifetime of combat. He'd served on the Vintar army. He'd been imprisoned in Somman, too formidable to die when Lianen was sent there to kill the excess in captivity.

Seeing the aftermath of such slaughter from his skill, though...

I felt a shudder run through me, an involuntary reaction to the gritty signs of death.

"I've got you," Kane promised roughly, tightening his arm around me.

He must have interpreted my shiver as fright from hanging lopsidedly.

He did. He had me. I didn't have room to fear him letting me go when he'd gone to such vicious lengths to keep me with him, to save me from that rapist.

Draped over him like this though, my stomach churned at the uncomfortable balance. With the stink of the monster increasing and the after-effects of the heffen dust causing nausea, I tried to breathe as steadily as I could and not vomit.

Running, his sword in one hand and me propped over his opposite shoulder, Kane navigated through the streets with confidence. My view was jarring and blurring, only the back of his shirt filling the majority of my sight. Beyond him, the scenery whipped by. Broken buildings, busted signs, and abandoned carriages. Puddles splashed up from his fast footfalls, and the stench of rot and decay wafted when he ran past dumps.

The monster's odor faded, though, and much later, it disappeared altogether. Somewhere throughout this battered town, Kane deftly ran and twisted in such a mix of turns that he'd lost the monster I'd detected. Likely one of those low-lying lizard freaks. I'd killed one the last time we'd been in Rengae, the day I'd met Ersilis and learned I was a tribis fae. My powers were harder to mask then, a force of life I struggled to command, much less understand. That night, my newly unbound magic had been such a fierce presence that I'd killed one of those long monsters that crept from the sewers.

I couldn't guess how far Kane ran, but he'd lowered me into a normal hold before I felt like I'd pass out. All that blood with my head hanging low. When he readjusted me into both arms, in front of him again, I felt dizzier than when the heffen dust first stuck to me.

Kane cast a series of worried glances at me. Concern was clear on his face but it wasn't as evident as the fatigue.

I'm sorry.

His dark-blue eyes screamed the thought in agony. I could see the frustration in his gaze. But I felt it too. I wanted to shout it right back at him. His having to carry me shouldn't be an obstacle in all this. Had I not been mad at him, had we not argued, perhaps I would've been quicker on my feet to avoid that couple blowing the dust on me.

No, Maren.

I wouldn't take blame. They'd tried to abuse me in the most carnal and worst way possible. It wasn't *my* fault. Yet, the warrioress in me hated the circumstances. Deeper down, furious anger burned. That I was deprived of the chance to kill that couple myself.

Focusing my anger on that *what-if* kept me in a lot safer mental space than replaying the memories of that brute's hands on me, the woman cackling as though the sight of a helpless woman about to be molested and raped was entertainment.

"Another?" Kane whispered. Again, I felt his fingers pressing near my dagger that pulsed. He'd felt it again, a "false" alarm, this time. The blade had been stimulated by my need to fight, the concept only thought out, not because of danger lurking.

No. Just my anger.

"We'll hide for now," he promised, striding beneath the rotting wood of a derelict frame. Ducking low, he carried me awkwardly toward a cellar, I figured. Then he turned, jogging up a short flight of steps.

He shouldered into a room. Bare but dry, it looked like a former family residence. Graffiti paintings and brandings marred the walls, and it seemed like whoever had called this their home had left with most of their possessions.

"The Scellins fled," Kane said as he carefully lowered me to the bed. "Those markings are from their largest gangs. Since this town is empty, this building has probably already been ransacked."

Although he told me that in a reassuring tone, he strode back to the door and locked it tight with a cross bar.

Still on my back, I couldn't do anything to let him know I understood. Through my peripheral vision, I watched him pace. Raking his hands through his hair, he seemed to decompress. To vent his exhaustion.

"Sleep, Maren." He approached me on the plain, uncovered bed. "I'll watch over you." His calloused fingers covered my hand. Without making eye contact, he stared at my hand as he gripped it.

My heart cracked at the agony in his voice. I wanted to thank him. An apology waited on my lips, to ask him to forgive me for lying about that sword. Then keeping that secret from him. I wanted to cry, to sob out and release the emotional reaction to what I'd almost endured.

I wanted to reach for him—to comfort myself in his protection and to soothe him that I *was* all right. That I would be all right. So many thoughts and wishes bottled up in my mind. All these raw emotions I couldn't bleed out.

He must have sensed my turmoil. Even though we seemed safe in here, sheltered and hiding for the moment, the illusion of peace opened the floodgates of everything I'd ignored in this numb status.

His thumb stroked over my knuckles. Sighing deeply, he lowered to sit on the edge of the cot. He faced the door, his free hand on his weapon, and he did as he said he would.

He watched over me. Under the touch of his hand on mine, I closed my eyes and hoped that the next time I opened them, I'd be able to return this gesture of comfort to him.

The patter of rain woke me. Stiff and sluggish after a weird sleep, I winced my eyes shut before trying to open them. Heffen dust was so potent because it took over the nervous system, but because the fastest way to absorb it was through the eyes, mine were dry and achy, even beneath my lids.

And the dreams. All the ordeals I'd suffered struck me immediately. Scary dreams turned to sobbing spiels, then at the end, fantasies that *I* had killed those gangsters, not Kane.

In a cycle—during my rest—I'd accepted it all. I wasn't sure if it was a healthy approach. Maybe it was the magic of the dagger, that fighter's sense that often lay dormant. Guessing that it worked on me during my dreams didn't seem too far-fetched.

Taps of rain thrummed against the roof, and it brought back memories. Would I ever experience anything else in Rengae? Both of my times here, I'd been in need of rest, drowsy and unconscious, then waking in a strange bed under the r—

Rain.

It hadn't been raining. Summer dried out this water realm.

I wrenched my eyes open to take in the dark room. Kane was slouched on the ground. He must have sat on the edge of the bed, then fell over asleep. A man could only be worn so ragged until giving in to slumber.

It wasn't rain making that noise.

I blinked. Once, twice. Then the third time, I stared at the horror that tricked me into assuming raindrops drummed on the roof.

It wasn't rain or any other precipitation making that pattern of taps overhead.

Feet.

Millions of feet. Shiny brown and yellow roaches skittered everywhere. Over the ceiling, down the walls, across the floor.

Oh, my g—

Kane jerked, his leg jumping up as a fat, wide roach rushed up his bare skin. Another one followed, from his boot to his knee.

He reared back again, slamming into the bedframe. Its legs scraped against the floor. "Wh—"

I jolted, not even thinking about what I was doing. Or realizing that I could move again. The paralysis was over. With the urgency to react, I dismissed that realization with a small hit of thanks.

I arced my hand out, spraying a wave of smoking steam in a circle.

They sure didn't like that.

"Over there!" Kane jumped onto the bed with me, holding on to my arm. As we stood together, our combined weight tipped the thin mattress to sink in. Wobbling, we maintained this "high" ground. I shifted my focus, catching sight of the largest insect that he'd directed me to notice. As big as a barrel, an enormous roach rolled from a broken window, the avenue for these things to creep in.

A shot of steam had it curling into a ball, hissing.

"More—" He pulled my shoulder back, redirecting me again. Through the gap at the bottom of the door, a fresh stampede of them snuck in.

"They didn't bite you, did they?" I demanded. Faint gray puffs lifted from their carapaces sliding together. The last time I saw that hoary hue was when Thea was bitten by the scarab beetle in Dran. That Somman fae mother fleeing north, she'd described the illusion as well.

Longuex. These insects carried the lethal hex.

"What?" Kane kicked at the medium-sized pests nearest us.

"Did they bite you?" I repeated impatiently. Over and over, I seared them with a hot mist.

"No." He grunted, stumbling on the uneven mattress with me.

They swarmed the room, trapping us in.

"The window," I said, quickly devising the best chance of escape we could hope for. My dagger buzzed at my back, and I felt raring to go. To fight. To kill. After the lethargy of the heffen dust confining my fae magic, I overcompensated with new, bold energy.

Kane leaned back, smacking the hilt of his cutlass at the remnants of glass through the opening. While I fended off the roaches, he beat at the square.

"Here." I formed a fat club of ice and handed it over. He accepted it without hesitation, a blunter, solid device to bash the shards away. I could heal his cuts, but this near the coast and racing to fight the Wetherones, I wanted to remain as uninjured as possible.

"Hold on," I said, steaming the room once more. The hot mist stalled them, but the freakish monstrosity at the opposite wall never ceased hissing, a call for *more* insects to come forth.

I flashed out a dome of ice, like a slide out of the room from the window. He clambered up first, buffered from the roaches, and I followed. I had no choice but to follow. He yanked my wrist up, lugging me after him as we fell out the window and left the roach infestation of longuex behind.

As we flew out, I switched to my Rengae magic, propelling us in a slight hurricane to land without any broken bones in a crashing drop. Still, we bumped into each other in a bruising tumble as we rolled to a stop on the muddy street.

"Are you all right?" he asked me. Jerking his face up, he flicked his hair back to frown at me. Crouching over me, on his hands and knees, he blocked out the view of dilapidated buildings with stained, moldy walls.

"Are you all right?" he repeated as a harder demand.

I sniffed as another odor neared. *Not yet.* A smirking kabol rushed up behind Kane. Larger than what literature showed in sketches, and similar to a tall goblin, the kabol giggled menacingly. It dropped on all fours, then lunged at us.

I ducked around Kane, clutching the cutlass at his side. As I stood, I swung the blade through the air and sliced the monster in half.

He climbed to his feet, dusting off his trousers. Facing me, he hesitated and stared at my hands.

When his brows rose, I frowned. "What?"

Catching his breath, he lifted a finger to point, then must have thought better, lowering it. "You're holding it wrong."

"Realm above," I muttered. "Then here." I thrust the hilt at him at the same time as I retrieved my dagger. "Behind you."

He turned his head, spotting a dozen of kabols running for us from the alley. But he tugged my hand to the side, too. "To your left."

Roaches swarmed from the exterior wall of the room we'd snuck into. Out of that broken window and from the rooftop. Even the cracks in the foundation. Those hexed insects raced for us. On the street, though, the kabols giggled and lunged faster.

We ran. Armed with my dagger and his cutlass, using blades or shots of my magic, we fled the double threat.

Chapter Twenty-Seven

The longuex bugs couldn't keep up. We lost them first. I almost thought the kabols had given up, but they were stealthier in these damp streets. As this poverty-stricken and war-ravaged town was mostly empty, we had clearance to hurry away. Some other stragglers showed. More gang members shouted at us in passing. Once they spotted the kabols on our tails, they rethought it and slunk to safety.

Not as bloodthirsty as goblins and sentient enough to be mischievous, kabols were determined pests of monsters.

A Reganean patroller almost trampled over one, but the rear kabol snarled and showed its demonic nature, claiming the horse by tearing its leg off midstride.

I didn't spare a look back. Following the instinct my dagger charged, I dropped into a sprint. A heart-racing thrill of fleeing propelled me to get out of there. With Kane's navigation, we eventually lost them.

Dawn had broken during our breakneck run. The sun rose and lifted in this balmy atmosphere, and with the sunshine better showing any dangers waiting ahead of us, we slowed to a walk. Then stopped. Hands on our knees, we agreed without words that we needed a break.

Out of breath, we staggered behind a pile of ice chunks. Likely pushed ashore from the miles of bergs that melted at the sea, they offered a spot to hide. Stacked and smashed against each other, the ice stretched high along the beach. It seemed safer to catch our breath here, further from the buildings and streets in the city. Too many nooks and crannies for things to pop out and chase us. While this resembled yet another ghost town, civilization sprang up with the curious few peeking out at us. These Rengaens seemed hardiest, not fleeing their homes like the common folk in the northern villages had. Perhaps their hold on the water protected them, making it more difficult for Devota's Somman soldiers to cruise through and burn it all to smoking ashes.

I straightened my back, standing fully when my lungs didn't burn for more oxygen.

"What happened to the elkhorns?"

Kane grunted, then coughed, sounding as ragged as I felt. "Ran off when..."

Can't blame them. I knew what he'd failed to say. When those Rengaen rebels attacked and I'd nearly been raped.

I'm not going back there. Mentally. I closed down that line of memories and soldiered on with what challenged us *now.*

Swallowing hard, my throat raw from the run, I lowered my hand. It didn't come back the same. With a frown, I glanced at it—now empty. The ice sword I'd formed had glued to the surface of a berg, the warmth of my snowy blade adhering to the colder chunk of ice.

I smirked, trying to wrench it free. Putting my boot to the wall of ice, I couldn't bust it off.

Huffing again from the exertion, I let it go and smirked. Trying to pry something from a frozen object reminded me of Sadera—when I'd stopped her in the swamp. Tugging like that sure was hard on the back. But I didn't pity that redhead. She had been asking for it, trying to order me around.

Using my magic as quickly as I could, then masking it, I molded another ice sword, thin like a rapier.

I looked up and caught Kane staring at me. I raised my brows at his cool expression. Almost judgmental.

"What?" I snapped.

"You're holding it—"

"Shut up!" I kind of liked the heft and ease of cutting down that first kabol. Silly me. In the rush of that escape, I'd fleetingly thought I might like to learn how to fight with a longer blade than my dagger. But if that meant asking *him* for guidance...

Focus, Maren. It was too easy to slip into the absurdly exciting challenge of arguing with him. Now that I was awake and ready to fight, I should. Bickering with him wasn't in the cards.

"Are we near Poround?" I asked instead.

"I'd say we've got a couple more hours to trek," he replied, looking away.

Facing the town, the scraps of civilization that still stood, he pointed at an ugly stone tower. Or the lower half of one. "That lighthouse is—was—a landmark for the largest marina on the coast." He turned to look the other way, toward the sea we couldn't view past the buildup of bergs melted in pieces.

"Which is still covered," he concluded.

This far to the southwestern coast, it seemed the icebergs and shelves of snow followed a shoved-aside current. Still, I could picture the Wetherones scaling them and reaching the mainland.

"So..." I turned to the east. "We'll go that way?"

He scowled, exhaling long and hard. "No."

I rolled my eyes. "Which way is Poround?"

He pointed. "That way."

"Then—"

Griping my hand, he stopped me from walking further.

"Now what?" I snapped. "They said to bring me. To deliver me there. I'm guessing the seas parted better there if the Wertherones already came ashore." The beach was probably lower there. Or a shallower bay had formed as the ice melted. Whatever the geographic reason, it didn't matter. "Which means we should go *that* way." I tugged, either to lose his grip or to yank him along with me.

"I'm not sure we should approach," he argued.

"Why not?" I flung my arm up. "That's the whole point of traveling south."

"I don't know if I trust that message," he admitted.

I shrugged. "I am *not* commenting on the topic of trust. Not with you."

"Because you abuse it?"

I shoved at his chest. Hard. Damn him, for not even budging.

"I lied. Once! I admitted it, and I'm sorry. Do you hear me? I've owned up to it. I've apologized. Holding that secret from you was torture."

"Then why'd you do it? Why'd you lie in the first place?"

"Because. Because Thea needs me. She has always needed my protection, and I will never, ever slack in that duty."

He glared at me, those cobalt pools of anger glinting in the sunshine.

"Just leave. Tell me where to go, and I'll do it. If everyone's looking at me as their best excuse of defense against those Wetherone freaks, I'll try my best. That's all I've ever done, Kane. Since the moment you came into my life and distorted it, I've tried my best."

Without a word, he stared at me so soberly. Beneath his stillness, I sensed the boiling fight he tried to hold in.

"Just go! I'm sick of your attitude. Of this annoyance you have for me. Of thinking the worst. I don't need it."

Once more, I waited him out. Not a word? I growled, beyond frustrated. "Leave if this is how you'll treat me!"

"That's what you want?" he asked, his voice low and threatening.

"No!" I shoved at him, wishing I could smack sense into him. "But you're not listening. I'm sorry I lied. That apology is a lot more than you ever gave me for playing with my head first." I dropped my chin to my chest, staring at the sand encased in a clear sheet of gritty ice that hadn't melted all the way through yet. I couldn't meet his gaze. I'd either throttle him or kiss him. "In case it's slipped your attention, I'm loyal. To a fault, Kane."

"To your sister. Nothing else. Not even the mainland—"

I gripped his shirt and pulled him close. "A *duty*. I am obligated to always protect Thea, and I will. I love her. She's my *sister*. Nothing can part the connection we have. It is a duty to keep her safe." I lifted my hand to join the other, and I shook the sweaty fabric. Beneath my knuckles, his heart raced. He was as riled by this confrontation as I was.

"But I *choose* to stand with you. To fight with you and try to end this chaos. I *choose* you even though you will always be the better fighter and know all these lands. Even though you can guess everyone's secrets faster than I will. Even if you can hold your damn weapons without error and face monsters without flinching. Even when you're a stubborn idiot with the most closed mind ever—especially where I'm concerned. I'll always choose you, Kane. I trust you to be my rock, my...partner. My protector. As long as I have you..."

I stared at him, trying to pry into his intense gaze and understand what the hell his problem was.

"If you can't get over the fact that I lied, *once*, then leave me. I'll go to Poround and die fighting a war I never wanted a part of."

He walked me toward a berg so fast I scrambled not to fall backpedaling. Clinging to his shirt, I remained on my feet. When he pushed me to the wall of ice, I was pinned.

What was wrong with me? Excited and turned on at him taking charge like this...

"No." He slammed his lips to mine and kissed me hard. At the first touch of his hot mouth, I dove into the urgency of it all. Fighting with him was a rush I never wanted to stop. This push and pull was the ultimate thrill. Kane challenged me like no other, in a way I only desired with him, but this was too important. We couldn't revert to something physically pleasing and ignore the argument we hadn't settled.

I couldn't handle the hot-and-cold and not know which way was what. Not when we needed to rely on each other against monsters and danger.

"No." He framed my face with one hand as I struggled to break apart and breathe. Setting his other fist against the ice, he caged me in. "I'm not leaving you." He angled down, his lips insistent against mine and his tongue claiming my mouth. Heat spiraled from my core, and I clung to him despite knowing better.

"Not now. Not ever."

"Then I'm not staying," I threatened, hating the breathiness of my weak protest before I kissed him back again. *Liar.* I could never leave him. "Not if you're going to be so angry with me every step of the way."

"I'm angry you lied. But I'm not angry with *you.*"

I pushed up for the space to wrap my arm around the back of his neck. "Then get over it," I growled, kissing him again.

"It's not that easy. I've never..." He faltered in his admission, too focused on kissing me harder and cupping my ass to lift me against him. "No one's ever mattered. Not like you. I've never wanted anyone to get half as close as you have."

My heart ached at the loneliness in his words. He'd lived without a family. Always hunted down. Even in friendship, he had rocky ties with Prince Lianen and Isan. They were almost like brothers, but at the same time, definitely not. Kane never having a relationship wasn't a concrete excuse for his ignorance of how this worked. But I could understand. He reacted with aloof anger, not working through a difference.

And with lies littering between us, this was bound to be a repeated challenge.

"I've never been consumed with worrying about someone like this. Terrified that I'll lose you." He caressed my face, ceasing the kiss to press our brows together. "That I wouldn't be there to save you."

Like in that shack. I saw it now. This resentment festered in him. *His* way of calming down from the fear of that moment when that man tried to take advantage of me.

"I will always forgive you, Maren. Just be patient and let me get there. I see— I understand why you didn't tell me about the Ranger sword at first. Once I thought back to how I'd held back explaining when we'd left Dran, it made sense.

I'd fallen too far in trusting you without stopping to consider how too many people abused the truth with you. Including me. And I hate how I did."

I smoothed my fingers over his cheek, then brushed back his hair.

He lowered his demanding mouth to mine again, growling into the kiss. "Be patient."

I resisted that idea by rocking my hips against him and sucking on his tongue. Reconciliation with Kane came with a potent dose of desire. Of lust. As thrilling as it was to argue with him, making up in a more physical way taunted me too.

It was a clear pattern. After a close call, we were only pulled tighter together. Reeling from the fact we'd been spared death from that Wetherone, we took the jarring leap to make love. To celebrate that we lived. Then, crawling back from the danger and horror of that man almost raping me, we dropped into hot kisses and barely constrained passion again.

Near death, to life. Again and again.

"I will always choose you too, Maren," he rasped, thrusting his hips against me in answer to me grinding down. "Even if you don't know which way to go and can't handle a proper grip—"

"*Proper?*" I reached down to grip him, stroking the hardness that thickened beneath his trousers.

He swore, groaning lowly as he pushed into my hand.

"Even if you're so gullible to be tricked into rushing to the shore."

What?

I stilled my hand and reared back.

Sweet confessions and honest explanations were over.

"Gullible?" I spat.

Back to fighting and insults.

His smoldering stare lightened as he regarded me, so submissive in his arms. "We're not going to Poround."

Chapter Twenty-Eight

If we weren't running from danger or attacking monsters, we were arguing. *Not true.* On the saddle, he'd shown me a loving pleasure. The same desire that warmed me now and had my core aching with need. It cooled fast.

Fighting did that to the libido—battling with each other or the enemy.

Or...

He lowered his hands from my ass, and I realized then that I'd wrapped my legs around his waist.

As our lust simmered, mostly because I reared back from his kiss, he sighed.

Fighting and arguing. *Or we can try something else.* We had to have more of a middle ground than this hot-and-cold. I strove for a calmer compromise now, not lashing out at him for making decisions on my behalf. *Again.*

"We're not going to Poround?" I spoke it like a fact, but he took it as the question it was.

Easy. Easy. I drew in another breath and sought a semblance of calm. My temper couldn't get the better of me. Not *every* time.

"No." He said it so simply. Matter of fact. And I fought down my temper harder.

I crossed my arms and leaned against the ice. Heated by the sun, it wasn't a shocking cold. More like a gentler cooling. A breather was always necessary with this man. "Because you say so?"

He rubbed his jaw, punching his fist against the ice without much force.

"How about this? Instead of trying to *tell* me what to do, ask me."

Turning back to me as he walked away, he sneered. "I tried that. When we rode here. And you got defensive and sassy."

"Sassy?" I spluttered as I pushed off the ice. I'd give him *sass*.

Sensing he'd said the wrong thing, he held his hands up. "If I refuse to leave you and you're deluded to think you want me, we can't do this. We can't go back and forth when there isn't much time."

"Exactly." I stomped away from the berg. "Don't tell me what to do. We can figure it out together." *Unless you're still hiding more things I should know.*

"I don't trust that message."

I knew this, even if I wondered if it was fueled by paranoia. "Because it was Ersilis's signature but came from Isan's bird?"

He nodded but switched halfway to shake his head.

"The *message*. It doesn't sound right. Like a ploy."

"How?"

"Everyone's been telling you to get the Ranger blade."

I nodded. "You. Isan. Baraan. Lianen."

"All the royals."

Again, I nodded. "Because everyone wants Devota gone."

"Then why would anyone expect you to do something other than that?" He glanced at me, confusion in his eyes.

"Because..." I shrugged. "Because I can defeat the Wetherones, and they're invading."

He propped his hip against the ice, much like I just had. "Did *you* know you could defeat the Wetherone?"

"I didn't know Wetherones were *real*. I thought they were a story."

"So did I, mostly. My grandfather never discredited them as a myth, but I was raised with the same generational conspiracy. That Wetherones were a false idea. Lore."

I frowned. "But you told *me* to defeat it. At the Somman palace."

His low laugh could have been sexy at any other time. "What, like *I* could have held my own against it? It infected me. It possessed me to kill you. You will always be stronger than me no matter what we face."

Warm satisfaction flowed through me, charmed by his praise. Even if I doubted it to be completely true.

"And watching you fight it, I realized that *you* could defeat it. You did. As a tribis fae. It reacted to *your* blade. Not Lianen's arrows."

I agreed. "Using one power didn't work either." Only after direct contact with my dagger, representative of all three realms of magic, did I have a way to kill it.

"Before witnessing it, I didn't know that," Kane admitted. "I was clueless."

I smirked. "Imagine that."

"I doubt Lianen knew how to bring it down, either," he said, plowing past my lame joke that he was a know-it-all. "He was most concerned about finding the Ranger texts—something I bet would explain Wetherones as more than an old folklore. Perhaps including ways to fight them."

I shook my head. "What are you getting at?"

"Who on the southern border of Contermerria would also know that a tribis fae can defeat a Wetherone? Who would know to request you to come and handle them?"

No answer came to me.

Isan? I discredited him. He hadn't signed the message.

Ersilis? How would she know a tribis countered a Wetherone?

Baraan? Sadera? Any of the Rengaens? Unless someone else told them, they weren't aware I *was* a tribis fae, assuming I was only a Vintar fae.

Word had to be spreading about my tribis might, but how fast word could travel was a different factor to consider.

I hated this twist that I couldn't understand. Nothing was clear. "I...don't know."

"Exactly," he said, mimicking how I'd spoken that word in argument. "We don't know. And that's why I'm not sure if you should go to Poround as expected."

"If *we* should go," I corrected.

He shrugged. I took that as a yes.

"Then where do we—" I raised my face, feeling and somehow scenting the gritty decay. Magic was being used nearby.

A stretch of shadows slithered along the edge of the ice that stood between us and the sea.

I felt Kane watching me. His hand lowered to his cutlass, and he raised it. I locked my attention on that edge. Along the jagged line of ice, I waited, not breaking my stare as I reached for my dagger.

I wasn't imagining it. It came. A shadow that shouldn't be there with the sun yet to rise that way.

With a grunt, Kane dropped to his knees. Covering his ears, eyes winced shut, he rocked forward. "Maren, no!"

A scream cut through my mind. It was happening to him too, this time.

"Maren! Come back!"

I'm right here!

"No!" He was stuck in a hallucination, but no inkiness wrapped around him. I dreaded to think of what nightmare he saw to make him cry out with such anguish. How could they do this? What dark magic did the Wetherones possess?

"Kane," I didn't take my attention off the edge of the ice up there as I walked toward him. "Kane." I repeated it firmer, louder. He rocked back and forth, breathing hard and covering his ears.

"Kane!" I grabbed his shoulder, and he resisted my grip.

Before I could try again, pounding hooves raced closer. I turned, facing the rundown coastal town. Along the path, an elkhorn galloped. Grunting with whinnies, the animal announced its arrival. Upon its back, the rider shouted commands to go, to go faster yet. Faster!

Red waves flowed from her helmet. Lips in a grim line, she charged forward along the thawing beach. Amaias squinted her eyes, daring one look back as she rode.

In a blur, she passed us, hidden to the side in this alcove of berg chunks. As she sped by, the elkhorn heaving and pounding its muscled legs to the cracking sand-ice, my head turned, tracking her. Trailing behind her was a shifting mass of shadows. Swirling like mist, the Wetherone rode a horse as well, its shadow snaking around them, rider and horse both. As a unit, they slipped in and out, from flesh to darkness again.

"Kane!"

I grabbed his arm, siccing a curl of heat along my fingers to jolt him out of this hallucination. He yanked free, then stared up at me.

Overhead, shadows crossed the sky, blanking out the sun. Following the Wetherone, this long streak of an extension left over us. It slithered as a lengthy shadow, tugged on a leash with the hulk chasing the princess.

I pulled on Kane's arm—hard. It was enough. Kane shot to his feet and ran with me down the beach.

We'd never catch up. Not on our feet. Instead, I skidded to a stop. My boots dug into the mushy slush soaking into the beach. I heaved in a deep breath and flung my arm forward. Like throwing something, yet not.

Ice burst out in a towering, flaky, frosty arch. It worked. I made contact. The second my ice touched the shadowed tentacle trailing behind the Wetherone pursuing Amaias, I felt the kickback. Like a filthy nudge of dirty power resisting mine. Lurching against the commotion, the Wetherone's horse raised on two legs. Midstride, the animal—possessed though it was—fell. The shadowy man tumbled off, intermittently morphing from flesh to darkness in a waving web.

He stood, a burly, stocky pirate. Flinging a rope of darkness toward Amaias, he stalled her. Then he turned back and scowled at me.

Come on. Do it.

I braced for the snaking spear of shadows to come at me. As soon as it did, I sprayed water at it and froze the liquid, gripping it like I had with the one in Somman.

But this one resisted, more shadows curling over my ice. Fire repelled those advances, but it would gain on me any second.

His efforts were split. He pulled Amaias closer, the shadow roping around her elkhorn's legs, at the same time that he challenged my powers.

"Kane! Get him."

He didn't delay, heeding my shout. I watched him pick up my dagger that I'd dropped on the sand. Focusing my magic at the point of contact I held with the Wetherone's shadow tentacle, I watched as Kane ran up to slice my dagger into its black mist.

No light burst out. Cyan. Red, green. Nothing.

I gritted my teeth, learning even with this setback. It wasn't my tribis blade that defeated it? It had to be *me* delivering the strike?

"Here!" Kane ran back, using his cutlass and my dagger to hack off threads of the shadows pulling at him. As though he sprinted from a cobweb, he cut at the air while the shadows slithered and changed.

Deep, throaty laughter filled my ears. The Wetherone disappeared, the shadow hovering faintly where it last stood. Then he phased into shape, half as a man and half as darkness. Back and forth, it shot through space, confusing me.

Amaias screamed, covering her ears. She nearly fell off her elkhorn as it neighed and grunted, bucking to break free from the shadows.

Thrown off by the Wetherone morphing in and out of view, but ever cautious of not letting the shadows touch my skin, I faltered. Panic crept closer. But I doubled down. I cleared my mind, seeking the mantras that grounded me.

Chin up. I rolled my shoulders, staying nimble as I used my magic—all three—to keep this thing from infecting me.

Face forward. "Which way *is* forward?" I growled to myself.

Hang on. That was it. *Hang.*

I used the trio of powers together, a contradiction that would otherwise never be possible. Fire spread from my hand with a glowing twine. Braided with it was a rope of ice. Both spiraled within a jet of water. All three at once, I whipped it out, catching the Wetherone's neck.

He bellowed, gripping the length. Counting on that force, I jumped up to follow.

I was flung through the air, and as I almost flew past him, I dove down and drove my dagger into his neck.

Black. A blanketing sphere of it at my strike. Then the blue. Red. Last, green. And with a groaning roar, the Wetherone was down.

Chapter Twenty-Nine

Amaias set her hand on her elkhorn's side, coughing after she dismounted.

"Thank you," she uttered once she caught her breath. It seemed her longuex infection was worsening, just as the Somman mother had explained it would. How this princess still stood, I had no idea. When she extracted a mint-green leaf from her pocket, a petal from the kalmere plant that she chewed, her respiration improved to a wheezing rasp instead of a lung-wracking cough.

Ironic. I'd set out to find the kalmere plant. It grew in abundance, but longuex was a bigger problem. That guilt would always pierce my conscience.

"Thank you," Amaias repeated, perhaps thinking her first attempt wasn't heard.

Kane approached me, his hand a warm comfort on my back.

I sighed. "You're welcome."

She scoffed at me, striding up close. "I wasn't talking to you."

I deadpanned, unable to react. That wasn't true. I was more than ready to talk back to her. But I was so stunned at her snubbing me like this, I couldn't begin to formulate a coherent response.

She wasn't thanking *me*? The person who'd just saved her life?

"I figured there had to be a reason they wanted you out of the prison," Amaias said in that same nonchalant yet cutting tone. "A tribis fae. Imagine that. You sure do find all kinds of oddities on your travels, don't you, Kane?"

I fisted my hand, and Kane drew in a deep breath. I recognized his stiff stance and heavier inhale as a tell. He was about to lose it, pushed to the limit of his patience. I'd let him.

Her gaze slid down to where Kane's hand rested at my hip as he held me to his side. "But I didn't think you'd actually go so far to seduce her to gain her cooperation." Her following huff would have packed more of a punch if it didn't devolve into another coughing fit.

"Seduce?" Kane gritted out.

Amaias flapped her hand at him. "Don't deny it."

I stood rigidly next to him. In my heart, I refused it. Flat-out rejected the idea that Kane duplicitously seduced me for a role in this war. But in my mind, a nagging, persistent doubt took root.

He growled, fisting his hand. "I don't—"

"Enough. You did what was necessary," she cut in, quicker with her words since the coughing had passed. "I knew you were conspiring with my brother about something, but I didn't realize you'd go through with it. I told him no woman would actually fall for the lies from your mouth." Again, she huffed at me, the best she could pass as a laugh. "But it seems I was wrong."

"You *are* wrong." Kane removed his hand from me and stepped toward her. "I—"

She lifted her hand to silence him. "And Lianen."

I narrowed my eyes, not sympathetic as she coughed more. "You saw him?"

"Yes. I ran into him on my way here. He told me you were tribis." There was the link of word spreading.

I gripped her hand, but she flung free of my touch.

"Was Th—a woman with him?"

"No." She scowled. "He was alone."

That doesn't mean she's not safe. That doesn't mean anything. He admitted he put her in a safe place and warded her. Still, worry spiked hard.

"We snuck into the same site seeking the books. That Wetherone chased me from it. Lianen said you were going for the Ranger blade. It's here?" She pointed down to the beach. "It's been in Rengae all this time?"

"No," I replied at the same time Kane argued, "I didn't—"

"You're not here to look for that blade? To kill the queen?" she demanded.

I pushed a jet of water at her empty sheath. "Where's yours? *You* kill her."

"Dragon fire." She shook her head. "I lost it in a fight with the dragons as Devota chased me through the swamp. After *you* left me at the castle."

My jaw dropped. "I didn't *leave* you there. And the first time, you told me to go."

She snorted. "Because I had to get Isan out. He's the only other one who ever believed me about the Ranger texts being out there somewhere." Shaking her head, she seemed to grow more frustrated. "If you're not seeking the Ranger blade here to kill the queen, why are you in Rengae at all? To hide while we fight the war?"

I slammed water into her chest, and she tried to double it back at me.

Hide?

"I just saved your life. Have some respect."

"For you? A commoner?" She spat water and the chewed-up leave onto the ground. "You might be tribis, but you're nothing—"

"Enough!" Kane shoved her back and took my hand. "She's fought more than any of you."

"Oh. Just because she spent a few months in the dungeons she thinks I owe her respect? She *caused* this war. She helped Devota kill the king!"

Guilt hit me hard, a niggling sensation I'd done my best to tamp down.

"Don't," Kane warned. "Don't. She tried to save him, not kill him. She didn't know, she didn't understand that Devota would use her to break into the castle."

"Yes." Amaias sneered at me. "She didn't know because she's just a commoner. From nowhere."

Again, I thrust my magic at her, and she fell. I'd be damned if I listened to this. From this ungrateful princess.

"I'm not wasting any more time with you," she snarled. "Twice, I've covered for you. If you won't find the Ranger blade to kill the queen, don't stand in my way."

"Your way of what?" I challenged as she stood again. "To whine? Just like your sister?"

"Don't ever compare me to her. Sadera..." She clenched her teeth, shaking her head.

"Your way of what?" Kane asked her, backing me up.

She narrowed her eyes at him, seeming surprised he would repeat what I'd demanded.

"To find the Ranger texts. Exactly what *my sister*"—she glowered at me with those words—"has tried to stop me from doing."

I frowned, picking at her words. She sure disliked being cast in the same light as Sadera. But it seemed it was a deeper affront than siblings not getting along. Sadera had ordered me to help get Amaias out of the castle. That was the only thing she'd demanded of me then. Baraan, though, had suggested Amaias could handle herself.

Kane stared at her, and I volleyed my gaze between them, trying to guess what he was thinking.

"Where is Isan?" he asked, his voice firm.

She pointed down the beach. "Poround. He teamed up with Baraan, but he's been fighting to keep the gangs from killing each other at the beach. Refugees and—" She sighed, shaking her head. "War. He's there because he wanted to help my brother in this war. Until *you* can get that sword and kill the queen." Her scowl was directed at Kane this time. Then she dragged her scathing glare toward our joined hands. "While you play with your tribis." She lifted a shoulder and dropped it. "Haven't had your fill of seducing her yet?"

"Don't—"

She cut him off again, haughty as she returned to the elkhorn and climbed on. Seated again, she blew a whistle, twice. "Make yourself useful," she snapped at me.

Corgas bounded onto the beach. When the pinkish-tawny one beelined for me, a small glimmer of joy hit me. The corga I'd lost! It was back, and I petted its round face as another darker and larger one approached Kane.

"If you've given up on finding the Ranger blade," Amaias said, "go help them stand their ground at the shore."

With that, she raced off, the elkhorn kicking up clumps of ice-glued sand.

She grew smaller in the distance as she left, but I remained there without budging.

Anger, frustration, and impatience. In familiar fury, they clashed and claimed my mind.

"I didn't seduce—"

I held my hand up. "What *did* you conspire with Baraan?"

"I didn't—"

I gripped his hand and twisted it until he faced me. "You did. You *did* conspire with Baraan."

"Not to seduce you."

I didn't bother rushing to tamp out the flames curling from my hand. I eventually masked it only because it was stupid not to. My temper flared regardless if I used my magic to show it.

"*What* did you conspire?" I narrowed my eyes. "Sadera mentioned it, too. When they found me in the swamp."

He shrugged. "To get you out of the dungeon. When we learned about the threat to Thea, we planned. Ersilis would help Amaias get in, and Ersilis would get you out."

I climbed onto the corga's saddle, and he did the same.

"Amaias wanted to get Isan out but couldn't do it on her own. So Ersilis joined her. To free you. That was the agreement. I wouldn't call it a conspiracy."

As we rode southeast, along the beach, I mulled over that. "Why Ersilis?"

"She...knew the castle. She was tortured there as a child. And she remembered the way inside."

I hated that she'd suffered. But I was grateful she cared enough to help despite it all.

"That's *all* you planned with the prince?"

"Which prince?"

I shot him a hard side eye. *Did he really just say that?*

He frowned, opening and closing his mouth.

"How many princes *have* you made plans with? When you weren't trying to kill them, save them, or steal their weapons?"

"Just Baraan. And Lianen. Isan..."

I nodded, teeth clenched tight. "All of them, then. Great."

"No," he argued.

I spared him a leveled look. He stared right back, his long hair whipping at the speed the corgas ran.

"You already know that I planned with Lianen to break in and kill the king. That was it. Baraan... he's mentioned some ideas that I've dismissed."

I shook my head. "Like seducing me?" *Too late.*

"No!"

"Then what? What were you planning with Baraan?"

"I love you, Maren."

I didn't reply. He was too damn stubborn to answer my question, determined to convince me seduction wasn't another way he'd tried to get to me. He had. But until now, I'd been positive it was true. Honest. Real. A genuine chemistry that we mutually felt and fell under the spell of.

"I love you," he repeated. "Even when you won't, because you'll never trust me."

"Leave it alone, Kane."

Love? Trust? Those two things would always be in the air between us, but now wasn't the time to discuss them. Not when we sped this fast on corgas bringing us closer to a battle.

The last time I'd let my love for him rule me, I'd raced into a trap. When I was convinced I had to obey the rules of affection for Kane and rush into the Vintar castle to save him, I'd unknowingly caused so many more problems.

I couldn't do that. Not again. And so long as we worked on this *together*, as long as we stayed united and tackled this chaos at each other's side, I could live with that sense of procrastination. Kane and I could address this later. Right now, it was war. And I'd face it with a level head and all the concentration and focus I could manage.

"Not now," I said, firmly but calmly. "What did you plan with Baraan? Aside from getting me out of the dungeon?"

"Nothing that matters now."

I gritted my teeth. Still with the secrets. "I'll determine that."

"When I served as a Vintar soldier, Baraan visited the king. I overheard him talking about a legacy. Something with a fight from long ago. I wanted to research it, and Baraan said his sister was interested too."

"An...interest in history?" I furrowed my brow.

"Basically. Something about an old battle. I was intrigued because I could have sworn my grandfather mentioned it before, or alluded to it. But the king had closed off any discussion about it. Like he was ashamed of it. I grew angry, thinking it had to be something about the Rangers the king wanted to hide, to protect his reputation and reign. At that time, I thought Isan and the king were responsible for my grandfather's death. So it...struck me. That's all. Maren, *I love you.*"

Damn this stubborn man.

"I didn't seduce you. Not to get you to help me with this war."

I shook my head and glared at him again. "I'm not discussing that right now." Because deep down, the very idea of him using me hurt.

I'd already erred with him. I'd broken into Vintar to save him because I couldn't bear the idea of him dying. Or even suffering. I'd learned too late that Devota used my affection for Kane as a way to get in.

And now? If he was playing with my heart *again*...

Never mind not trusting *him*. I first needed to trust myself and not let my heart be a weakness when deciding who to fight with. Or for.

Chapter Thirty

Kane didn't push. He didn't repeat that plea to hear him out as he confessed his love. He didn't speak at all as we rode the corgas toward Poround. Either he'd finally learned the lesson of knowing when to shut up or he became afraid that more insistence would backfire.

It didn't matter to me. Without wondering what his feelings were for me, I focused on the task at hand. Namely, the battle waging ahead.

Poround, it seemed, lay at a lower elevation. Just as I'd guessed. Water was visible as we rode down the slope toward this key location. From above, we saw it all. Boats floating in the water. Bergs had been shoved aside, creating a tunnel—a canal for the waves to lap at the beach.

Never before had I witnessed liquid water touching land. Surreal. It was all foreign and awe-inspiring. I'd imagined it from stories Thea and I read in the basement in Dran. I could picture it from a tub of soap, the ripples ebbing and flowing in a wash bin. But to witness waves on land, on a beach?

Incredible.

And terrifying.

With access to water, no longer restrained by an impenetrable wall of ice, the Wetherone pirates could breach Contermerria. And they did. Men gathered on the shore, wading through the waves to swarm the beach.

From a distance, I followed the streaking shadows that came off the Wetherones. Like tentacles of mind control, their dark magic waved from them. But many more backed them up, and it was then that I realized the Wetherones I'd met—and killed—were their *fae*. Pirates of the human variety accompanied these sea-faring invaders. Tall, brutish, and swift with cutlasses and clubs alike, the pirates made up the majority of this invasion.

As we rushed closer, I wanted to have faith. I couldn't see the elkhorn Amaias was riding, but the Rengaen forces had other steeds. Corgas. Elkhorns, even ashirs. From what Baraan and his scouts had shared in the swamp, I'd suspected Rengae was emptied. From floods, gang infighting, and Sommans sweeping through to capture folk for internment, I figured this would be a barren land the Wetherones could easily take over.

Not so.

Rengaens fought everywhere. From saddles and on land. Yet as I watched a shadow-man sic his tentacles of darkness on a crowd, those fighters turned on each other. Just like they'd done in the Somman camps. And just like Kane had turned against me and tried to kill me, possessed.

They'd be overtaken in no time, despite their larger numbers.

"If you go find Isan and keep him safe," I started, assuming he could live and resume a reign of winter to block the Wetherones from Contermerria with ice again. Not because Amaias ordered us to help him. And not because I still felt guilty that I'd accidentally played a hand in his father's death. "I'll—"

"*No.*" Kane pulled on his corga's reins to slow alongside mine. "We're in this together."

"Then—" I paused, stilling at the feel of magic in the air. Ignoring the stagnant stink of the Wetherones and the salty pulse from the Rengaens at the shore, their magic weak the Somman summer reigning, I focused on something else.

Chilly. Minty. Refreshing. I sensed it, and it stood out.

Someone used Vintar magic nearby. I jerked my face in the direction of where it came from. The source was a tall, ramshackle building falling apart from rot.

"There."

It had to be Isan.

I slid off my corga's saddle and ran toward the structure. Kane didn't question me, rushing with me. He burst through the door first and immediately started cutting his way through. Kabols, goblins, and even frecens scurried in here. Frecens! The pale-blue bloodthirsty monsters that had terrorized Dran. Only two fought in here, and against the kabols and goblins, it was a bloodbath.

"Nasty," I muttered under my breath as Kane and I cleared them out. In a small, plain room on the second floor, we found Isan. He lay in bed, gaunt and struggling. A kabol's wiry hands gripped his throat, strangling him as he giggled.

Ice chips had fallen to the bed alongside the former heir prince. He'd used his power all right, but it wasn't enough to save him.

I blasted a geyser of water at the monster, and he shot out the window, screaming.

Drawing in a deep breath, I approached the blond man gasping on the bed. Between his worsening longuex disease and that kabol squeezing his throat, it was a wonder he lived.

"Easy," I told him as I laid my hand on his arm. My magic healed him. Blue light rose in a vapor where I held on, and he breathed easier, his eyes closing in relief.

"Help Amaias," were his first croaky words of a greeting.

Kane slammed the door shut and rested his back against it, panting. "What did he just say?" he barked out, incredulous.

I slapped my hand to my brow. "No."

"You have to help her!" He sat up, improved with my healing but still looking like he was at death's door. "I found her. She escaped the castle, too, and—"

"Yeah." I held my hand up to stop him. "We just ran into her."

"Then help her find the Ranger texts!" he implored. "She can find the books."

"The same ones Lianen is looking for?" Kane jeered.

Isan grimaced. "I don't know if we can...trust him. I encountered him too, on my way here. He seemed...flighty. Nervous."

That news comforted me. If Lianen was flighty, maybe it was because he wanted to hurry back to where he hid Thea. Nervous, because he worried about her.

"Funny. I thought the same thing of the sisters." I paced, peering out the window at the battle. Chitchat would have to wait. If Isan was alive for now, then I could go out there, kill some Wetherones, then come back here and heal him again, then...

"Amaias?" Isan scowled at me. "She's not *flighty*."

Kane held his hand at me. "Maren, let it go."

I shot him a scathing look. "You're telling me what to think now?"

"No. I—" He retreated, hands up. "Never mind."

"She can find the maps," Isan insisted.

I frowned, turning toward the weak man on the bed. He coughed again, but Kane didn't wait to ask, "What maps?"

"Maps to where?" I added.

The door opened and slammed shut. We turned together as Isan struggled to breathe.

Ersilis hobbled in quickly, starting when she saw me. Her signature smirk creased her leathery face. "What are *you* doing here?"

Kane and I shared a look.

I shrugged. "You...told me to come?"

Her face wrinkled further, the lines increasing with the depth of her annoyance. "No, I din't!" She bustled past us to lay a hand on Isan's forearm. After a moment, she snorted. "Ah. You already healed him."

"Didn't you send me a message?" Kane asked.

"Yes." She slanted her brows at him. "With his bird."

I nodded. "And...you requested that I came here."

"But the Wetherones are here!"

I gaped at her. Kane covered for me as I floundered in confusion. Not complete confusion. We had proof now that Ersilis *hadn't* sent that messenger bird to us, or she hadn't penned and signed that specific request for me to come here.

"You didn't send that message?" Kane asked.

"I sent *a* message. But not for her to come here!" She swatted the back of his head. "Idiot."

"What message *did* you intend to send?" I asked.

"To end the legacy!" Her double chins strained with how tightly she clenched her teeth after that outburst. "The legacy of the Riverfall!"

Kane huffed. "Ersilis, that's..."

"It *must* be true!" She stomped her boot, and oddly, I was impressed. Even with her limp, she could still be *that* imposing to slam her foot down, not fall, and intimidate me.

"Which is why you *must* help Amaias," Isan insisted. "The Ranger text must reference the legacy."

Once more, I cut him off by holding my hand up. "That woman—"

"Princess!" he argued.

"—does *not* want my help." I turned to Ersilis, looking her straight in her one eye. "What's the legacy of Riverfall and how does that matter?"

It seemed I'd never know. Or at least that history lesson—story time, perhaps—would have to wait.

Pirates crashed down the door, and we all fell into the fight.

"Keep him alive!" I told Kane, gesturing to the prince in the bed.

"He ain't the one who matters!" Ersilis argued, using her Rengae magic to fight the pirates. With magic, my dagger, Kane's now-broken cutlass, and a broom Ersilis grabbed, we fought the invaders out of the room. "Stay with him!" I told Kane again.

At least they're only humans. No shadows lurked or stretched out from these pirates. Their eyes were bloodshot, but blue, green, and brown, not covered with a swirling blackness. They weren't possessed, but that didn't mean they were easy to kill or stop. Over the bodies of the kabols, goblins, and frecens we'd slain on the way up the stairs to find Isan, we tripped and fell back down, pushing the Wetherones to the first floor.

Baraan rushed in, too, and upon spotting us in battle, he joined.

"Maren?" he asked, surprised. "Why are *you* here?"

That's what I want to know! Clearly, someone intercepted that message for us.

"Ersilis sent a scroll to warn you to stay *away* from the shore," the Rengae prince shouted over the clash of fighting. I slammed my shoulder into a pirate and sliced my dagger across his gut. We fell onto the street, and the others followed out of the building they'd seemed to have designated as a rendezvous point.

I gritted my teeth as another pirate banded his arms around me. Lifting into his chest, I kicked both of my feet at a skinny one trying to stab Ersilis. "That's not the message we received!" I shouted back at Baraan.

We didn't have a chance to discuss this miscommunication any further. Outside on the dingy streets, humidity clung to us. Sweat poured from my face as I fought pirate after pirate. Ersilis and I were separated from the others, and all I could do was strain to stay afloat in the violence that came in never-ending waves.

After Ersilis sent forth a final burst of water that knocked back a pirate I stabbed with a spear of ice, we staggered toward a chunk of ice for shelter and support. We gulped in air, drained from fighting. I had so many questions. Too much confusion.

Ersilis gasped, and I feared the worst. I had no idea how old she was, but she wasn't young, that much I could tell.

Was she dying? Was this it?

I gripped her hand, sending healing magic into her. But she thrust my hand away, annoyed as she pointed. "Look!"

Frowning with a double-take, she looked back at me and took my hand, healing *me*.

I squinted, peering ahead, and when I noticed what stunned her, I sucked in a hard breath too.

Chapter Thirty-One

Striding up from the beach was a "royal" woman I didn't look forward to facing.

She gripped a blade, the metal sparkling with magic, as she strode with confidence.

From the beach. Not *to* it.

With a slowly curving grin, Sadera stalked toward the town, holding what had to be a royal Rengae blade.

"Where'd she find *that*?" I pushed away from Ersilis.

The haggard woman called out to me, frantic. "Maren? No! Maren!"

Sprinting forward, I fended off the pirates that tried to reach for me. Grubby hands groped and swords slipped past. With my dagger and ice sword knocking back their attempts, I forged ahead.

Another fae blade! A sword that could also be used to end Devota! Kane and I didn't have to go hunting for the Ranger's weapon. One was right here!

"Sadera!" I yelled as I hurried toward her.

She didn't turn. Didn't acknowledge me at all. With cries of war all around, I wasn't surprised. Waves crashed to shore too, another sound that carried so far.

"Sadera!"

Now she turned, sending a wave of water at me.

I blocked it, frowning at her action. The woman was antagonistic. Both Rengae princesses had an issue with me. I knew that. But—

"Where did you find that?" I demanded. A circle of frosty stalactites spiked into the beach from my Vintar spell, lining her in a cell.

"Leave me!" she ordered. A tidal spin of water from her hands cleared down my ice cage.

"We can use that sword," I argued. "To kill her and end her reign!" *And block off these Wetherones again!*

Sadera laughed a sinister, nasally cackle. "*I* will use it."

To kill the queen? It was the ending we wanted. "You will?"

"Leave me!" she ordered again. A higher wave flowed over me, catching me off guard enough that I floated further from her before I could resist her magic.

She intended to flee. But I didn't trust her. How could she have withheld that sword when all the royals—other than the wicked one on the throne—had tried to unite and end the current disastrous summer?

Did she intend to use it to dethrone Devota?

With fire, ice, and water, I tried to trap her and get an answer. My efforts were wasted because, soon, she wasn't the only thing I focused on.

Shadows cut through the waves. That darkness was back. Screams and wails stabbed at my mind, the sounds locked in my skull as their dark spell slowed my actions.

Not again. No.

A hulking Wetherone slowly advanced, zeroing in on me with wicked, chortling laughter. One moment, shadows coiled around and from him. The next, wrinkled, sunburned flesh and ragged stained garments dripped from his enormous frame.

My breath caught. The dagger buzzed in my hand, reacting to my fear. "No."

He chortled louder and shot out streaks of darkness. They careened at me like a net of ill will. All I could do was slice at the air. At the nothingness of his shadows. The blackness wasn't real. It wasn't a physical surface to sever. With more speed than the first two shadowy pirates I'd fought, this one seemed to rely on the presence of the sea to trap me within its tentacles of despair. The liquid cast a buoyancy that enabled him to slip around me.

"No!"

I fought, resisting and attacking as fast as I could. Frantically, I forced my legs to brace against the waves and my arms to lift again, again, and yes, again, wielding my dagger and ice sword.

The Wertherone wouldn't let me use my ice to grip its obsidian tentacles of dark mist. My fire was extinguished with steaming sizzles. Any use of my water magic was melded into the force of the sea. I couldn't find a single advantage. No moment of an opening came. Surrounded by the tentacles of shadowing circling more and more, I felt isolated.

Alone on this beach in an impossible fight.

Ersilis was back there where I'd left her. Kane was guarding Isan. I thought. I had no clue where Baraan was.

Sadera? She was the last one I'd spoken to out here.

I had no help, and the idea of failing because I wasn't strong enough on my own ate at me.

Chin up! Face forward, Maren! And—

A dragon's wing blanketed the sky. I spat out a mouthful of water as I landed on my back, tossed aside from the Wetherone's kick.

I blinked, squinting up at the clouds.

A dragon?

That sure wasn't a sign of help. Yet, it did assist me. The Wetherone slapped up streaks of darkness, combatting the dragon that swooped too close. Large wings stretched wide, and great rolling breaths of fire pushed down.

I'd wondered why we hadn't seen them since Somman. And I couldn't make sense of why one came now. Here. But I'd take this unexpected break to slip back closer to safety, further from this Wetherone that seemed impossible to kill. Before I could be pulled into the waves, I staggered away.

Retreating up the beach, I tried to catch my breath and not trip on the dead that lay strewn everywhere. I doubted my heart would ever slow. On rubbery knees, and with shaking arms out to balance myself, I concentrated on not falling flat on my face.

Realm above.

When would this terror end? How?

Behind me, I spotted Sadera striding away. She'd remained, watching me fight like it was a special feature to enjoy as a spectator. Unscathed, her blade glowing, she turned her back to me and left the beach on the back of the darkest, largest corga I'd seen yet.

As she departed on the swift animal's back, another familiar voice called out to me.

"Maren!"

I cringed, turning toward Devota. She must have come on that damn dragon.

Her red robes flapped with the wind as she ambled across the beach, regal and proud, chin lifted high. Magenta bangles rattled on her slim wrists as she pumped her arms in a graceful pace of athleticism. She didn't smile. For once. Maybe she'd finally lost that cockiness. I didn't care.

Her lips twisted as she neared. "You will bow—"

"To no one!" I screamed it at her. I was sick of this stupid, *stupid* goal of hers. My servitude. My respect. She deserved neither. I wouldn't grant her anything but death by my sword. I didn't have time to repeat this ridiculous argument, now or ever.

The Wetherone lunged forward. Before a streak of dark shadow circled my ankle, I sliced it free with a sword of ice.

"You will work for me." Devota cowered, then screeched as the Wetherone approached her, too. Her blasts of fire hardly deterred it from claiming her, but she did redirect it back toward me. "My servants told me. I returned to the palace, and they said they saw you kill it."

Snarling, she sent more useless fire at the Wetherone. We weren't battling together. She wasn't helping me defeat it. She merely kept it away from herself, pushing its focus toward me.

It didn't seem to care who it targeted, lashing out shadows at us both.

"You will work for me, tribis," the queen declared.

I narrowed my eyes, bracing for another volley of strikes from the Wetherone. The way she said that. Scathing and with malice, of course. But addressing me by my fae lineage?

Tribis? I was. But I had a name, too. She damn well knew it.

The last time I'd been addressed by my fae power was in that message.

Bring the tribis.

Like I was a thing. An item. A tool. She wanted to utilize me as one, that was obvious. Devota enjoyed a sick glee in demeaning me. Making me inferior and squashing me down with her thumb. She'd taken great pleasure in torturing me and reminding me what I was to her in the dungeons at her castle.

A toy to torture. A slave to punish. A prisoner to loathe.

And now, a tool. *A weapon.*

Without a doubt, I knew Devota had done it.

"Did you request me to come here?"

She grinned, baring her teeth in a way that likened her to a demon. "Glad the message was received."

She had. She'd intercepted that message and manipulated it. She'd changed it to bring me here just so she could ask—no, demand—that I agree to be in her employ.

As a tribis fae to fight the Wetherones for her.

"You will," she vowed. "You will serve me. You will kill these pirates for me."

"Over my dead body," I snarled, still fighting the Wetherone. A trio of pirates waded through the waves, storming at me too.

"How about over *his*?" She clutched the hem of her robe and flung it to the side. It was likely supposed to be a dramatic flair of a gesture. Grand and suspenseful. But I'd seen this show. I'd experienced this quest before.

Kane.

A pair of Somman guards brought him close. His hands were tied, and fresh cuts marred his face as his head hung down. He walked, his long, lean legs moving on their own. They weren't dragging him.

I inhaled a deep breath for patience, reassuring myself he was alive. He—we—could handle this. Relying on the fervent hope that practice really did lead to perfection, I tried to take faith that we could manage this challenge.

Unlike the last time she'd tasked me with the thought of saving this man's life, we were in it together.

He lifted his face, and his hair fell back to show me that steely, serious gaze. With that simple, sober stare, I understood. He'd handle her. Somehow. We wouldn't be parted again. We wouldn't be split by her manipulative ways.

I believed it. For all of one moment, I believed it.

Until a Wetherone leaped further up the beach and shot out streaks of nightmarish inkiness. One stroke snagged the first Somman guard. Within a moment, he turned toward Kane, punching him and trying to grapple for his throat.

"Stop!" Devota cried out. "Stop!" She blasted her soldier with fire, but the possessive Wetherone shadow had already claimed him. "Don't kill him yet!"

The Somman didn't heed her order. He didn't even react to the fire she shot at him.

I formed a short sword of ice and launched it into the air. Throwing weapons wasn't a skill I'd mastered. At least it didn't pierce Kane's leg. It stabbed into the sand, and I hoped he could use it to free and defend himself.

I didn't have a chance to watch and see. The Wetherone attacked me. Then Devota. But mostly me. The queen retreated, running at times to escape the far reaches of the shadows.

I willed my body to hold on, to stay on my feet. Screams and wails sounded in my head, competing with my sanity.

Baraan rushed up, too, and I caught a glance of him fighting with Kane, trying to hold back the possessed Somman guards. Kane swiped the ice sword, clearly having slipped out of his ties.

Without faculty of their minds, though, it seemed the Wetherone's shadows changed the Somman guards into unfeeling killing machines, impervious to pain.

Devota screeched and screamed at me. *Bow to me. Serve me. You will work for me.* Over and over. I tuned it out, or perhaps it mixed in with the hallucinogenic sounds of misery the Wetherone's presence caused to echo in my head.

One look back showed me Ersilis in a heap on the ground. But the next time I had a chance to look back, nearly getting caught in a rope of shadows at the distraction, she wasn't there.

Just when I thought I'd fall, that I couldn't take another moment of nonstop fighting, I heard Kane threaten Devota. She'd cowered in the background, fisting her hands to yell at *him*, too. Her frustration knew no bounds. She wasn't getting her way. Her possessed men were trying to kill her bait—him.

As long as he fought, I would too.

"Chin up," I muttered to myself, spiking out fire and ice at this awful pirate fae. In the shallow waves, it was too confusing. Those disappearing and reappearing acts were infinitely harder to follow in the water rolling back and forth.

"Face forward," I rallied, rotating my shoulder. Before the circuitous cycle ended, my elbow was yanked back.

"Forget the queen!" Ersilis's scratchy voice came in quiet, the screams in my head ballooning into a din.

"What?" I blinked, finding her at my side. I wasn't wounded too badly, but her fingers clutched me and she healed me nonetheless.

"We've got"—I panted—"to stop meeting like this."

She scowled at me, reinforcing my guess that she truly lacked any sense of humor. "Forget the queen."

Nodding at the Wetherone, she tipped her chin. She lifted both hands, sending twin tidal bursts of water, clearing the seas from him. Without the water touching him, easing his phasing-out disappearance acts, my ice could seal around him. I used my Vintar might and shackled him in a corset-like hold. As he writhed and bellowed, I ran for him. Ersilis still parted the water, keeping him clear.

He braced, snarling at me as I came close. Because he assumed I'd jump, I slid instead. Skidding across the sand, digging my knee in with a burn of friction, I punched my dagger up into his lower stomach.

I covered my head with my arm, protecting my face from the show of colors. Depressing matted blackness was blown apart by blue, green, then red.

This Wetherone was gone. I wasn't sure I'd listen to Ersilis's idea to forget about Devota. I wanted off this beach *now*. Before another freak could challenge me.

"You will serve me, Maren!" Devota cried out, a macabre grin on her face at the sight of how I'd killed this Wetherone. "You will kill them and protect me. Or else he dies!" As she pointed at Kane, he swung the ice sword at one of the two possessed guards.

His head didn't roll, but with that amount of bloodshed, he was gone. The man dropped to his knees, then fell the rest of the way to the sand.

Without the Wetherone's active possession, it seemed his infected prey ceased to exist, too. The other one still raged, battling between Baraan and Kane.

Devota snarled, increasing her blasts of smoke, fire, and sparks at Kane to capture him.

Again, Ersilis caught my arm. "Forget the queen!"

I shook my head, worried Kane wouldn't survive the deranged guard—even with Baraan's help—and Devota's strikes. It became a trio of too much danger. Baraan countered her fire with his water. Kane stopped the guard from killing him, then also deflected Devota's strikes. Devota alternated between Kane and Baraan. If I—and Ersilis—joined them, the odds would be in our favor to overcome the queen.

"Come on!" I urged her. For an ancient woman, she was *strong*, digging her feet in.

"No!" she protested. "I told you. Kane is fighting the *right* war. I thought he was!"

I shook my head, tugging to break free of her. "I don't know what that means."

"You must stop Sadera!"

I stilled, mid-pull, and furrowed my brow. "What?"

"She will rule."

I flung my hand at Devota trying to kill Kane. He groaned under the fierce pressure of fire she cast over him, Baraan's water the only thing stopping him from being charred alive. "*She* is the ruler. Right there!"

Ersilis shook her head, her one eye squinted in seriousness. "The river."

I groaned. "What river?"

"The river! The legacy of Riverfall. It rules."

I tore my attention from her, frowning back at the fight. "Kane!" I sent a blast of ice to help shield him from her fire.

Ersilis must have sensed I was about to abandon her with this crazy talk. She jerked down on my hand, and I faced her directly.

"The river calls the power. *Not* the person."

I shook my head. "That makes no sense!"

"You must stop Sadera," she repeated.

I spluttered, teetering between the urge to scream at her and groan at this riddle I didn't have time for.

Chapter Thirty-Two

I refused to stand by and watch Kane burn alive. Despite Baraan's forcefield of water, Devota's magic was stronger. She was the queen, the mightiest fae of her realm. Never mind the nonsense Ersilis gabbed about. Devota *was* the ruler, and if I didn't help, she was going to kill Kane.

"Baraan!" Ersilis must have sensed she was losing me as an audience. The old woman released my hand and hobbled closer to the sand. "Baraan!"

He grimaced with the oppressive effort of countering Devota's magic. Through slitted eyes, he glanced at us.

I ran. I'd wasted enough time already listening to her.

"Go stop your sister!" Ersilis yelled. She pointed north. "Stop your sister from reaching the Riverfall!"

I sent out more ice, casting a short, domed structure just above Kane's head. He was crouched so low from the fire, he was almost flat on the sand. Baraan frowned, but upon noticing that I'd taken over the force of magic against Devota, he stood, breathing hard.

"Sadera...?" he said, utter confusion on his face.

"Stop her," Ersilis ordered him. "At Riverfall."

As soon as she yelled those words, Devota sneered and flashed a band of flames at her. Ersilis fell, avoiding the hit as she slipped under the waves.

Nodding at me once, Baraan accepted that I had taken over helping Kane. He bolted up the beach, running toward a corga that he whistled for. Once he jumped onto the saddle, they took off.

"What—" Kane eased out of the ice dome, kicking off a large chunk to hold as a shield as I approached him. "What did she say?"

"To forget about Devota," I replied, taking up a ready stance to fight next to him.

"*What?*" He scrunched his face, shaking his head as he clearly didn't understand either.

I shrugged, licking my lips as I buffered ice against Devota's flames. "That the river rules."

"What does that mean?"

"I don't..."

I lost track of what I was going to say. I was too startled. Bewildered even. I closed my mouth and tilted my head up slightly. A chill swept through me, the sunshine hiding behind heavy, thunderous clouds hanging low. They crossed over the harsh brightness that had shone so harshly a moment ago.

Soft, cleansing drops of rain dropped on me. Gently, they trickled into my hair. Goosebumps spread over my flesh as the cool beads of moisture sped up. They collected in a stream, streaking down my face and removing the grit of sand and sweat.

Rain.

It was *raining*. Such a simple, basic thing that hit me with enormous meaning. When I was drugged from the heffen dust, I marveled at the lack of it. Summer heat and nonstop sunshine had overruled the moisture-laden nature of this southern realm.

With its return...

"What's going on?" Kane asked, frowning at the new change in the air. Not only did rain fall, but the temperature also dropped. A cold front breezed through, erasing the constant heat that seemed to dog us every minute of the day and all through the night.

Devota screamed. A ghastly, bestial trill that cut through the air.

Rain fell with more intensity, putting out most of Devota's flames. Embers burned. Sparks sizzled and arced toward us, but the water pouring down on us changed the situation.

Curling her fingers, Devota raised her hands. Trembling with the strain as she gripped the air, she gaped, chugging in hard inhalations. Her eyes went round as her brows slanted down. A feral snarl tautened the skin on her face.

She lifted her right arm, a punch into the air, and only a mediocre blast of flames pushed up with the motion. "No!" Her simple cry stretched out, dragging into the precipitation.

Lightning flashed, a bold streak in contrast to the darkening skies. Thunder rumbled overhead.

It was no longer summer...

Devota's power waned drastically as she tried, again and again, to thrust her hands out and project the magic of heat and fire.

It seemed the season had changed—again. It was raining, a dreary, soaking sensation replacing the dry heat.

"What happened?" Kane asked. "What..."

"No!" Devota cried out again. "No!"

She couldn't raise flames. Nothing sparked as fearsomely as it had when she'd arrived.

"What's going on?" I muttered.

"She rules," Ersilis answered, hobbling closer, her weaker leg dragging more noticeably in the soft sand.

"Not well," I quipped. Devota was fading before our eyes, her magic diluted.

Devota's brows arched up, and she howled at me. She drew her sword. A simple blade she must have requested from her soldiers since I'd ruined the one she'd been carrying. Her hand closed around the hilt, and she swung it up at me. Rage danced in her glittering eyes, her muscles tense. Tendons showed in her neck, she ground her jaw so tight.

Before she could charge at me, Kane stepped in, fighting her with the cutlass a pirate had dropped. Metal clinked and clashed as their blades hit and held. When she grunted and increased her strikes, she again proved that she had been trained well. She could handle her blade deftly and with upper body strength that never wavered. Kane matched her, though. After picking up a staff of wood, likely busted from one of the many buildings destroyed close to the shore, he seemed to have another advantage of two weapons against her one.

Waves rose. Swelling higher, thicker, and with shorter breaks between them, tidal pulses crashed onto the beach. Forced further back, I clutched Ersilis's hand and shot bursts of ice to block Devota's flames. None of her uses of magic matched the intensity of what she had delivered earlier. As her power receded, Kane's confidence to fight grew.

She lifted her arms, one in a block and the other to angle her sword at me. "You must bow—"

The largest wave rolled to shore right at that moment. Tripping, she lost her balance, so much that Kane had an opening. A moment to strike. He drove that staff of wood forward. The point wasn't primed and whittled. It wasn't designed to impale anything. Happenstance rendered it a piercing point.

But it was enough.

As she struggled to regain her footing, trying to spear her sword through me, the wood stabbed her. It was a lethal wound. Poking out her upper back, the weathered staff cut all the way through. Flesh, muscles, bones, and heart. It darted through it all.

Choking on air, she staggered, her hands going to the bar shot through her. "No." It was a weak mumble of protest lacking the rage and defiance of her previous shouts of that one word. "No." This time, it didn't offer any semblance of the authority she relished.

Blood spread slowly from the opening of her wound. With the wood stuck tight, it prevented a free-flowing gush of her life's essence.

Her death came swiftly, though. With staggered breaths, similar to something I would have expected from a poor soul suffering from longuex, she drew in wheezing, wet, and laborious inhalations. None of them filled her lungs, her chest barely rising as she canted forward. Jammed at a diagonal angle, the wood staff sank a few inches into the sand.

Devota gasped as she slid down the coarse stick. Blood dribbled out her mouth, frothy with the last of her air.

Another violent wave swooshed at her feet, and that mere pressure turned her from that slow drop of gravity. Twisting on the impalement, she fell to the side, then landed on her back. The wood staff flung up, ending like a flagpole rising from the beach.

Her eyes remained open—glassed over and vacant as she passed.

I stared at her, making sure those lids didn't blink. That she didn't bounce back again. Didn't return and attack once more.

She didn't. Lying there in the waves with the thunder booming and lightning flashing in the distance, she remained dead. Unmoving and slowly covered with more and more water lapping the shore. Murky seafoam covered then revealed her. Her dead stare remained unchanging, so eerie under the surface, looking up at the dark, storming sky.

Ersilis grunted. Clutching Kane's arm, she kicked at the first queen's foot.

Nothing. No reaction at all, save for the waves swaying her into the sand beneath.

"Dead." Ersilis grunted after she voiced her simple consensus. Bold and blunt.

I swallowed, my mouth dry. War cries and battle sounds continued in the distance, the pirates and Rengae fighting nonstop. More Wetherones hadn't approached since I'd killed that one, but I knew they weren't gone.

It felt like this struggle was only beginning. Whereas this one with Devota had finally ended. Shielding my face with my hand, but still squinting to see through the rain, I looked up at the drumming tune of a chant out at sea. Dotting the surface, more ships approached.

"Who..." Kane cleared his throat. "Who rules now?"

The deadpanned glower Ersilis sent him was a scolding.

"That wasn't a fae blade." He needlessly pointed at the dead queen he'd just killed with an old, weathered stick of wood.

Panic, or if not that, confusion, covered his face. Rain plastered his hair to his face, and he shook his head to clear his vision. Glancing at me, then staring at Ersilis, he seemed to wait for an answer.

"Does the throne go to Lianen?" he asked next.

"She didn't have any children..." I added. "Are *you*—"

He shook his head vehemently. "No. I wouldn't be..."

"Well, how does it work?" I wiped the rain from my face, peering at them both. "Only a fae blade can end a reign." That was what I'd been told all this time.

"Rengae," Ersilis replied dryly. "Rengae rules." As she lifted her palm to the sky, the pelting of raindrops on her skin emphasized that point. Summer had indeed changed to rain. But the ruler...

"The river calls the power. Not the person."

"Sadera is queen," I said, testing the words out on my tongue. They tasted acidic, like an admission I'd rather never make. All they'd focused on was removing Devota. Just like everyone had concentrated on the act of taking out King Vanzed and the reign of winter.

No one seemed to have looked ahead to who should rule instead.

Other than Lianen. He'd considered it. He'd thought ahead and begged us to find a fae blade not only to end his sister's torture and destruction, but also to return Vintar to the throne. To reinstate winter for the critical reason of blocking invaders from taking over Contermerria.

Like they do now.

"Sadera," Kane repeated. A statement and question for clarification in one.

Ersilis nodded. "Sadera is queen. That fae blade ending a reign was jus' a tale. An ol' tale. Probably to scare them royals and keep 'em in line for hundreds of years."

When Kane and I lagged to reply, slotting this news in, she grunted. "A tale, I'm tellin' you. A dumb ol' tale." She gripped my arm, this time to kick at the corpse of the first queen. "She's a dead body. Flesh and bones. Anything kills it, it'll die."

That did sound logical. Simple. But... "Then how is Sadera..."

"Because of the legacy of Riverfall." She hobbled to Kane. "I know he taught you that one. I know he raised you right. Your grandfather tol' you 'bout the legacy."

"I..." Kane gripped his hair. "It's a story, Ersilis. Just a story I thought I dismissed as a boy."

She slashed her arm through the air. "No!" Pointing at Devota, she growled. "*That* was a story. Ain't true. It ain't true that a fae blade ends a reign. A blade jus' kills a person!"

"Then how the hell does the reign end?" I shouted.

"The river." She enunciated it slowly like I was a moron. "The fae blade. In the *river*!"

She shook her head, swatting the back of mine. "Think, Maren. Think 'bout when the king died!"

I didn't try to rehash that memory. It haunted me in my dreams plenty. Guilt harbored in the recesses of my mind, and I hated that I couldn't have known enough then. That I wasn't aware of *all* the details to avoid falling into Devota's game. I fisted my hands and drew in a deep breath for patience. "Just explain it!"

"The fae blade wedged into the Riverfall bed," Kane answered, his face solemn as he seemed lost in a memory as he figured it out. His stare remained distant as he gazed at the approaching ships. "*That* determines the reign of the land."

AMABEL DANIELS

Chapter Thirty-Three

The blade stuck *in* the bottom of the river?

I blinked, then wiped my eyes as sweat burned. Even with the constant rainfall soaking me, it had yet to rinse out the grime?

"The fae blade standing from the riverbed," Ersilis agreed with Kane's conclusion. "Yes."

"*That's* the legacy of the Riverfall?" I asked. Doubt hung in my words. Blunt skepticism. After the mess from believing what everyone said before, that a fae-forged sword would end a ruler's reign, I wasn't quick to jump onto *this* theory. Not without proof.

Ersilis scratched her head. "Part of it."

Realm above.

"Soon as I saw Sadera with that blade and heading north, I jus' knew. I knew it had to be true," Ersilis stated. She pointed at Devota. "It ain't the other idea. Cuz you jus' killed Devota. The seasons changed *before* ya killed her. Summer ended before she died."

Drumming mixed with chanting, the combination low and frightening. Those ships came closer as we spoke. As we stood around like targets. I didn't want to stick around to face any more Wetherones right now. The last fight drained me. Ersilis had healed the few wounds I'd collected, but my mind, my spirit—they were tired. I was emotionally spent and now more confusion was piling on.

"Then is Sadera going to..." Again, I looked out to the sea. "Is she going to stop them? Somehow?" We'd been rooting for Isan to reclaim the throne to protect Contermerria.

Ersilis passed us, hobbling away from the beach. She gained her footing better as she climbed the slight slope up the sand. "No. She ain't gonna stop 'em. I watched her get that sword of hers *from* them. Off one a them boats!"

Kane grabbed my hand and ran up after her, cursing the whole way. "We went from a sadist to an ally of the Wetherones?"

Ersilis pulled a whistle from a cord hanging from her neck. "Long as Sadera's sword is wedged in that river, it sure looks that way." She blew three times, and corgas came running.

I narrowed my eyes, peering north. It still didn't add up. "Sadera was *just* here, though. You mean to tell me she rode out of here, managed to cross the entire Hunann Swamp *in minutes*? Got into the Riverfall Chamber alive, removed the Somman sword Devota stuck in the riverbed, and jammed *her* Rengae blade in?" I snapped my fingers, leaning to ease onto the corga's saddle. "Just like that?" I added when she didn't reply, getting onto her corga.

I didn't know how mine knew to choose me, and I guessed it remembered my scent. I didn't care. I appreciated the convenience. And loyalty.

"I ain't sure how she got there that fast, but I'm tellin' ya. That's what she done."

"Then we can take her sword out." Kane ordered his corga to run, and we filed into a line, rushing through the remaining battles spread out sporadically further from the beach.

"But ya ain't got a Vintar blade to stick back in!" Ersilis argued.

Because I...broke it.

"A troll, Maren," Kane reminded me. "A mountain troll destroyed the sword. Not you."

I both loved and hated that he *knew* I'd be assuming guilt for it. But neither would make it any less true.

"How does this work, though?" Kane asked once we entered the swamp. In this region of the continent, the swamp stretched the thinnest. We weren't looking at days of a ride. Hours, but not minutes like Sadera somehow accomplished. "How does this legacy work? Why does a fae's sword being stuck in the riverbed change the seasons?"

"An ol' spell." Ersilis shrugged, hanging on tight as she rode. "My mother tol' me when I was jus' a babe. Like ya said, a story when ya young. Somethin' that gets lost through time."

I bet those Ranger texts would explain it.

We rushed through the swamp the best we could. *We*, as in the people in the saddles. The corgas excelled in this terrain—any terrain, it seemed. Slitting our eyes and angling our heads down, we tried to see ahead. It was impossible. It wasn't a deluge, but a steady rainfall that, with the impressive speeds the corgas galloped, it was like riding into a sheet of precipitation.

Before us was a fae. Someone used a trickle of power. Ersilis noticed it at the same time I did, glancing at me. "Rengae," she announced.

Kane took up the rear as we rode in a single line and approached the man lying on the soggy land. He rested a pace away from a quickly rising river. His face was not easy to see with that thick auburn beard, but I recognized him even in this drenched state.

"Baraan," Kane said as he lowered to the ground. Ersilis remained on her saddle, but I dropped down to heal him.

The simple cutlass in his chest had done too much damage though. I could *heal* someone, not raise them from the dead.

"No," he told me weakly. "Don't bother."

I gagged but recovered, seeing that his leg had been ripped off as well.

"Go," he told us. "Go help them."

"Them who?" Kane asked, looking in the direction of where Baraan pointed.

North. Of course. To the castle.

"My sisters..." He drew in a shuddering breath, and I hoped it wasn't his last. I winced at his grotesque position, and I laid my hand on him. Not to heal, but to numb the pain.

"*Both* of them?" Kane asked.

"Sadera..." He paused for a moment. "She reversed the river. I watched before she noticed me following her. I don't know where her Rengae sword came from. She claimed she'd never known where it was. That she lost when she was a child. But she held it and stabbed it into the river."

"What happened?" Kane urged.

"It stopped." Baraan closed his eyes and lifted his brows. "She stopped the river. Then reversed it. When her sword touched the bottom of the stream and stuck in the rocks, she... controlled the river. She withdrew it and her corga jumped into the stream—backward."

Countering the power of the Somman sword ruling from the top?

"I followed her and watched her do it three more times. I couldn't catch up. Each time she reversed the river, it would eventually correct itself, but her sword in the bottom would change it. I reached her." His finger trembled as he pointed down. "And she..."

Killed her own brother.

"Amaias came by just when the lernep took my leg. I was stuck in place and it..." A tear crept down his face, washed away by the rain. "Isan—"

"He came with Amaias?" I asked. I thought he was about to die.

"She kept healing him to get him by. Isan blasted the lernep, and I told Amaias where Sadera was headed—with the sword we thought she didn't have." He gripped Kane's hand and held it tight. "Please. Help her. We never trusted Sadera, and now..."

Now, she proved why they shouldn't have.

"Let's go," Ersilis said.

No fanfare? No farewell? It tore at me to just *leave* him here in the wild.

"I don't have long, Maren. Go. Please help her. That's my last wish."

I nodded at him and with a sob clawing at my throat, I got back on the corga and raced onward again.

Kane wasn't shocked when these odd animals swam as well as they ran. Upstream, they covered a great distance. And I only hoped it wouldn't be too late—both to fulfill that dying prince's wish to help *one* of his sisters. Hopefully to stop Sadera from calling herself queen, too.

Chapter Thirty-Four

Unlike the first two times I approached Contermerria's highest castle, it was unguarded. All the Somman soldiers and staff lay dead. On the steps leading to the open gates. In the foyer where I once fought the mutant hur-wolves. Throughout the palace, staff members and guards remained lifeless on the ground where they seemed to have fallen. No wounds or marks showed on their skin, but I didn't have time to puzzle out the cause of their deaths. Not now.

We didn't bother dismounting from the corgas. They slinked along even the narrowest hallways and bounded up the many stairs—or down—five at once.

I thought I would have felt more anxiety rushing into this grand palace again, but with Kane and Ersilis as company, and knowing Devota and her most loyal minions were dead, my confidence didn't diminish.

Sadera was irksome, but was she as bad as Devota? Worse?

Something killed everyone on their way in... She wouldn't be a *good* leader if she dropped staff in a wake of death. I had no grounds to trust the princess if she obtained her blade *from* a brutal invader delivering it to shore.

"Flooded it."

I frowned at Ersilis's comment before we neared the turn to the colosseum.

"She flooded it all, I think." She pointed to the walls and floor, the evidence of excess water not from Devota's days of décor. Now that she'd mentioned it, all the gaudy trappings the Sommans flaunted as ornamentation were absent.

Washed away.

I wasn't sure how Sadera could have "flooded" the guards out in the open, but it must have been a hit of water somehow. Once we reached the colosseum where I'd been a slave for four months, I saw how right Ersilis was.

Water churned high, and the floating debris at the surface had my stomach clenching in despair. Bodies—of slaves and dungeon masters—knocked into boulders of ice that still hadn't melted even in the summer. I didn't look down, steeling myself against the memories, tuning out the cries and whips and fire and hell.

Face forward. I'd never needed that reminder more than I did right now. Steadily focusing ahead, I led Kane and Ersilis along the narrow path that would bring us down deeper into the Riverfall Chamber I'd escaped.

We heard the fighting before we reached it. The corgas were ready to gallop on this narrow bridge that dipped into the chamber. Without so much as a slip, their webbed, nimble paws ate up the distance and delivered us to the one room I never wanted to see again.

Quieter than the sisters fighting and the whirring drone of the cyclone in the middle of the chamber, our corgas sped down the stairs without anyone the wiser. Sadera was quick to take this castle and the reign, but she hadn't set up any reinforcement for security. We ran right in, but that didn't mean we could count on a simple fight.

Sadera and Amaias fought on the smooth, soaked patio space. Sadera wielded the Somman blade—Devota's—that she'd pulled out of the riverbed. Amaias held her own, something without magic she likely picked up somewhere, smacking and striking at her sister.

Beyond them, Isan stood at the cyclone. One hand up and the other hanging low as he coughed.

Positioned over the narrow river that cut straight through this once-regal and revered room in the castle, a tall, furious hurricane of water spun. Within it, barely visible through the spiraling water, was the Rengae sword, standing firm and clear of the moisture within the eye of the storm. Sadera had jammed the tip into the rocks at the bottom, and she'd erected a spiraling force to encase it.

"Help 'im," Ersilis ordered me.

I followed the direction of her pointed finger, and I understood at once.

Isan was trying to freeze the cyclone. Likely to pause it long enough to remove her fae blade controlling the land.

Kane nodded at me. "I'll help her," he said, tipping his chin at the dueling sisters.

Ersilis hobbled after me, muttering. "I'll heal 'im as ya go."

I ran to the former heir prince and set my hand up to join his use of Vintar magic. Together, we blasted ice at the spinning current, but it revolved so fast, the curled sheets of ice we forged were too thin to sustain the pressure.

"It won't work," Isan said, gritting his teeth.

"It...might." I cringed at a piece of ice flinging *out* of the cyclone. Once more, another thin slate shot out, and if I hadn't shoved Isan back into Ersilis, they would've lost their heads.

"Keep tryin'!" Ersilis ordered.

Kane's shouts up near the sisters' fight distracted me. Every time I glanced at the other side of the patio, I worried he'd be killed.

I was accosted by the memories of all the times I'd felt crushed under this specific worry. Each occasion meshed into a gut-twisting agony.

When he nearly froze to death in the sleet out of the swamp.

When he'd been beaten in the Somman dungeons.

When he'd been extradited here and I thought the king would execute him.

When he'd fallen over the waterfall.

When those spiders had spun him in a web and a troll wanted to eat him.

When the Wetherone possessed him.

When Devota faced him off at the beach.

Every time. Each incident chipped at me, sending the idea of being with him further astray.

And now, as he fought the new ruler of the land, that same gripping anxiety wouldn't let go.

All I could hear, all my mind could replay, was the last time we'd had a moment between just the two of us.

"I love you, Maren."

He'd promised it. He'd even remarked that I was incapable of the same sentiment. A false comment if he'd ever shared one. I *chose* him. I loved him so much that it scared me, especially in this life of death and danger. Especially *here*, where I'd lost him once before.

I hadn't been brave enough to put myself on the line and argue how wrong he was. That of course, I loved him. I cherished him, and deep down, regardless of my temper clashing with his, I did trust him.

"How'd she know?" Ersilis asked Isan, ripping me from my thoughts. "How'd Amaias know to come? And you?"

Isan clenched his teeth as he tried to freeze the cyclone. "She came to the rendezvous with more... kalmere for me. She said she went to her rooms. Sadera's. She found a book she'd been looking for."

"A Ranger text?" I asked.

He nodded. "Not...an important one, but it mentioned the legacy. That the sword was key..." His coughs interrupted his explanation. "Amaias always looked into the tomes in the library. Over time, Sadera must have spied on it all. Pieced it together. She wants to kill her."

"Amaias wants to kill Sadera?"

Kane groaned, taking a hit on the arm. I faltered, not concentrating on my power. "I have to help—"

"No! Stop this and get her sword out of the river," Ersilis argued.

"Sadera," Isan said, panting, "wants to kill Amaias. Because she knows. Amaias knows what the Ranger texts look like."

"Which means Sadera wants to hide them?" I guessed.

He nodded, a jerky, feeble motion.

"Because...she wants to rule..." He cleared his throat. "With the Wetherones."

Amaias flew back, landing in a heap. Sadera had blasted her with water. While Kane was knocked out from the same push of a wave, still climbing back to his feet, the Rengae ruler stalked toward her sister. Rotating her wrist, the sword slicing through the air, she readied to kill her other sibling.

"Family," she spat. "Who needs them?"

I ignored the cyclone and sent a blast of fire at her.

She turned, brows raised as she smirked at me.

"Maren, don't!" Kane had climbed to one knee, shaking his head at me. "Get her sword out of the river. I'll handle her. Just get that sword!"

She scoffed, turning to jet a hard hit of water at him. "You'll handle *me*?"

I intercepted her strike, freezing it still.

"Maren, *don't*," Amaias begged weakly.

Do this. Don't do that. These constant orders. I owed no one my obedience. When would they let *me* make a decision for once?

I ran toward Sadera, but I didn't get far. Water rose from the river. The cyclone remained in form, encasing her sword stuck into the riverbed. Pumping my legs to run hard, I got nowhere, lifted as she raised the water in the room.

I resisted, forcing a field of repellence around me, but she was too fast. Water gathered in the chamber, raising us all. Higher and higher, we swiftly floated toward the ceiling.

We were suspended. Amaias glowered at me, swimming hard for Isan. Ersilis formed a bubble around herself, half of a sphere below her body as she floated at the choppy surface climbing toward the ceiling.

"Kane!" I found him.

He swam toward me, his arms cutting through the waves that circled within the chamber.

"I told you to leave her to me!" he yelled.

Still? Even now he'd pick a fight with me?

I grabbed his hand, pulling him close to shape a pocket of air to protect us.

"She threatened to do exactly this," he said, hugging me close. "I didn't want you to challenge her. Not with your temper. Not until we had that sword!"

Water shot up to the ceiling. Every inch of the chamber was filled. Corgas swam furiously, and I worried they'd drown. While the cyclone swirled so fast, the space within it remained dry and undisturbed. Her sword remained wedged in firmly.

Sadera's protection seemed flimsy, a weakly trailing halo by her head, but it was all she seemed to need to breathe with ease. As she floated, pushing onto her back to look up, she grinned.

Lowering one arm, she gripped her sister's sword. As she raised her other arm, her hand flat and pointed at me, she manipulated the water to spear toward me.

Chapter Thirty-Five

Kane clutched me in his arms. "She's going to—"

Our bubble popped. My magic was beaten. One by one, as I held my breath, I witnessed the other Rengaens lose their hold on their spells. Sadera's mouth moved as she cut through the water, likely casting a spell on all of us to override our attempt at protection.

Just like Devota's mastery of fire was the strongest in her reign, Sadera's control of Rengae magic would beat ours. She'd reversed the direction of the spells we'd used, and our heads were surrounded by cold water.

Ersilis flailed her arms closer to the cyclone. Amaias and Isan held hands, their sphere gone now too.

I clamped my lips shut, a scream of anger locked inside. As Sadera propelled through the room filled to the brim with water, she turned. Her other arm joined the first, and together. Changing her mind, she shot toward her sister.

That blade would pierce Amaias in a heartbeat. Isan tried and failed to cast a block of ice to shield them, but it disintegrated, overwhelmed by Sadera's magic in this sacred room.

Ice was out. Fire had to be too. Unlike them, I had one more power to rely on, even if this new queen was stronger with it.

Instead of trying to secure a pocket of air to breathe, I called forth more water. I *added* to this flood, riding on the spell she'd cast. I banked on my Rengae magic and spelled the water to stream into the room even more. Pressure increased. My skin felt tight as the hydraulic intensity ticked higher. There was only so much room in here. Only so much volume.

Sadera paused, whipping around and treading to stare at me. Her brows dipped down as she registered *I* was the one toying with her brand of magic.

Cramming more water in here wouldn't last. A point of too much pressure would be reached.

She clenched her teeth and swam for me.

The tip of the sword shot through the water as she aimed at me, her mouth pinched. Unwavering despite the violent swirling within the room and the ever-growing pressure as I pulled more water from the river to further flood this chamber, she held that blade tight and targeted it at me.

More. A little more...

Any second now. It had to work.

She'd started the spell, and I'd tinkered with it. If she wanted to flood this room, I'd do it better—to the point it would burst. If it didn't, if I miscalculated, we'd all die.

My lungs already burned for oxygen. Darkness edged in from the frame of my vision. My heart raced, and my limbs tingled.

More.

She was nearly to me, the sword aimed at me no matter how I treaded and tried to remain immobile. I was the target.

Hang on.

I willed my spell to speed up. More water. More pressure. The old walls of this chamber had to give!

Kane's hand gripped my arm. He pulled me behind him, barricading me and keeping me back.

The sword pierced him, instead.

No!

I felt his body jerk at the impact. His head fell forward with the whiplash. His legs shook outward too. Sadera had thrust that sword clear through him. The blade slid free as she jerked it back out. My mouth dropped open as I screamed and held him to me.

Then his body jolted again. Mine did too. Our limbs stretched in a suspension of gravity as it changed around us.

With a heaving suction, the walls gave way and exploded. I closed my eyes and hugged Kane to me as we were forced out of the Riverfall Chamber on a tsunami crashing down from the mountainside.

All thoughts vanished. Time didn't register.

But I held on tight, determined and convinced, that once and for all, Kane and I belonged together in the face of certain death.

Even if it would be the end.

To be continued ... in FOREVER RULE.

Acknowledgments

For editing, I thank C.J. Pinard at www.cjpinard.com. For the cover design and photography, I thank Kellie Dennis at Book Cover By Design at www.bookcoverbydesign.co.uk. For proofreading, I thank PSW.

About the Author

Amabel Daniels lives in Northwest Ohio with her patient husband, a trio of adventurous girls, and a collection of too many cats and dogs. Although she holds a Master's degree in Ecology and is a science nerd at heart, her true love is finding a good book. After working as an arborist and park technician, it's not surprising that her fascination with nature shows up in her YA fantasy titles, especially the Olde Earth series.

Follow Amabel at her website and on:

Facebook, Instagram, Bookbub, Goodreads, and Amazon.

Other Books by the Author

Olde Earth Academy
Secrecy
Discovery
Mastery
Victory
Challenged
Threatened
Endangered
Attacked

Olde Earth Boxset Volume I (Books 1-4)
Olde Earth Boxset Volume II (Books 5-8)

Revenged
Retrieved
Remade

Legacy of Riverfall
Last King
First Queen
Forever Rule

Made in the USA
Las Vegas, NV
05 February 2025